DISCLAIMER:
Any and all thoughts or ideas put forth in this trash issue should not be accepted as scientific fact or quotable as such. While some research was done to ensure we presented concepts in the proper light, we may still have inadvertently misrepresented facts due to our own ignorance in pursuit of providing a fun reading experience.

FORBIDDEN FUTURES 14.4
ISBN: 978-1-960213-48-8
© 2025 FORBIDDEN FUTURES is a trademark of ODDNESS. All rights reserved. Nothing may be reprinted in part or whole without permission from the publisher and creator. Any similarity to real people and places in fiction and semi-fiction is purely coincidental. All material in this issue is copyright to the respective creators. The publisher assumes no responsibility for unsolicited material.

ODDNESS | PUBLISHER
MIKE DUBISCH | ALL ARTWORK

SLEEP
THE ANCIENT PORTAL

The kingdom of sleep is one of the most mysterious realms of our very existence, for each night we surrender control as reality dissolves and our minds drift into an unconscious state. All of nature's creatures share this strange ritual.

THE BRAIN EATS ITSELF WITHOUT SLEEP!

Sleep is a necessary biological maintenance routine. Microglia (the brain's immune cells) become overactive during prolonged wakefulness, consuming both damaged cells and healthy neurons. Beta-amyloid, a protein cleared during deep sleep, accumulates and chokes synaptic function, and the brain begins to digest itself.

After 24 hours without sleep, emotions begin to swing. After 48 hours, the brain misfires with hallucinations, and perception distortions begin. Within 72 hours, memory formation begins to deteriorate. Beyond 96 hours, the boundaries of self start to blur as your personality begins to fragment.

THE TWO SLEEPS OF OLD HUMANITY

For thousands of years, humans followed a biphasic slumber pattern before the invention of artificial light: a "first sleep," followed by a quiet, liminal wakefulness, and then a "second sleep." In between the two sleep cycles, people used the time for praying, conversation, or even visiting a neighbor.

Historian Roger Ekirch traced the decline of biphasic sleep to the rise of gaslight lamps, whose artificial light extended the waking day, resulting in sleep being compressed into a single uninterrupted session.

REM SLEEP: RESET OR GATEWAY?

Sleep is far from rest. During REM sleep (the stage associated with dreams), the brain is as electrically active as it is when awake. The limbic system, which governs emotion, lights up. The prefrontal cortex, which handles logic and self-restraint, goes dark. The result is a state of vivid, unpredictable activity.

Researcher Francis Crick claims sleep exists to clear mental clutter, while Harvard's Allan Hobson argues dreams are just the cortex's best guess at deciphering random neurological noise.

HIBERNATION

Now, imagine a very long sleep cycle, such as hibernation, which is simply life stretched across time. In deep space, where years pass between destinations, this kind of sleep might be the only way forward.

If we could safely enter such a state, sleep would become an endurance trial unless completely placed into a "null state," so you don't experience time. Researchers will need to answer the question of what happens to the mind in that stillness. If thought slows to a crawl, do dreams stretch into epic intervals? Would hibernation require mental hardening to undergo the freeze?

Explore this concept and more in Mike Dubisch's graphic novel "Weirdling."

MIKE DUBISCH:
WEIRDLING
ISSUES: 1-4

MIKE DUBISCH (Artist & Author)
JEFF ECKLEBERRY (Lettering)

MIKE DUBISCH
WEIRDLING
1

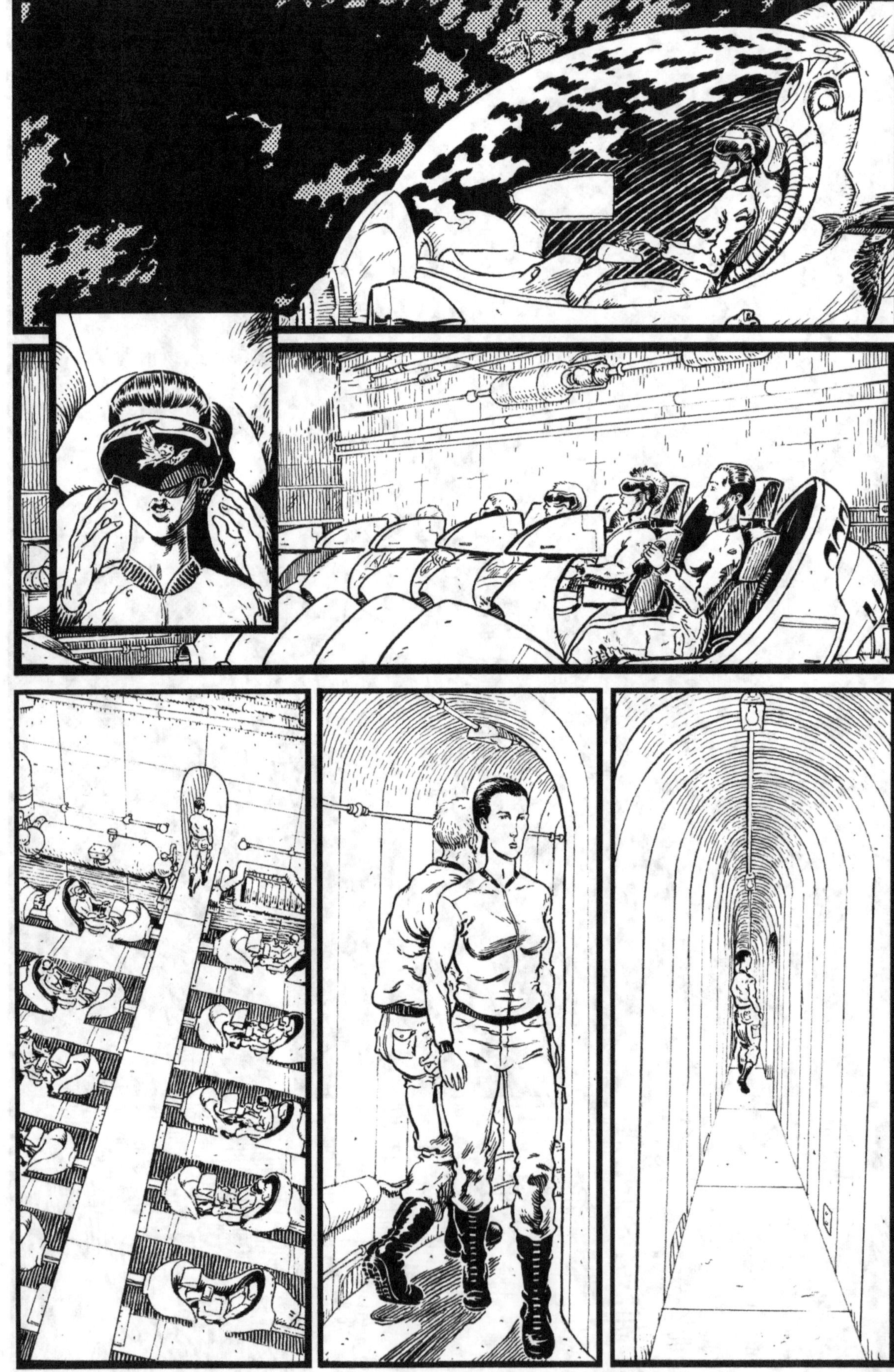

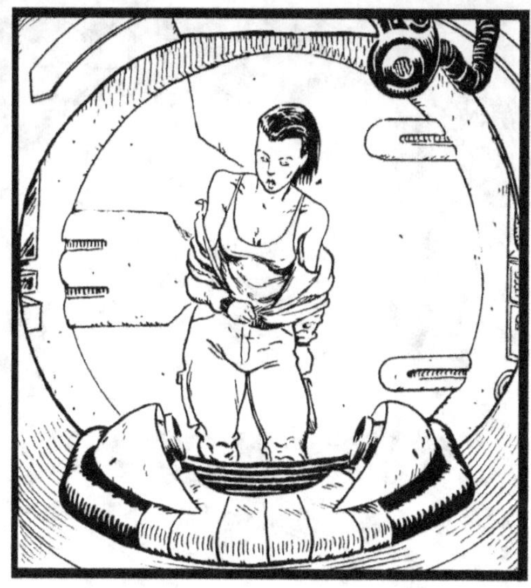

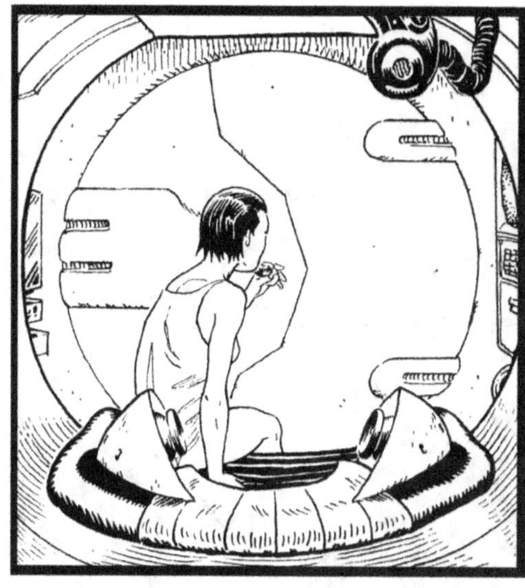

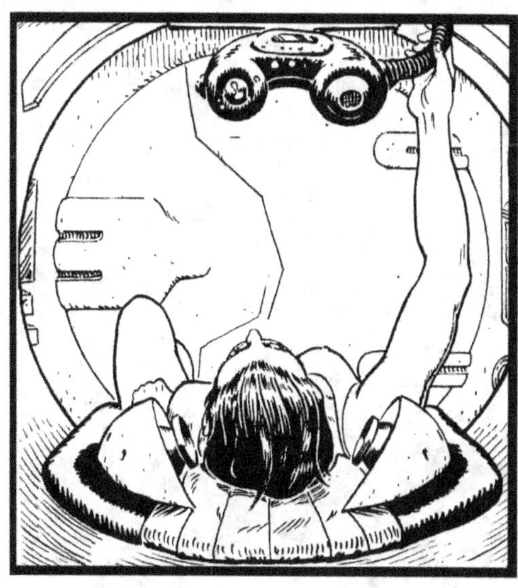

DOCTOR!
DOCTOR
MANDRETTA!

HIS FATHER IS A MAN FROM THE VILLAGE, JOSEF VESSELL – THE BABY, ADAR, HAS SLIPPED INTO A COMA, THE APPARENT CAUSE A LARGE EXTERNAL GROWTH.

THE GROWTH HISSES AND WHISPERS AS IT DISPLAYS A FORKED TONGUE!

HE LIVES BUT BARELY BREATHES -
IF ANYONE CAN SAVE THE BOY'S LIFE, IT'S ANNA MANDRETTA!
I SHALL BEGIN WITH AN INCISION AT THE APEX OF THE GROWTH -
DUBISCH -AFTER- Calle
THAT UNCANNY SOUND AGAIN - IT'S SICKENING!
MMMEE
MMMMEE
OH MY GOD - IT'S GROWING!

JOSEF? I AM THE SURGEON WHO OPERATED ON YOUR SON.
I'M AFRAID-I'M VERY SORRY...
MY SON...? IS HE...?
I'M SORRY SIR... THE GROWTH'S RAPID PROGRESSION AND ITS STRANGE PROPERTIES... WE COULDN'T SAVE HIM.
MY SON... DEAD?
I'M TRULY SORRY, SIR.
NO... NO, IT'S NOT TRUE.
MY SON IS NOT DEAD!
MY SON IS DESTINED TO LIVE FOREVER AND RULE THE WORLD!

NICHOLAS, HELP! HELP!
YOU ANNA. YOU'RE THE ONE WHO WILL HELP HIM. HEAR ME ANNA... HEAR NOW THIS WORD I SPEAK TO YOU...
FOOLS! THE GLORY OF MY SON'S RULE FILLS YOU WITH DREAD!
HIS IS THE POWER OF AZAG-THOTH...
DOCTORS! TAKE A LOOK AT THIS.
MY GOD, ANOTHER TUMOR! DR. VAN HISE, WHAT DO YOU KNOW ABOUT THIS FAMILY?

HE HAS A WIFE, MARNA. THEY LIVE IN THE SWAMP WEST OF THE VILLAGE.
WE MUST GO TO HER, TELL HER WHAT HAPPENED AND BE SURE THAT SHE IS NOT ALSO AFFECTED.
JOSEF'S BEHAVIOR HAS BECOME ERRATIC IN THE LAST FEW MONTHS. MARNA SPOKE OF IT BEFORE SHE TOO BECAME WRAPPED UP IN JOSEF'S DELUSIONS.

SHE SPOKE OF AN AFTERNOON PICNIC BY THE LAKE. JOSEF STOOD UP. SUDDENLY THE EARTH BENEATH HIS FEET CRUMBLED AND HE SLIPPED INTO THE BRACKISH WATER.
HE DID NOT EMERGE FOR AN UNCOMMONLY LONG TIME. MARNA WAS CONVINCED HE HAD DROWNED UNTIL HE FINALLY AROSE FROM THE LAKE WATERS, SEEMINGLY UNHARMED.
IT WAS THEN THAT HE BEGAN TO BEHAVE STRANGELY AND PROFESS UNUSUAL BELIEFS.
HE BELIEVED HE HAD BEEN CHOSEN BY AN ANCIENT GOD THAT DWELLED BENEATH THE SURFACE OF THE LAKE.
HE BUILT A HUT AT THE SITE. NO ONE IN THE VILLAGE EVEN KNEW ABOUT THE BABY— CONCEIVED THAT VERY DAY!

MARNA?
MARNA VESSELL?
I'M DR. ANNA MANDRETTA FROM THE MISKATONIK UNIVERSITY HOSPITAL.
MARNA?
NGHIZ IDDA, BENEATH NINNKIGAL, IA KANTAL AMAKKYA.
MARNA, I'M SORRY, I HAVE TERRIBLE NEWS.
IA DAG! IA GAWT! IA MAR GOLOBA SUHGU RIM! MANDRETTA AR UTUK! SHE IS HERE!!

YOUR CHILD, ADAR, SUCCUMBED TO THE EFFECTS OF THE GROWTH. YOUR HUSBAND HAD TO BE SEDATED.
MY SON WILL BREATH AGAIN... YOU, MANDRETTA, WILL FACILITATE HIS REBIRTH!
HE SHALL RETURN WITH HIS FULL POWER! IT WAS MEANT TO BE!
WHAT DO YOU MEAN?
THE WORD WILL BE HEARD BY YOU THIS DAY.
THE WORD, THE WYRD!
WHAT- WHAT ARE YOU DOING?
THE WORD ALONE WILL BIND THE HANDS OF YOUR ENEMIES AND SHIELD YOU FROM HARM. HEAR THE WORD INSIDE.
ON YOUR INNER LANDSCAPE...

IT'S COMING RIGHT TOWARDS ME! WHAT AM I DOING HERE?
WHAT DID THAT WOMAN SAY TO ME?
BZZMMMMM
!
WHERE AM I? HOW DID I GET HERE?
MY GOD, I'M IN A STORM!

IT WAS A WORD--
WAIT, I HEAR IT NOW, WITHIN ME!
I KNOW THE WORD!
WEIRDLING!
I DID IT! WITH THE WORD I STOPPED THE STORM! ME, ANNA MANDRETTA! NOTHING CAN TOUCH ME!
--Lucidream interrupt--
All personnel report to battle stations! All personnel report to--

THE HOWL OF THE BATTLE KLAXON TORE ME OUT OF THE NIGHTMARE.

READOUT ON THE LUCIDREAM EMITTER SAID SHIP TIME WAS 0600.

I DON'T KNOW WHERE DAWN WAS ON THIS WATERLOGGED WAR MOON.

IT SURE WASN'T HERE.

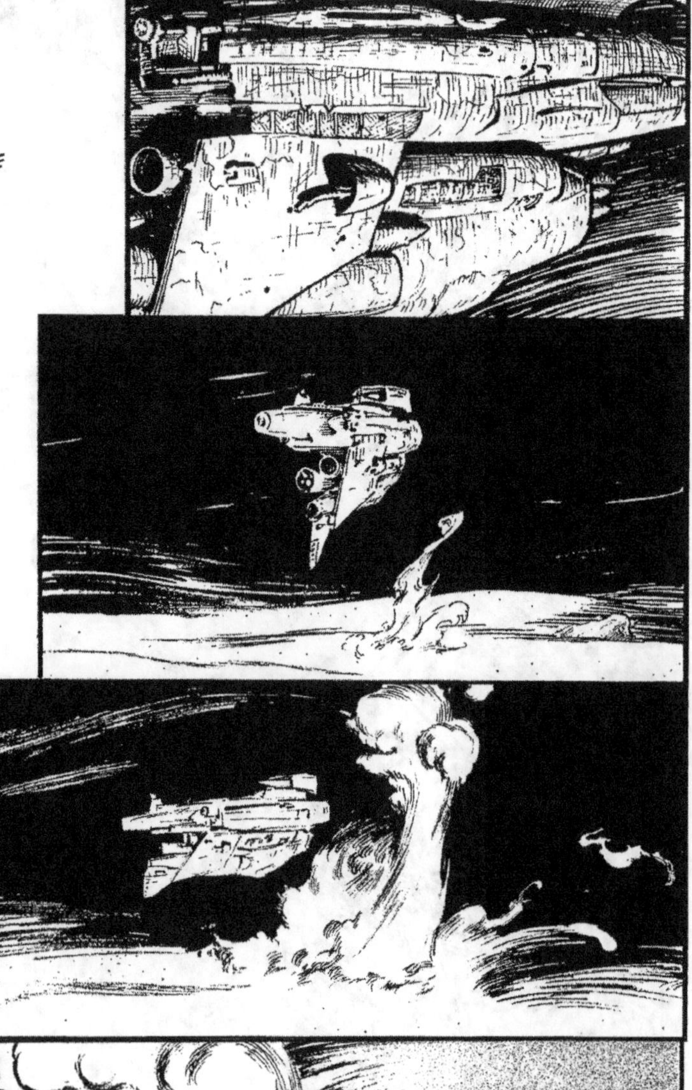
WE'VE BEEN DOWN HERE IN THE OCEANS OF TALLIS I, FIGHTING A WAR IN THE DARK.

ALL THAT WATER ABOVE US, THAT INKY LIQUID SHADOW, SEEMS TO BE COMPRESSING THE ALREADY RAT-HOLE NARROW HALLS OF THE XII DREADNOUGHT CLASS WARSHIP.

I HATED BEING UNDER WATER WORSE THAN VACUUM - IT'S THICK AND IT'S HEAVY AND IT ECHOES THROUGH THE HULL.

BUT CLAUSTROPHOBIA WAS THE LEAST OF MY PROBLEMS.

MY NAME IS ANNA. ANNA MANDRETTA. THE TERRAN REPUBLIC NEEDED ME TO HELP DEFEND ITS INTERESTS AGAINST THE XAX.

THEY YANKED ME RIGHT OUT OF MY MOP-SLINGING JOB AT THE MCSOYBURGER AND I WAS FLUNG INTO DEEP SPACE.

SO I SIGNED A WORK ORDER AT GUNPOINT, HAD A SIX-HOUR CRASH COURSE IN MEAT-CARVING AND WAS PART OF THE CONSCRIPTED CIVILIAN WORKFORCE DEFENDING HUMANITY.

A-ROOGA-RO

PERSONNEL – REPORT TO BATTLE STA

SONNEL – REPORT TO BATTLE STATION

PERSONNEL – REPORT TO BATTLE STA

SONNEL – REPORT TO BA

WEIRDLING
continued on page 48

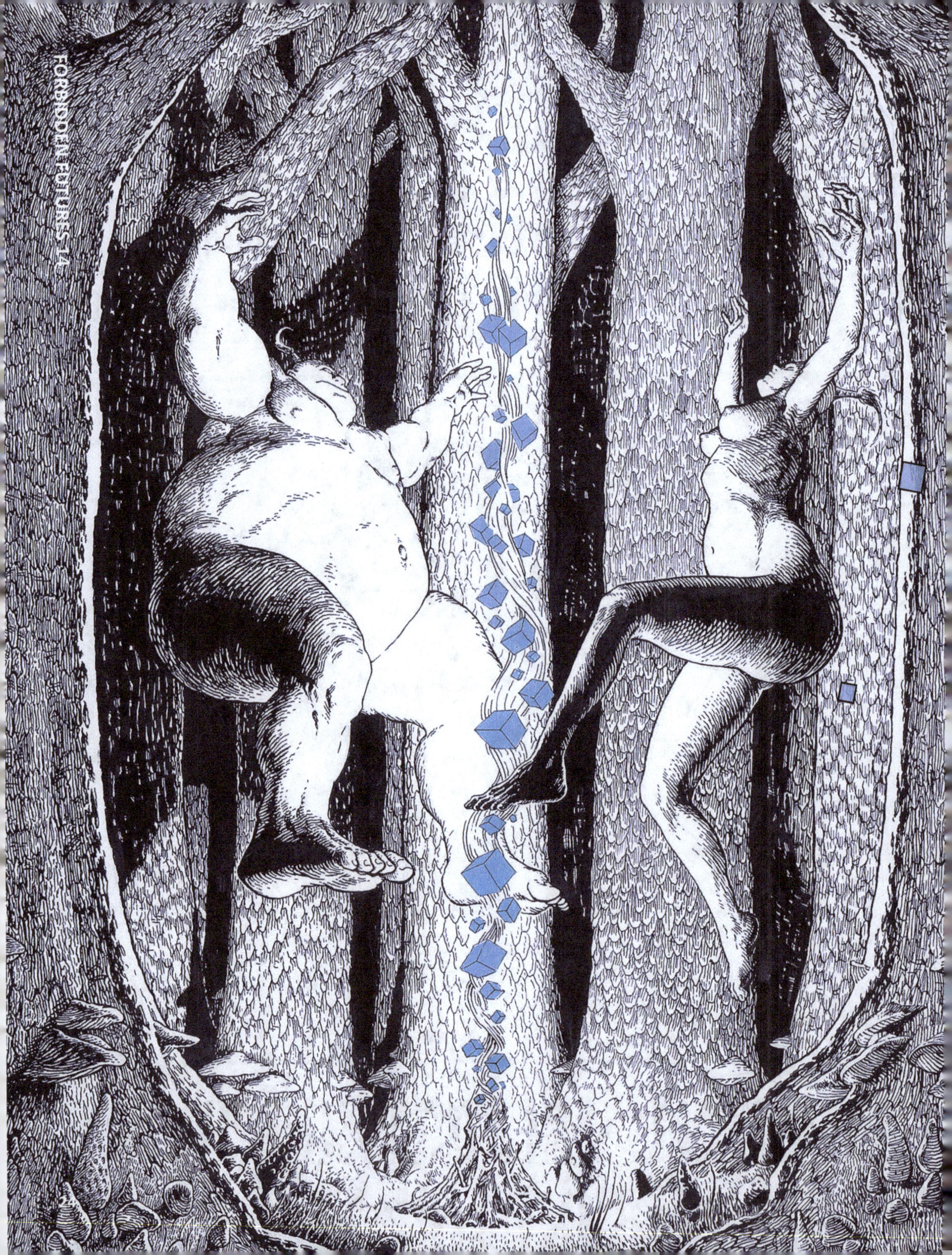
FORBIDDEN FUTURES 14

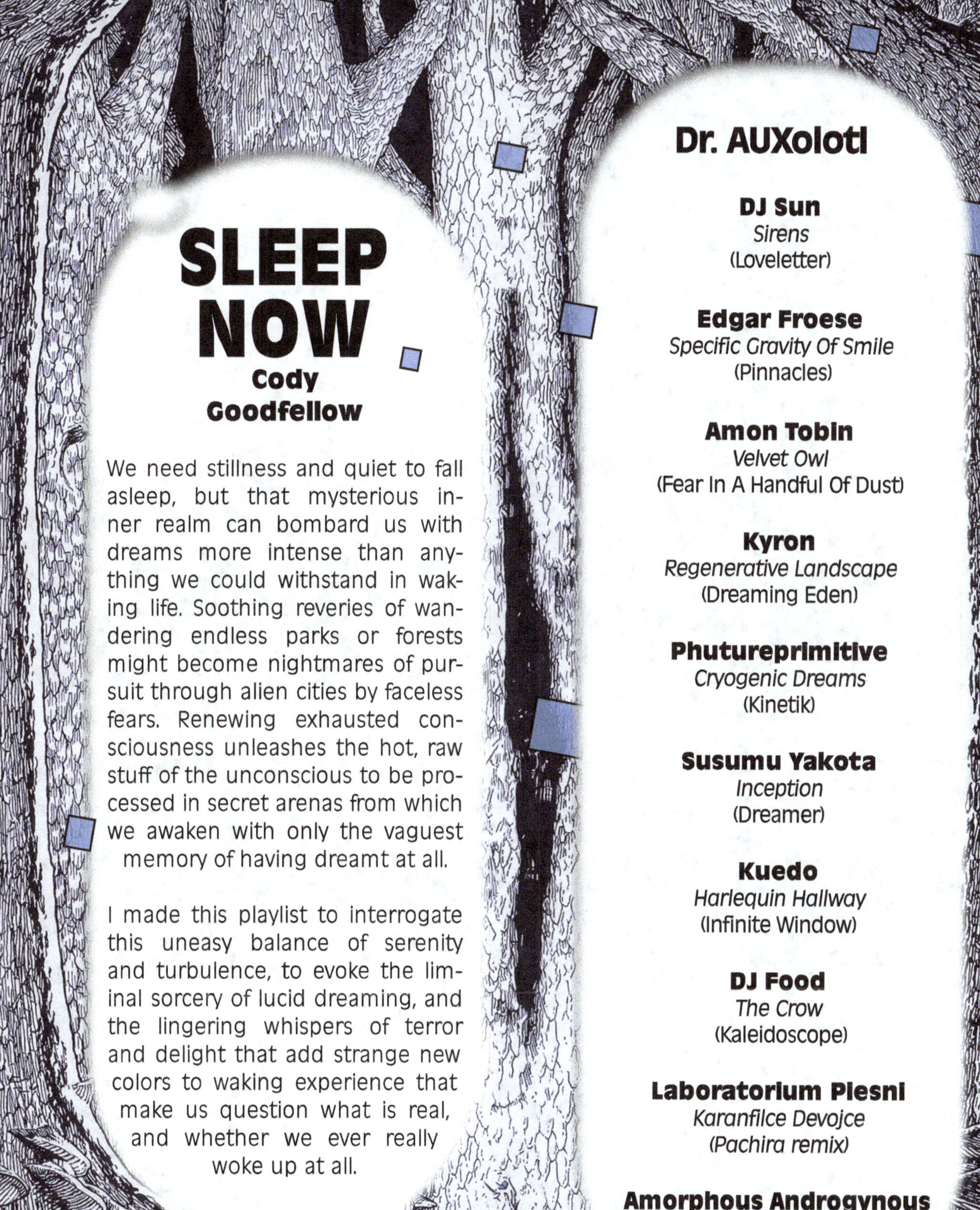

SLEEP NOW

Cody Goodfellow

We need stillness and quiet to fall asleep, but that mysterious inner realm can bombard us with dreams more intense than anything we could withstand in waking life. Soothing reveries of wandering endless parks or forests might become nightmares of pursuit through alien cities by faceless fears. Renewing exhausted consciousness unleashes the hot, raw stuff of the unconscious to be processed in secret arenas from which we awaken with only the vaguest memory of having dreamt at all.

I made this playlist to interrogate this uneasy balance of serenity and turbulence, to evoke the liminal sorcery of lucid dreaming, and the lingering whispers of terror and delight that add strange new colors to waking experience that make us question what is real, and whether we ever really woke up at all.

Dr. AUXolotl

DJ Sun
Sirens
(Loveletter)

Edgar Froese
Specific Gravity Of Smile
(Pinnacles)

Amon Tobin
Velvet Owl
(Fear In A Handful Of Dust)

Kyron
Regenerative Landscape
(Dreaming Eden)

Phutureprimitive
Cryogenic Dreams
(Kinetik)

Susumu Yakota
Inception
(Dreamer)

Kuedo
Harlequin Hallway
(Infinite Window)

DJ Food
The Crow
(Kaleidoscope)

Laboratorium Piesni
Karanfilce Devojce
(Pachira remix)

Amorphous Androgynous
Indian Swing
(Alice In Ultraland)

DREAMER

By Joshua Sky

You've gotta be kidding. Of all the times for the technicians to screw up, they've gotta do it when they activate my cryochamber? They accidentally froze me half-conscious. Schmucks!

I've got no motor coordination. I can't scream, let alone open my eyes. All I've got is me, myself, and my thoughts. Luckily, the plotted trajectory for the good ol' starship Hammerfall, is only, give or take, half a millennia (Earth-time) to its destination. So, it all comes down to simply entertaining myself for about 500 years. I'm not even sure how much time has already passed. Five minutes? Man, I knew I should've tipped the sleep tech better.

Talk about being fucked.

Think positive. I'm not dead, right? Or maybe I am, and this is what happens when you bite the big one. All you've got is your floating consciousness, for all eternity. Stay positive. Ride the upside. Dead or alive, I know that I exist and I can still dream, which means I can go anywhere and do anything within the far-flung bastions of my mind. So there's hope. Even more, there's vision. I can plot out any story, relive any memory.

Not to brag, but I've gotten pretty damn good at dreaming. With nothing else to do but practice, I've been able to focus, painstakingly enhancing the fidelity of my every fantasy. I'm certain anyone can fold time in their mind if they just index their thought patterns correctly. A moment, if spent right, can last a lifetime. I've lived quite a few journeys, unfurling mega-epics that I was kicking around in the back of my mind. From the wars of Ogdaria, where kingdoms wage battles in order to control the Haitaro, a hyper-intelligent race of flamingos, cursed without hands. To the astral adventures of Topper and Zero, about a man and his dog who perished in a tragic accident and travel through the afterlife, helping to heal the trauma different angels endured when they were alive. Countless fantasies. Countless universes.

Sometimes, they allow me to forget my cosmic predicament. I wonder if this is what it's like to be a processing computer. No extra-sensory, just mental computation. Though a machine is a lot smarter than I am.

I'm really worried about my family. Alicia and the kids are in the same row of pods as me. Lord, I'm hoping they don't have the same problem. Though, she'd be better at handling this. She always has the right attitude; she is comfortable in her own skin, with her own thoughts. Hell, would she even miss me? I used to joke that she'd make me wait an eternity in the afterlife. Maybe that's what's playing out now. "Oh, don't worry about Daryl, he's just taking a long nap. Always lazy, that one."

I miss her and our kids.

What if there are other problems with the ship's computers? That would endanger the family. I can't think about that. Because there's literally nothing I can do. The worry will corrode my innards if I let it, and this is definitely a marathon across parsecs, not a sprint. Our destination is the Paradise System. It harbors a string of verdant ocean worlds without continents, but instead, vast constellations of lush, gorgeous island archipelagos. I've always dreamt of living on a tropical island, and these, being part of the new colonial frontier, are quite affordable. All the isles back on Old Earth are untouchable price-wise, and overpopulated too. So this presented a chance for a better future for our children.

I keep reflecting on all the special times we've had. Simple things, like taking long drives across the hover byways. Strolling through supermarket aisles with Hannah, who loved staring at the colorful cereal boxes. Food would be pretty sweet right about now. Oddly, I'm not hungry, but it would be great to enjoy the sensation of taste. The only thing I can feel, outside of an undulation of emotions, is cold compressed, canned air. I keep picturing the last time we all went out for ice cream, how I stained my new shirt with a dollop of Rocky Road. Marshmallows. Chocolate. Almond fudge. Drool.

The brave man dies once.

The coward a thousand times. But the dreamer, ah, lives innumerable lifetimes. I've been reliving my life. Every moment. All the triumphs and tragedies. Playing out what could have been. What was and is. How I didn't have the guts to go out with Cory Ellers during the Sophomore Dance when I was 15. She even asked me out, but I stupidly told her that I was busy working. At the library! What kind of an idiot was I? We ditched school once to see a show at the robo-theatre, and she later complained I was so into it that I didn't notice how she was hoping I would make a move.

Or, other fantastic follies, like when my old neighbor Tyler, when we were 12, knocked on my door to take one last walk before his family moved off-world. I was too busy being jacked-in to the latest shoot 'em up that I passed on hanging out. I can still see the disappointment on his face. It was the climax of our friendship, and I would rather spend it playing video games. That's the thing adults don't tell you when you're a kid, that the decisions you make, no matter how old you are, affect you later. They teach that mainly in the teenage part of growing up, but it still applies to childhood. I would run into Tyler again, but 26 years later, in our late 30s. When we had been battle-worn by work, obligations, and time.

Time. Time. Time.

Tick. Tick. Tick.

My biggest sources of guilt have followed me everywhere, including this predicament. Like blackholes, they have an inescapable gravitational pull of their own. The first end-less void of remorse was not being a better son to my father. He walked out on the family. It caused a lot of damage and hardship. But in the end, I still could've been better to him, especially when he kept reaching out near the end. I should have been kinder. I was told that on his deathbed, he was screaming my name. That scene often enters my mind, and it haunts me.

Then there was my other folly, which was cheating on Racquel. I was young and stupid and horny. I was 22, okay? There were unrequited feelings for my ex. But still, it was wrong. I broke character. And though it was never meant to be, I hurt someone, and I've come to learn that I really don't like doing that. I just wish I never caused any pain or suffering. Friends have accused me of being a people pleaser. But so what? Couldn't you say that Superman is one, too?

All the alternate realities of doing what's right, or following a different path, have been lived through before my mind's eye. Again and again. Oddly, it hasn't made me feel better. I suppose I need to take satisfaction in the life I've lived.

I do.

Reframe.

Looking at my current situation, it's the opportunity of at least five lifetimes. I'm still unsure how much time has passed, but I don't think that matters anymore. All the answers are here. Within. They always have been, lying in wait. All the progress humanity has achieved, every invention and breakthrough, was around since we first stood upright, we just needed to crack the knowledge behind the discoveries. The same goes

for each of us spiritually. Our truths are present, we can uplift them so long as we try. The machines can do anything we can, but better, except for being human. Inward, there's a multiverse. A cosmology of feelings and self. There are more memories to be made, stories to create. Instead of half consciousness or purgatory, I've been frozen in a state of zen.

Why can't I just fall asleep?

WYRMQUEST
BY JEFFREY THOMAS

To this end, he calculated what he expected to be the next stop in the Wyrm's long, circular migration through the galaxy, setting forth in his one-man craft. Of course, his main objective was to defeat the mindless starbeast before it could circle back to his home world again to wreak further destruction, vacuuming up whole villages as it was wont to do. Yurn couldn't follow the creature through the wyrmholes it slowly burrowed through spacetime in its travels, and thus he calibrated his ship's cryopod so that he would awaken several years from now at his destination, just as the Wyrm arrived there itself.

Of course, his calculations could not be expected to be perfect right down to the day, let alone hour. When he arrived at the first world where he planned to confront the starbeast, he found it had already emerged from its wyrmhole and swung its immense, pulsing body low over the planet's surface, sucking up whole hordes of the gentle sentient ungulates that grazed its vast grasslands. Still, he jetted forth through the air from his hovering craft and attacked the starbeast with beams fired from his gauntlets, burning long tracts through the Wyrm's membranes and causing its purple blood to rain upon the savannah. Wounded, the creature fled back into space, tunneling a fresh wyrmhole, and the grateful survivors of its attack watched Yurn jet back to his craft and chase after the Wyrm in the hopes of arriving at the next stop in its migration earlier this time, before it could inflict so many casualties. Once again he calibrated his cryopod and entered suspended animation, for almost a dozen years on this jump.

He did in fact arrive at the next planet before the Wyrm, but much too early. He spent nearly two years waiting for it to catch up to him, befriending the indigenous race of fragrant plant beings and even taking a wife among them. When the starbeast finally emerged above their forested world, an army Yurn had trained was ready for it. The Wyrm was already furrowed with scars from Yurn's last battle with it, and now in addition to his gauntlet beams the monster was met with volleys of poison-tipped spores. The Wyrm sucked up only a few plant beings before it plunged back into the fabric of spacetime. Yurn bid his new wife farewell, knowing that he was too far along in years to ever pass this way again, but then he had left a trail of wives behind him during his decades of space battles.

On he jumped, sometimes arriving after the monster, sometimes before, never quite at the same instant—as to be expected. Again and again he engaged it, the crystals in his gauntlets becoming increasingly depleted. He was too far from home by now to have the gauntlets replaced, so he hoped they would retain enough power to finally overwhelm the increasingly wounded starbeast before it could cycle back to the planet of his own people.

Yurn was encouraged, though, knowing that the next world in the monster's journey was home to the giant green Cyclopi, a proud warrior race with whom his own people had sometimes traded. Yurn knew generations of Cyclopi had been ravaged by the Wyrm, and expected them to welcome his assistance in battling it. According to his calculations, he figured the Cyclopi would just be awakening from their deep hibernation, which lasted for about a decade at a time.

Indeed, though he could not communicate with the silent Cyclopi verbally they welcomed his arrival, and together they engaged the Wyrm. However, once again Yurn had miscalculated. The Cyclopi hadn't just emerged from hibernation, but instead dropped into their long slumber right there on the battlefield in the middle of the fight. In horror, Yurn could only continue to do battle with the ravenous monstrosity alone...even as the last of his gauntlets' power drained away.

THE SLEEPDOM'S LOTTERY

by Anna Tambour

The sleepdom's lottery is rigged. So crooked that a stroke of lightning has hung suspended, thundering away in jelly-shaking snores for so long, only Chair Stone mightn't think the sky always had that obnoxiously loud light-polluting split.

Not that anyone knows what Chair Stone thinks, it having slept so long, a red-hatted army of soldier lichen bristles from it, headrest to feet, lest anyone forget.

For winners earn the right to sleep as long as their wont and wish.

And sleep, to the rest, is just a fantasy, though one returned to the woke to tell the tale of living in the glittering castle built of Snail's slime.

"It doesn't add up," snapped Hypatia, weighing a heavy egg. "Tell us the truth, or that sleeping bubble will get it. Whyever would you leave that castle? Didn't you say it had nasturtiums growing up the walls and fields around it filled with lettuces?"

She had never won so much as a catnap, so Snail refrained from a foot-jerk reaction.

"It did at that." Snail's foot slid embarrassingly down Bigbrain's skull.

The fairy noticed nothing, but she was never observant. just confident. "So you were living the dream!"

"Dreaming a living, your Excellentia. There is a distinction."

"Not in the winnings."

"In the small print."

"Who reads—"

"Precisely," Snail said sadly.

"But those views."

"Of the sea."

"Yes! Sea breezes instead of this muggy—" She hurled the egg at the bubble, which twitched, only enraging her more. "You threw away the greatest prize any of us can have. For what?"

Snail shrugged dream-grown wings. "Life" was too obvious to say.

"And those ridiculous wings! A snail with wings is like a fish with—"

"Actually, I had the choice of a bicycle or wings." Snail didn't feel comfortable revealing the pain of slime dryup, and the shame of muscle attrition to this most critical, unobservant critic—someone who hadn't even noticed how weak and wandering Snail's eyes had become.

Hypatia leapt off her seat, but not before throwing back without looking at Snail, "The lottery's rigged. You won, and what a waste."

"I'd never come back," she swore. "I'd never come back," she said, kicking Bigbrain, swearing her oath and sealing it with a kick at everyone else in her path.

OH, EY. What would you reckon? The lottery isn't rigged. Hypatia won—fair and square, as she insisted. It all added up. She who had never even blinked, won! "I am humbled," she crowed.

That was, like Chair Rock's win, before my time. So long, a sleeping snaketree has melded its roots with her tresses.

It's a hike to her, as she lies in the dankest most sound-muffled patch of the sleepdom. We can't have children running into her, or when they grow up, the sleepdom will never be able to sell a lottery ticket.

THE GODDESS OF DREAMHEAVEN

BY CHAD STROUP

I dream I am a devil who yearns to be an angel but in real life only exists as a common man, and I do not favor it.

However, like any man with a sharp sense of ambition, I set about to change my circumstances. I have a singular goal, daunting as it may seem, and I plan to achieve it.

It takes far longer than I expect to locate God—or the being who claims this title as its own. I must transcend the waking world of Earthhell and enter Dreamheaven. Per the suggestion of a local street miscreant claiming to be some sort of witch doctor, I need to enter the dreams of a true believer. The alleged witch doctor scrawls the obscure instructions on the back side of a handbill for a sober living home. To my surprise, his instructions are a success, though they come complete with a frustrating learning curve. On my first three attempts, I leave the hosts in a state of perpetual nightmare. One reliving the premature death of his pubescent daughter at the massive hands of her soccer coach, the next trapped in a thick loop of silverfish skittering in and out of every flesh orifice, the third grounded in a universe that was devoid of unconditional love.

For this I will be eternally sorry.

The fourth host becomes my treasured vessel. A woman. I did not know I would have to assume her form, her essence, for my plan to work, and so I must adjust. I know it will matter not once I plead my case to God, as neither devils nor angels nor other denizens of Dreamheaven possess genitals or chromosomes or anything else on the spectrum that assigns one the unchosen role of a man or a woman. In this unknown world exist only those who fall in between. To call them androgynous, however, would be a gross understatement. Gender is a human concept, one that is not granted passage in Dreamheaven. These beings have defeated what it means to be human, to be slaves to the bodies they were granted at birth, and they are all the better for it.

The first thing I see upon entering their domain is an orgy—or a mockery of one, the likes of which would result in several arrests and law-

suits on Earthhell. Though they possess no orifices nor anything with which to penetrate them, they have still discovered ways to derive pleasure. Their moaning is music, notes so beautiful were they heard in the waking world they would cause eardrums to blister. Then, once healed, these damaged drums would blossom, bearing flowers boasting colors that should not be allowed to exist.

The angels and devils beckon to me, inviting me to join in their merry faux fuck. Something stirs in me, a sensation I do not understand, perhaps because I have spent so much of my life socialized as something I am not versus the being I have now become. They move toward me, hesitant, brandishing crude weapons constructed from bone and human leather. I recognize it as human leather because there are faded traces of tattoo work on the flesh of one weapon.

Before I can change direction, they attack. I scream, expecting the wail of a bitter banshee but only hearing the distinct emptiness of no sound at all. I have never felt so helpless. They tear at what little clothing I wear upon my breasts and hips, and I go tharn. Though once they discern my body is that of a waking woman possessing the pretty little details they do not, the parts they have no use for, they quickly lose interest. And so I press on.

I pass through a thin, wet membrane. Pieces of it trail behind me like persistent cobwebs. The next realm I reach is no less erotic, though it disturbs me in a way I cannot quite fathom. The ground is riddled with corpses, each of whom are missing some key body part. Yet they are still living, or whatever passes for life in Dreamheaven. They moan in orgasmic distress, similar to the beings I encountered in the previous space. However, these corpses wear no masks of pleasure, and for that I find them to be infinitely more honest. They smell like honeysuckle. But then I remember that

the sense of smell does not exist in dreams. I am assigning my own scented memories—or perhaps my host's memories—to events that have yet to occur. The promise of death, of immolation, always lurking.

These beings, too, beg for me to join them. But it is not yet my time.

To die, to enter a state of perpetual ecstasy. I still need to finish my quest to find God.

I kneel as close as I can stomach to the fetish corpse nearest to me, body spread supine, jaw hanging askew. I ask where I can find my adversary. With chattery teeth and livery lips it informs me that God is a human construct and that if I continue my search for something that does not exist, I will become lost in Dreamheaven forever. Instead, I must learn its real name and call out to it in the abyss.

I should have known this quest would prove to be more challenging than I initially assumed. I do not know how soon I will encounter this strange abyss, but I expect it will be most unpleasant.

I trudge into the next realm. The ground is the texture of undercooked scrambled eggs. The sky is lilac and finite, defined by a jagged black border. And the air is too thick and dust-ridden to breathe comfortably. Small creatures writhe in the crevices of existence. And yet another sensation runs through me that I cannot name. It is beyond the five senses of wo(man). It is then that I realize I have already reached the abyss. I have arrived at the end of Dreamheaven, the kingdom of God.

Or whatever its name might be.

I call out the first pseudonym that comes to mind, and it is a familiar one.

Mykel.

It rings a powerful bell because I feel as if it belongs to me in some way. It may be my name back on Earthhell. I have already forgotten. Or is it my host's name? Perhaps it is both.

Perhaps I have been God all along. Wouldn't that be a riot? And also far too thin of a web to be woven.

But then a sound soars from the abyss, sliding shivers through my soul. Mykel answering my call. Singing in a language of spiritual climax. Burning through my Dreamheaven body like dry ice that has been clutched a few seconds too long.

Somehow, I can discern what Mykel says to me, despite it not being spoken in any language that could be deciphered on Earthhell, although I do not understand the implications. I am unsure whether I am set to transcend my former self and become what I was always intended to be—a dreamborne chrysalis—or if I am to remain in my given husk and bones.

To learn my fate, I must step into the abyss, enter Mykel's embrace. The ultimate trust fall. And so I do.

I am weightless. For a moment, for eternity, who can say? Time is relative in Dreamheaven.

I enter the deepest pocket of black, a womb I would rather not be ejected from. If only I had the choice. But dreams and nightmares are not about choice. They are about discovery.

Black fades to grey bleeds to blinding white.

I awake from Dreamheaven, choke upon my return to Earthhell, if it in fact does exist. I heave myself from my bed, hobble to the bathroom and peer into the medicine cabinet mirror. I see what hideous mistake God/Mykel has made of me, return to my bed, and cry myself back to sleep.

TO SLEEP, PERCHANCE TO DREAM

BY JESSE ROSE

Hey there….have you been getting enough sleep lately? Looks like you've been burning the midnight oil lately, my friend. I know the signs all too well: the dark circles under the eyes, the drooping eyelids, the constant yawning…they're a dead giveaway. Why don't you take a seat over here and rest for a second, maybe enjoy a nice cup of chamomile tea?

There you go. That's much better, isn't it? Well, now that you're comfy, why don't we talk about sleep? The nature and mysteries of it have beguiled us for centuries. From early Greek philosophers like Alcmaeon and Aristotle proposing hypotheses about sleep deriving from a lack of blood flow to the brain or being part of the digestive process, to ancient peoples from Egypt, Rome, and Greece worshipping gods like Isis, Somnus, and Morpheus as lords of the realm of slumber, we've had some interesting ideas about how sleep works and why we do it for eons. Centuries later, we know more about these questions than ever before, and sleep has become a multi-billion-dollar business, giving rise to a plethora of sleep aids ranging from medications and breathing apparatuses to specialized mattresses and noisemakers that emit relaxing sounds of all colors of the rainbow.

Sleep has figured prominently in various artistic creations over the ages, including literature, plays, paintings, and music, but it seems that perhaps the most appropriate medium to explore the subject is film. After all, what is a movie but a waking dream one can get lost in for a while? For that reason, let's cover 13 of the most essential cinematic offerings that either focus on the concept of sleep or use some aspect of it as a creative narrative device. Hey, couldn't hurt, right? Maybe it'll put you into a more relaxed mood to help catch some winks tonight.

THE WIZARD OF OZ

There might be no better movie to start with than this 1939 classic, not only due to its beloved reputation over the decades, but also because it's one of the earliest and best examples of dream-based cinema. It's argued that the narrative trope of "It was all just a dream!" is the most despised storytelling device, seen as lazy, devoid of thought, and negating the power of everything that had transpired before awakening, but Oz is one of the few examples of a movie that employs this device successfully, so much so that it's considered one of the most charming elements of the movie. The land of Oz that young Dorothy (Judy Garland) and her little dog Toto travel to is a magical, visually-stunning landscape that already feels like a dream thanks to its vibrant colors and surreal architecture, and the fact that many of the actors who first appear as residents of Kansas later fill the roles of Oz denizens like Scarecrow, Tin Man, Cowardly Lion, the Wicked Witch, and the Great Wizard himself hints to the audience that while we're not in Kansas anymore, Toto, we might not be as far away as we think, either. And as Dorothy's arc goes from wishing she was anywhere else than her farmstead to tearfully exclaiming "There's no place like home!" in a bed surrounded by loved ones, awakening from a dream still feels like a satisfying and emotional end to the journey. Any film buff desiring to dip their toes into sleep-based cinema should consider making their first step on the Yellow Brick Road.

SLEEPING BEAUTY

Though Disney had previously explored the concept of sleep playing a crucial role in a fairy tale setting in their first full-length animated feature, 1937's Snow White and the Seven Dwarfs, it's elaborated upon even further in 1959's Sleeping Beauty, an adaptation of the centuries-old fairy tale about a princess cursed to eternal slumber at the prick of her finger on a spinning wheel's spindle. Interestingly, sleep is reframed here as more of a saving grace than it is in Snow White, as the curse is originally intended to deliver death upon Princess Aurora before one of the three kindly fairies changes it to one of everlasting sleep that can be broken by true love's kiss. Additionally, the fairies later cast a spell to put the entire kingdom to sleep to allow more time for them to save the day with the valiant Prince Phillip. Thanks to its beautiful, stately animation and the popularity of Maleficent as one of Disney's best villainesses, Sleeping Beauty has withstood the test of time as one of the company's most beloved features, and viewers should give it the chance to cast its own pleasant spell over them.

INVASION OF THE BODY SNATCHERS

Quality horror movie remakes are hard to come by, but this 1978 update to the original 1959 Body Snatchers film is one of the best. Moving the setting from a small town to San Francisco, it follows two health department workers who begin to suspect that the population is being replaced with emotionless doppelgangers, later found to be creatures derived from alien plants that duplicate human beings while they sleep in order to replace and dispose of them…the dreaded "pod people", in the parlance of our times. Snatchers is a tight and disturbing thriller, instilling the paranoia of being surrounded by malevolent beings but having no way to know who they are or who is left that can be trusted. The notion of the creatures striking once a human is asleep taps into a primal fear, given that we are most vulnerable while we sleep…. and we all have to go to sleep sometime, don't we? Thanks to both its frightening audio/visual effects and thought-provoking themes about politics, conformity, and humanity, Snatchers is a film that any horror fan should allow to take root in their viewing schedule.

THE LATHE OF HEAVEN

This 1980 PBS adaptation of Ursula K. Le Guin's novel tells the story of a young man cursed with the uncontrollable ability to change reality by dreaming. He is assigned to a dream specialist who is initially skeptical of the man's claims, but when the doctor discovers that the man is telling the truth, he quickly endeavors to take advantage of this newfound power. Lathe deals heavily with the classic theme of people playing God when they shouldn't be, even if they are doing so for altruistic reasons, but it also throws in the element of the doctor's directives backfiring in a "Monkey's Paw"—like fashion—after all, dreams notoriously operate according to their own bizarre subconscious logic, so why would anyone think that they wouldn't cause some chaos? Shot on a shoestring budget from a public grant, Lathe comes up with some creative solutions to bring some of these dreams to life, and it stands as proof that an intelligent, thought-provoking film made with miniscule means can easily top an empty-headed blockbuster any day.

DREAMSCAPE

Multiple movies on this list deal with the concept of a person entering another person's dreams using some kind of futuristic technology, but 1984's Dreamscape was perhaps the first to do so, paving the way for later films like Paprika and Inception. Dennis Quaid stars here as a young, handsome rogue with psychic powers who is recruited into a secret government project that involves treating sleep disorders by infiltrating a person's dreams, but trouble arises when the president of the United States is admitted as a patient and an assassination conspiracy is brought to light. Dreamscape is a fun action sci-fi tale that knows what its audience wants in a lighter offering and delivers it well. A great deal of its success lies in its various dream sequences, especially those belonging to the president, where ruins of nuclear holocaust and radiation-burned victims are used to terrifying effect. Mix in a solid cast of character actors and some enjoyable, slightly-cheesy creature special effects, and you've got a delightful popcorn flick in Dreamscape.

A NIGHTMARE ON ELM STREET

After the breakout success of John Carpenter's 1978 film Halloween, slasher movies officially entered their Golden Era at the box office, but by 1984, they had to start feeling stale—how many times can you replicate the formula of a silent masked killer stabbing and slicing through nubile teens before it starts to get old? Horror maestro Wes Craven struck gold by adding his own spin on the concept, inspired by cases of Asian refugees who died unexpectedly in their sleep after experiencing nightmares: What if the killer stalked and murdered you in your dreams, where you are at your weakest and most vulnerable? Therein lies the brilliance of Freddy Krueger (Robert Englund), a disfigured, wisecracking specter who slays teens from beyond the grave using both his iconic knife-bladed glove and his powerful ability to manipulate the dream realm. Multiple films on this list include the concept of dying in real life after being killed within a dream, but only Nightmare advances the idea of the injuries sustained in the dream being replicated in reality: slashes from Freddy's glove, strangulation by bedsheet, or drowning in a bathtub. Made for a mere $1.8 million, Nightmare made the most of its budget, offering some creatively surreal sequences that captured the fear receptors of audiences, and it gave birth to an enormously successful franchise. The enduring legacy of Freddy can't be denied, and the original movie that brought him to life deserves its title as one of the finest horror movies ever made.

UNTIL THE END OF THE WORLD

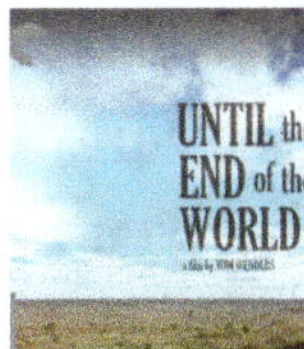

It's not often that the genres of ruminative arthouse picture and science fiction are combined, but Wim Wenders proved that it could be done in this sprawling 4.5(!)-hour-long 1991 sci-fi epic, a futuristic tale that centers around a love triangle of people (Solveig Dommartin, William Hurt, and Sam Neill), the winding cast of characters chasing them around the globe, a bag of stolen money, an experimental visual technology that allows people to experience the memories and dreams of others, and a malfunctioning nuclear satellite that threatens to destroy the world. Fans of Wenders' loose, relaxed style should find much to enjoy here, including beautiful cinematography of cities and landscapes shot in a variety of countries, a genuinely sweet and moving portrayal of humanity, and a soundtrack loaded with killer music from U2, Nick Cave and the Bad Seeds, Lou Reed, Julee Cruise, Neneh Cherry, Patti Smith, and Depeche Mode. The movie touches on a variety of themes, but it's the description of a recurrent dream that opens the film, and a key section of the plot involves addiction to the imagery of dreams, perhaps as a commentary on how dreams should be enjoyed but not pursued to the exclusion of reality. End is another magnificent entry to Wenders' stellar filmography, and viewers should endeavor to seek out its many pleasures.

DARK CITY

It's strange knowing that Alex Proyas' 1998 film Dark City and The Matrix were released so close together when they share so many key narrative concepts (and even some of the same sets), but what's even stranger is that while Matrix went on to worldwide recognition and acclaim, City remains unknown to many today despite being a masterful fusion of dark sci-fi and film noir. It follows an amnesiac man (Rufus Sewell) who wakes up in a mysterious city where it's always night and a group of otherworldly beings called the Strangers—pale, hairless humanoids clad in black fedoras and trench coats—use their powers to put the city's population to sleep every midnight, transform material surroundings, and inject new memories into inhabitants' minds, all in a grand experiment to further understand what makes us human. City is bolstered by its amazing cinematography and set design, with the shadowy city covered in Art Deco and German expressionist flourishes that recall other sci-fi stunners like Brazil, Metropolis, and Blade Runner, and the labyrinthine plot will have your head spiraling. It's a criminally slept-on offering, and lovers of cult sci-fi should definitely make time for it…perhaps even with a midnight viewing.

THE MATRIX

Exploding onto screens back in 1999, it's hard to understate what an effect the Wachowskis' masterwork The Matrix had on audiences at the time, blowing minds with its groundbreaking special effects, elaborate martial arts sequences, ultra-cool fashion aesthetics, and gripping narrative about an underground hacker (Keanu Reeves) whose existence is upended when he realizes that our reality is actually an elaborate virtual reality program created by machines to enslave and harvest human beings, and that he could be the prophesied figure known as "The One" who will free humanity from this digital prison. Matrix's elaborate mythology draws on a rich variety of thematic sources, but it works on a wider level that resonates with the majority of the population: Who hasn't felt like we are all just wandering about in a sleeping world, drifting aimlessly through a carefully-woven dream of commercialized banality masterminded by shadowy forces, waiting for someone to wake us up and take us to the "real world" where we can serve a greater purpose? The results of subsequent sequels have been mixed, but The Matrix easily deserves its crowning as one of the finest sci-films ever made, with many even considering it….The One.

PAPRIKA

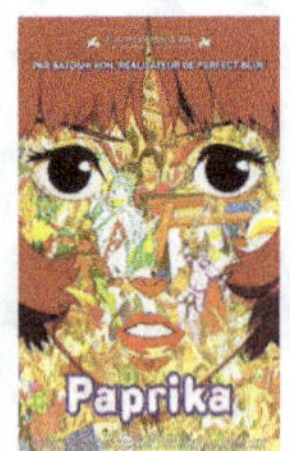

Japanese anime director Satoshi Kon, who we unfortunately lost at the age of 46 in 2010 to pancreatic cancer, managed to make a large impact on the world of mind-bending cinema, expanding craniums with offerings like Perfect Blue and Millennium Actress that explore the shifting depths of memory, consciousness, and mental illness. His influence is evident in the films of Darren Aronofsky like Requiem for a Dream and Black Swan, and it seems likely that his 2006 film Paprika was a crucial source of inspiration for Christopher Nolan's Inception, which came out just a few years later and shared similar concepts and visual references. Continuing forward the idea of using tech to enter the dreams of others, Paprika adds a few more ideas of its own, including exploring dreams via an alter ego, multi-level access to different areas of the subconscious, and attacks of "dream terrorism" that infect victims with madness even when not directly linked to a dream device. Filled with sorts of fun and inventive visuals, Paprika is a smart, flavorful addition to dreamy cinema that should not be missed.

PANDORUM

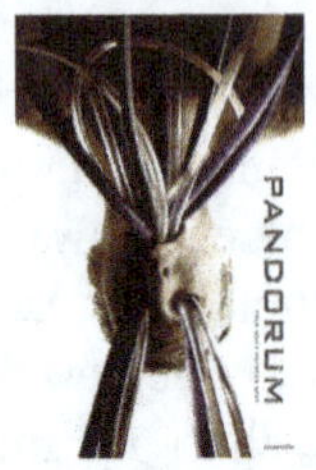

Suspended animation, whereby humans are induced into years-long slumber via the freezing temperatures of cryonics or some other means, is a handy literary device that helps explain how humans can endure the huge amounts of time needed to traverse space without aging, but it can also be used to add a twist to a story when something in the suspension process goes awry. 2009's Pandorum is one of the latter, following two astronauts (Ben Foster and Dennis Quaid) as they unexpectedly wake up from cryosleep on a large spacecraft, unable to remember who they are or what happened prior to their awakening. Much of Pandorum's power lies in the amazing set design, depicting most of the ship as grimy, industrial, and covered with debris, and the surroundings are often bathed in darkness pierced by colored lighting in hues of blue, red, and green, which also add much to the atmosphere. Critics and audiences initially rejected Pandorum, but it's more entertaining and effective than people give it credit for, and it deserves a second look.

INCEPTION

Christopher Nolan has rightfully taken his spot as one of modern cinema's most captivating dream-weavers, combining his dark cinematic style, knack for thrilling action sequences, and affinity for high-tech gadgetry to bring a mainstream blockbuster appeal to high-concept sci-fi stories that stretch the imagination to mind-melting degrees. 2010's Inception is perhaps the strongest demonstration of all of these qualities at work, starring Leonardo DiCaprio as a thief who specializes in the "extraction" of secrets from the dreams of others who puts together a team of specialists to perform the inverse of it—placing the "inception" of an idea in the mind of their target—despite harboring some dark secrets that threaten to unravel the entire operation and put everyone's lives at risk. Nolan expands even further on the "dream-linking" concept, adding new elements like layering sub-levels of dreams within dreams, the exponential expansion of time in each level, and motion in one dream altering the physics of another, all of it cleverly wrapped around the classic heist film plot to give things another fun twist. Other filmmakers might be content to produce tame or unchallenging fare, but Inception is Nolan's way of saying to them: You mustn't be afraid to dream a little bigger, darling.

ANIARA

This 2018 Swedish film follows the cruise-ship-like spacecraft Aniara as it sets off to trans-

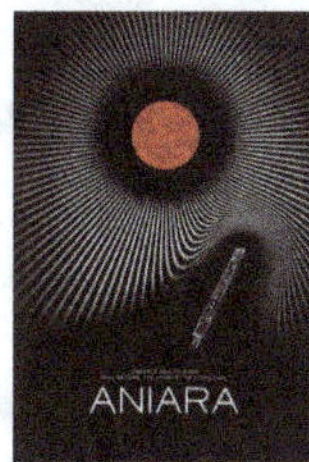

port hundreds of passengers from an uninhabitable Earth to a new settlement on Mars. After the ship is knocked off course and forced to jettison its fuel, the passengers must come to grips with the reality that they are now uncontrollably drifting through the endless blackness of space. Aniara is not the kind of film where brilliant minds rush to beat the clock and figure out a genius solution in the nick of time; it's established early on that there are no options to correct course or call for help, so we instead focus on the passengers' attempts to cope with this realization. At first, they begin to rely on the Mima, an AI program that allows them to escape into a dream-like trance that fills their minds with visions of a pristine, nature-filled paradise, but when it is destroyed due to overuse, they turn to other methods: some positive, others self-destructive. Aniara is an unrelentingly bleak movie with much to say about having to reckon with an unavoidable fate, and it will surely linger in the minds of viewers well after it's over.

All right, that's 13 films–plenty to get you started on the journey to explore the world of sleepy cinema! Now get yourself to bed and catch some Z's, won't you?

Sweet dreams…

THE RANDOM BOOK CLUB™

ONCE A MONTH, we send you two inches of books. Not the ones you wanted. Not the ones you expected. NOT even books we publish...maybe! Just... two inches of books. New or used. Pulled blindly from the ODDNESS bookshelf. No curation! No refunds!

Join at your own risk!

FOR NO ADDITIONAL INFORMATION, VISIT ODDNESS.US

PART II: DREAMS

In Webster's 1828 Dictionary, a "dream state" is defined as the thought or series of thoughts of a person in sleep, often wild and irregular and not under the command of reason.

DREAM TYPES

REM DREAMS *are a byproduct of intense neural signals in the limbic system and visual cortex during sleep.*

NON-REM DREAMS *during slow-wave sleep are fragmented and thought-like for the sleeper.*

LUCID DREAMS *are those in which the dreamer becomes aware that they are dreaming. In some cases, dreamers can even control their actions.*

DOWNLOADED DREAMS *are a machine-rendered interpretation that coexists alongside your memory of the event.*

Humanity now lives in the digital future predicted by science fiction authors, ushered in by the era of dream downloads! Did you know scientists can now generate imagery of what someone may have seen in a dream?

In 2013, researchers at Kyoto University used fMRI scans and machine learning to flag visual elements of dreams with an accuracy of up to 60%. To gather data, the test subjects were stirred during the early sleep stages and asked to describe their dreams so their brain activity could be correlated with visual word categories. These results were reverse-engineered to infer patterns and symbols from brainwave data, enabling statistical predictions.

In 2023, scientists at UC Berkeley and Osaka University demonstrated that fMRI patterns can be used to train AI image generators and generate videos of crude dreamscapes.

Dream downloads may become the preferred form of self-expression, allowing users to selectively replay a highlight reel of their favorite REM sessions for friends. If dream data can be captured and replayed, it is also possible that it can be stolen or altered. Tech giants have already normalized biometric tracking via apps, raising important questions: Could law enforcement subpoena your dream file? How long before you can buy dreams off the shelf? Could we earn money daydreaming?

MIKE DUBISCH:
WEIRDLING
2
X-11

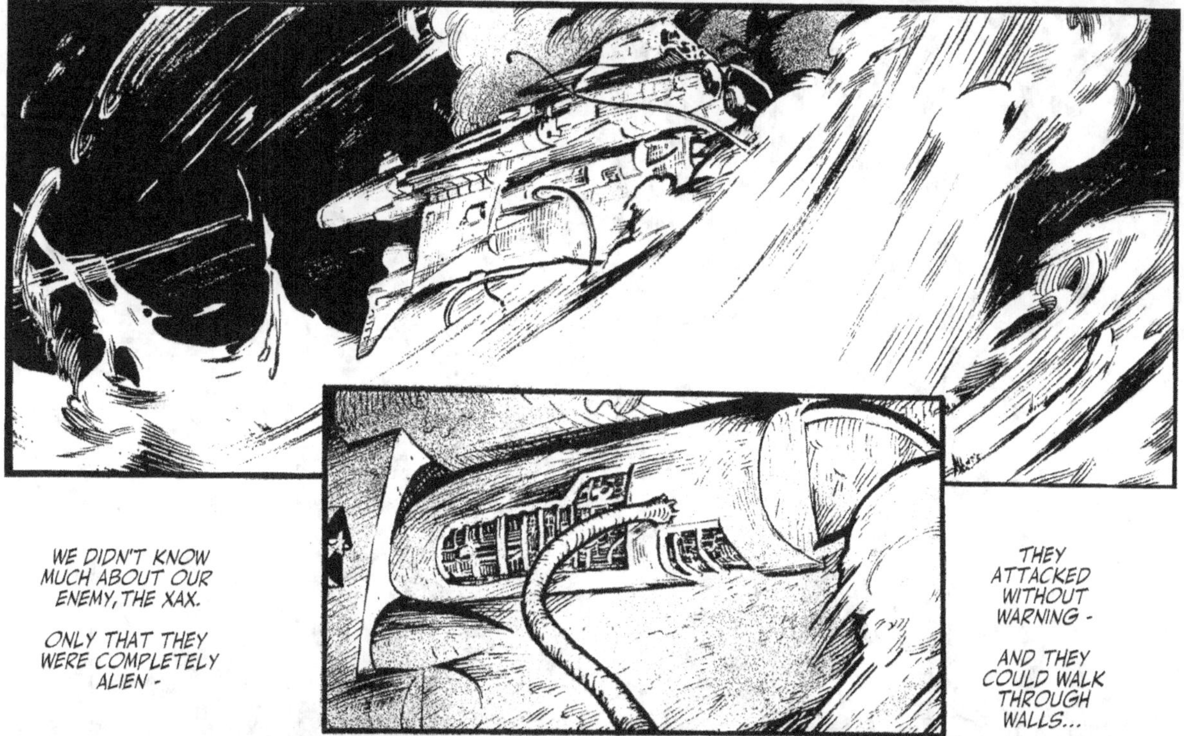
WE DIDN'T KNOW MUCH ABOUT OUR ENEMY, THE XAX.

ONLY THAT THEY WERE COMPLETELY ALIEN -

THEY ATTACKED WITHOUT WARNING -

AND THEY COULD WALK THROUGH WALLS...

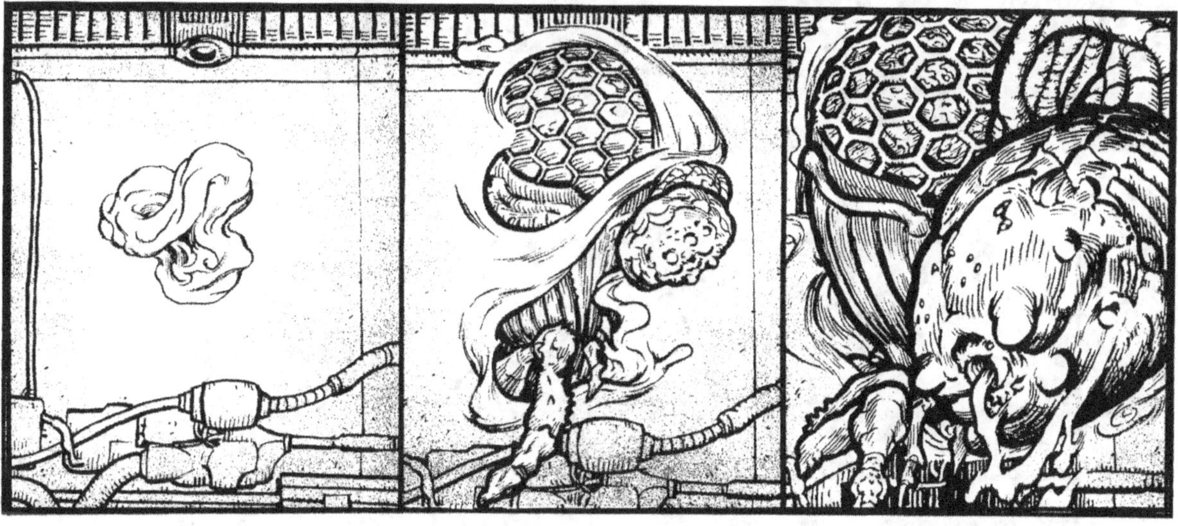

ANY WOUNDED? ANY MEN DOWN?

BACK THERE - WE HAD TO LEAVE BACH...

THE AIR WAS FILLED WITH THE SMELL OF GUNSMOKE AND STEAM JETTED FROM VENTS AT MY FEET, BUT I DIDN'T SEE ANY SLIME.

I FOUND THE GRUNT NEAR A SEAL ON LEVEL FIVE.

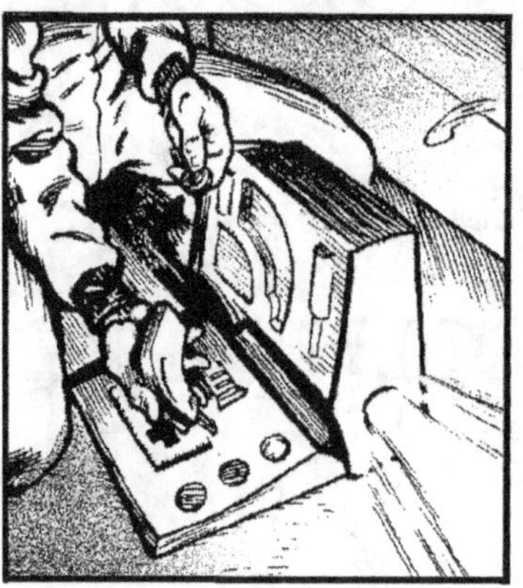

I TOOK OUT THE SMART SCALPEL AND AN M.T. -

HE'D BEEN SLIMED PRETTY BAD.

THE MEAT TENDERIZER TURNS HIM RIGHT OFF.

THIS WAS GONNA HURT ME MORE THAN IT HURT HIM.

THAT IS, NOT AT ALL.

THE SCALPEL HUMS IN MY HAND.

ONCE REMOVED, THE AFFECTED FLESH MELTED QUICKLY INTO THE SHREDDED REMAINS OF HIS BOOT.

I PULLED OFF THE M.T. AND DRAGGED THE SOLDIER TO HIS FEET.
BACH STILL GRIPPED HIS WEAPON, ALERT FOR THE ENEMY AND FOR—
SPLAT
SLIME!

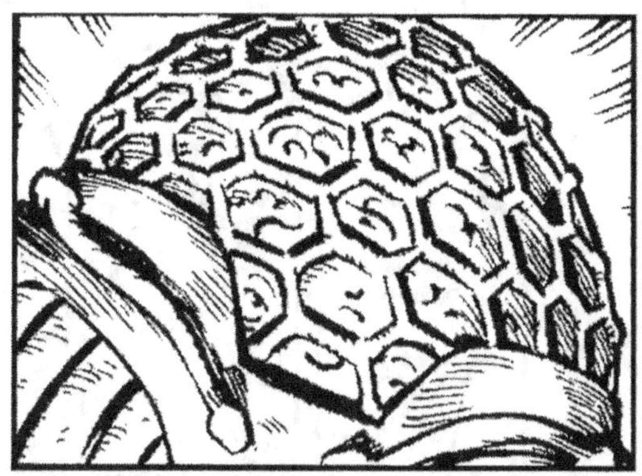

WE COULD BOTH STILL LIVE IF WE JUST BACKED AWAY—BUT I WAS FROZEN WITH HORROR AND INSECT FEAR.

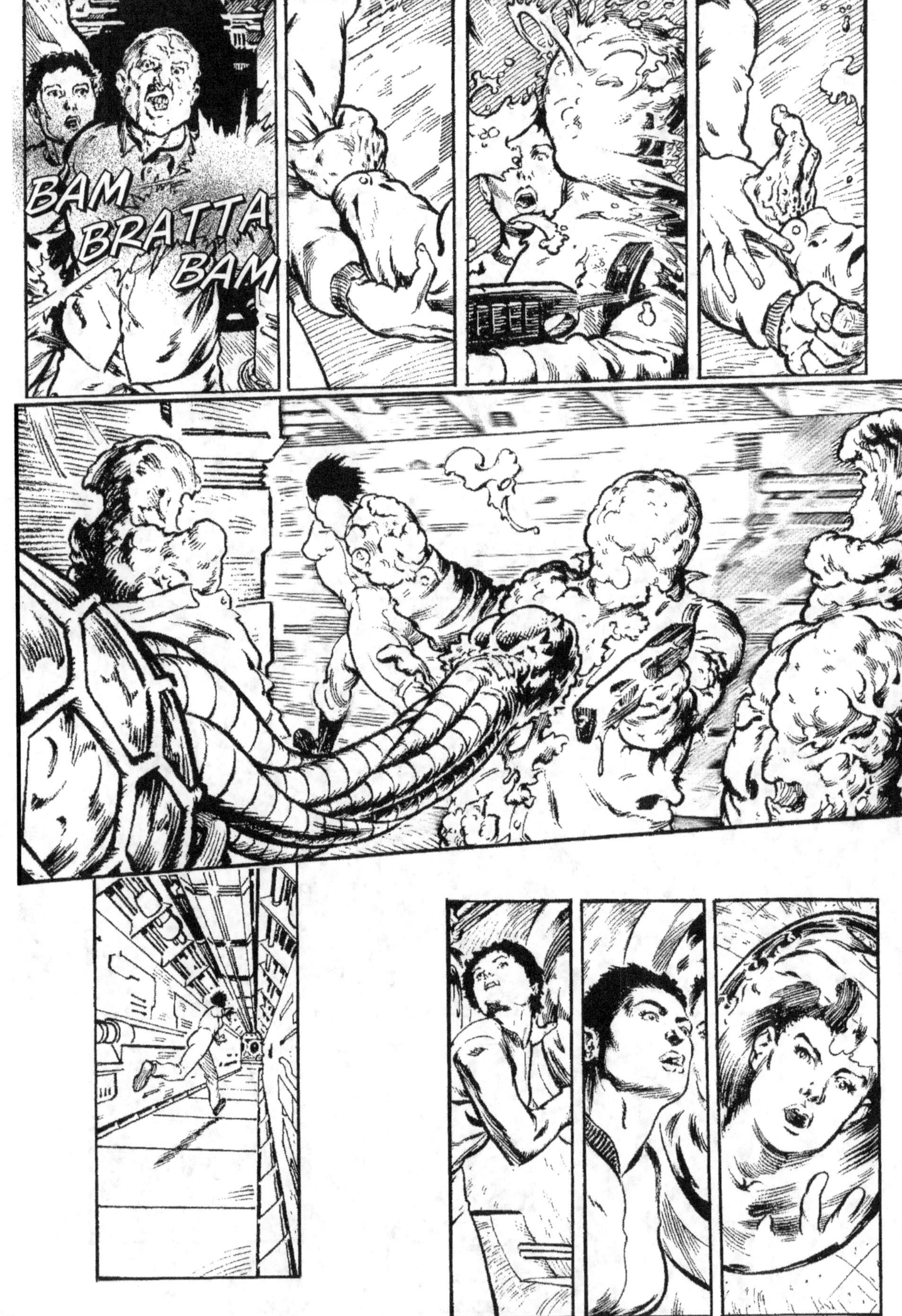
BAM
BRATTA
BAM

SAFE - FOR NOW... I'D DROPPED MY MED-KIT. I HAD TO MAKE MY WAY TO A WORKSHOP. PROCEDURE.
BACH, THE OTHERS, THEY WEREN'T HUMAN ANYMORE. BUT THERE WERE OTHERS I COULD STILL SAVE.
HEY -
HEY, SOMEBODY DOWN THERE?
THE TURBULENCE WAS A GOOD SIGN - WE'D BE STILL AS STONE IF THE XAX CENTIPEDE HAD MANAGED TO WRAP US UP.
SOMEHOW, I KEPT MOVING.

IT'S THE CONDITIONING.
I COULD HOIST THE GRUNT, GORMAN, UP ONTO MY BACK, CARRY HIM THROUGH TREMBLING PASSAGES TO THE WORKSHOP -
I COULD FORGET ABOUT THE OTHERS, STEPPING INTO THE UNKNOWN - THEY WERE LOST NOW - LOST AND FORGOTTEN.
THEY WOULD NOT, COULD NOT, LOOK BACK.
AND NEITHER COULD I.

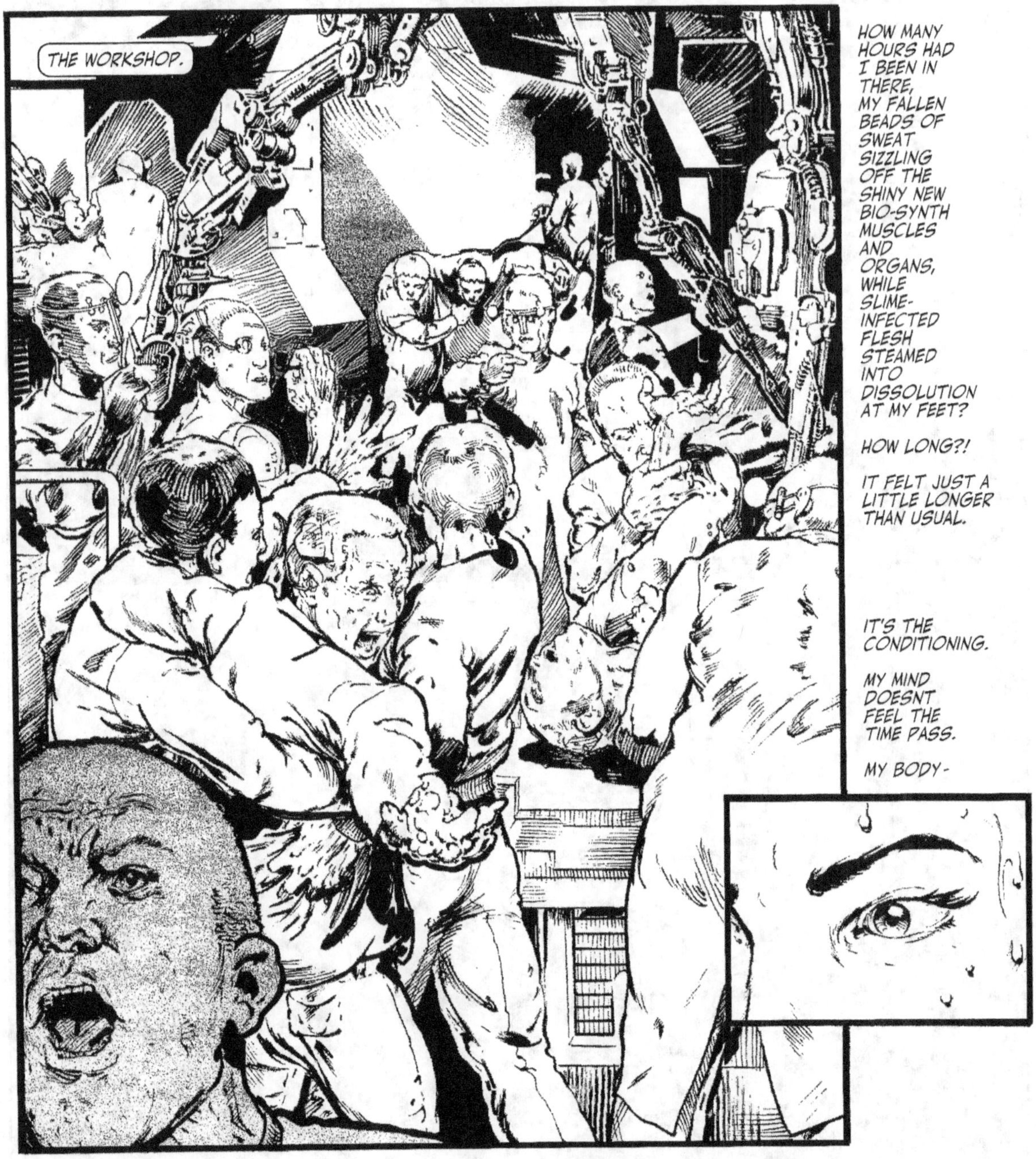

HOW MANY HOURS HAD I BEEN IN THERE, MY FALLEN BEADS OF SWEAT SIZZLING OFF THE SHINY NEW BIO-SYNTH MUSCLES AND ORGANS, WHILE SLIME-INFECTED FLESH STEAMED INTO DISSOLUTION AT MY FEET?

HOW LONG?!

IT FELT JUST A LITTLE LONGER THAN USUAL.

IT'S THE CONDITIONING.

MY MIND DOESNT FEEL THE TIME PASS.

MY BODY—

OH GORMAN! I DIDN'T S-

I'M SORRY, DO I KNOW YOU?

I'D NEVER HAD A NIGHTMARE WHILE UNDER THE LUCIDREAM EMITTER - I DIDN'T EVEN KNOW IT WAS POSSIBLE.
THE EMITTER WAS THE CONDITIONING METHOD.
MANDATORY.
IT WAS NECESSARY TO AVOID SPACE DEMENTIA - IT ALSO HELPED US TO SHAKE OFF THE BATTLE AND REMAIN -

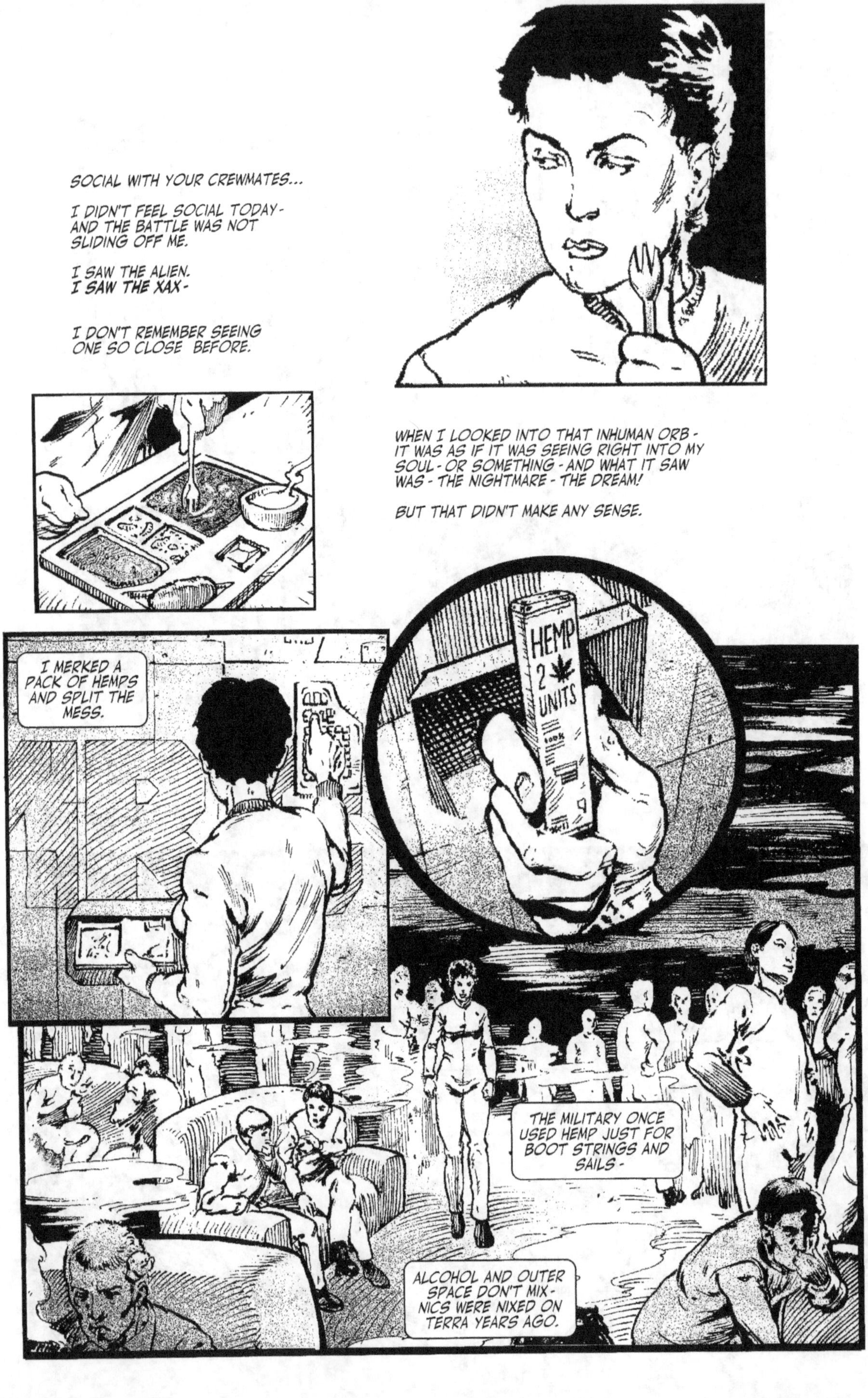

SOCIAL WITH YOUR CREWMATES...

I DIDN'T FEEL SOCIAL TODAY - AND THE BATTLE WAS NOT SLIDING OFF ME.

I SAW THE ALIEN. *I SAW THE XAX -*

I DON'T REMEMBER SEEING ONE SO CLOSE BEFORE.

WHEN I LOOKED INTO THAT INHUMAN ORB - IT WAS AS IF IT WAS SEEING RIGHT INTO MY SOUL - OR SOMETHING - AND WHAT IT SAW WAS - THE NIGHTMARE - THE DREAM!

BUT THAT DIDN'T MAKE ANY SENSE.

BUT YOU COULD SMOKE ALL THE HEMPS YOU WANTED IN THE SMOKING ROOM.
IT SPARKED UP ON EXIT FROM THE TWO-PACK. I DRAGGED HARD, AND THOUGHT ABOUT THE DREAM.
I'D ACTIVATED THE L.D.E. LIKE EVERY NIGHT. REGULATIONS.
BUT THE DREAM WAS DIFFERENT. I WAS DIFFERENT. A DOCTOR. THERE WAS SOMEONE -
NICHOLAS. MY ASSISTANT. AND I WAS THE HEAD OF NEUROSURGERY - AT THE MISKATONIC UNIVERSITY HOSPITAL.
MY TALENTS WERE HONORED AND APPLAUDED - IT WAS A WORLD OF WONDER AND DISCOVERY, AND I FELT IT WAS MINE.
BUT MY POWER AND SKILL WERE NOT ENOUGH.
I WAS SUMMONED TO OPERATE - BUT WAS UNABLE TO SAVE THE LIFE OF THE CHILD.
EVEN AS HE EXPIRED, THE HIDEOUS GROWTH TWISTED AND MOANED.

HIS NAME WAS JOSEF VESSELL. HIS SON, ADAR, CONCEIVED, I WAS TOLD, BY NICHOLAS, AFTER AN ENCOUNTER IN THE DEPTHS OF THE LAKE.
NO! MY SON IS NOT DEAD!
MY SON IS DESTINED TO LIVE FOREVER AND RULE THE WORLD!
NO ONE KNEW WHAT HE SAW DOWN THERE, WHAT HAD PULLED HIM UNDER —
BUT HE BELIEVED THAT HE HAD BECOME LITERALLY THE VESSEL OF THE LAKE GOD - AN ANCIENT EVIL, LONG SUBMERGED HAD INFUSED HIS SEED WITH ITS DARK ESSENCE.
WHEN HE EMERGED, ADAR WAS CONCEIVED.
HIS WIFE SHARED HIS BELIEFS - INCLUDING THAT THE BOY WOULD RISE AGAIN AND RULE -
AND SHE BELIEVED -
YOU, ANNA MANDRETTA, WILL FACILITATE HIS REBIRTH!

THE WOMAN-MARNA VESSELL-SHE WAS ALSO AFFLICTED, AS WAS JOSEF. AND WHEN SHE TOUCHED ME - I DON'T EXACTLY REMEMBER - JUST A SENSE OF THE DREAM, AND EVERYTHING IN THE DREAM, BECOMING FLAT AND FLOWING INTO MY MIND - THE TATTOOS ON HER SKIN AND THE MARKINGS ON THE WALL BECOMING PART OF WHO I WAS, AND THE ONLY THING OUTSIDE OF ME WAS HER CAT, STARING INTO MY EYES.
AND THEN - I WAS SOMEWHERE ELSE... IT WAS COLD AND DARK AND I WAS ALONE...
AND THEN - THE WORD.
THERE WAS - A WORD - A WORD BURNING IN MY BRAIN - A WORD THAT ENCOMPASSED ALL THAT HAD JUST SPILLED INTO MY MIND - A WORD I SPOKE -
AND I HAD POWER - POWER LIKE NO OTHER - POWER LIKE I NEVER BEFORE DREAMED...
WHAT WAS THAT WORD?

THE TETRA-HYDRA-CANIBINOID MOLECULES HAD ATTACHED TO THE THC RECEPTORS IN MY BRAIN.
A BUZZ HAD BEEN CAUGHT -
DRIFTING - DRIFTING OUT OF THE SMOKING ROOM, A SMILE PLAYED ON MY LIPS AND I WAS NOT THINKING ABOUT WHAT I WAS NOT THINKING ABOUT ANYMORE...
I STILL DIDN'T FEEL LIKE SOCIALIZING - I HEAD FOR THE WORK STATIONS - VIRT EQUIPPED.
I WANTED TO GET AWAY... I PUT ON THE HEADSET AND THE VIRT LOADED UP -

AND I WAS GONE...

2200 HOURS - WELL PAST MANDATORY L.D.E. ACTIVATION. I'D LOST TRACK OF TIME INSIDE THE VIRT. OR MAYBE I'D BEEN AFRAID TO RETURN TO THE DREAM.

BUT AT THE EDGE OF MY VISION THE SHADOWS SEEMED TO TWIST AND BREATHE AND I KNEW IT WAS TIME FOR REGULATION DEEP SONAB.

I WOULD HAVE TO HOPE THAT THE NIGHTMARE WOULD NOT RETURN - THAT I HAD DREAMED THE LAST OF THE MISKATONIC HOSPITAL AND -

WEIRDLING!

ANNA?
ANNA?!
ANNA, CAN YOU HEAR ME?
UHHH... NICHOLAS?

AHHH - ANNA, YOU'RE CONSCIOUS. HOW DO YOU FEEL?
WHO ARE YOU?
I AM DOCTOR SCHRECK -
YOU FAINTED - POSSIBLY DUE TO AN ACUTE CLAUSTROPHOBIC EPISODE. DO YOU REMEMBER ANYTHING?
NO-NO, I DON'T... I-FAINTED?
YOU'LL BE FINE. HOWEVER -
FOR SECURITY REASONS YOU MUST BE MONITORED. FOR THE SAFETY OF THE SHIP.
I SHALL BE YOUR REGULAR CASE WORKER. WE WILL MEET DAILY - TO TALK.
DISMISSED.
I DID REMEMBER - DIDN'T I? I HADN'T SIMPLY FAINTED - HAD I? NO - I REMEMBER!
BUT THE DOCTOR - DID HE KNOW? IF HE DIDN'T, THEN WHERE WAS IT?
WHERE WAS -
THE ALIEN - THE XAX!
IT WAS HERE! IN A HOLDING CELL, BEYOND THAT DOOR - SOMEHOW I KNEW. I COULD FEEL IT IN THERE.
I COULD FEEL IT.

IT WAS HERE! STILL ON BOARD THE SHIP - AND ALIVE!!

I REMEMBERED NOW!

I'D SAID A WORD - AND I'D BROUGHT IT DOWN.

THE ALIEN, THE XAX - THEY WERE... AWARE OF ME!

THEY WERE AFTER ME!

THERE WAS SOME SORT OF CONNECTION BETWEEN THE ALIEN AND MYSELF -

I COULD FEEL THAT TOO - IT KNEW ABOUT ME - AND I KNEW ABOUT IT.

SOMEHOW, FROM THAT BRIEF ENCOUNTER, I KNEW MORE ABOUT THE XAX THAN ANYONE ELSE ALIVE -

BUT WHAT I KNEW WAS JUST OUTSIDE OF MY CONSCIOUS THOUGHT -

IT KEPT SLIPPING AWAY - LIKE TRYING TO CATCH A FISH IN THE STREAM WITH MY BARE HANDS...

I - I WAS AFRAID TO SLEEP. BUT -

I WAS MORE AFRAID TO STAY AWAKE.

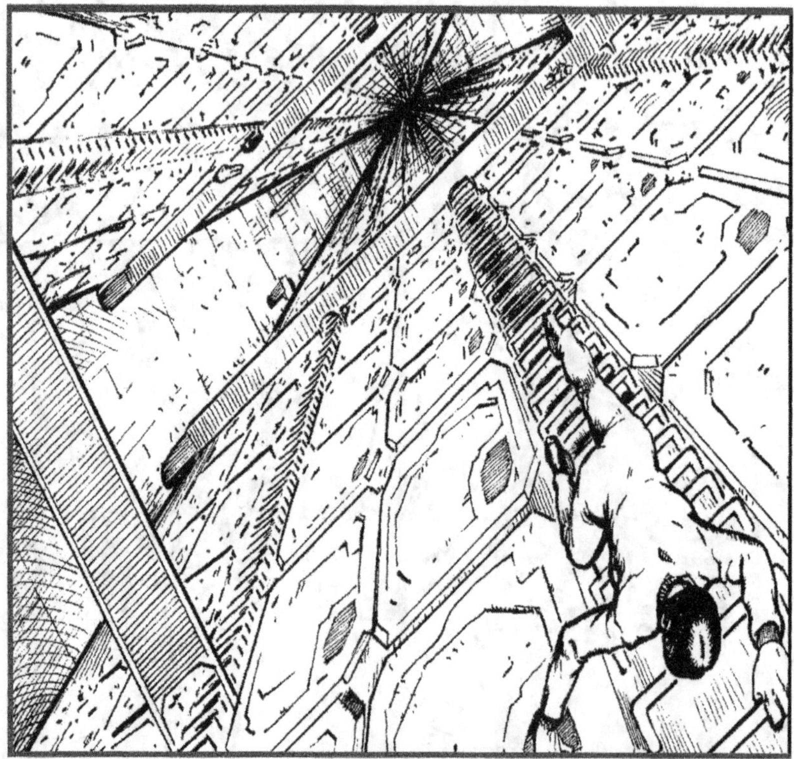

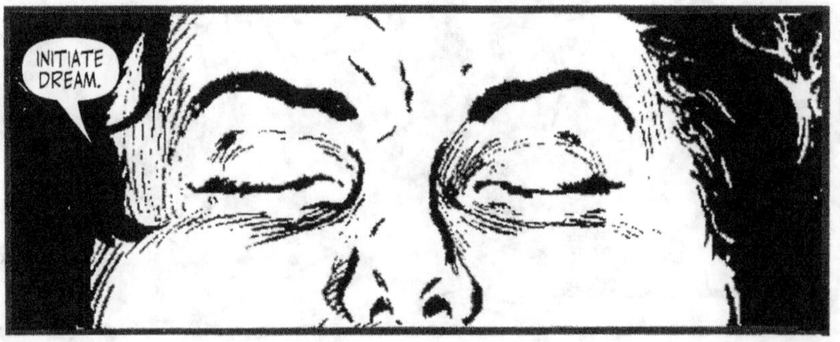

ANNA? ANNA, IF YOU CAN HEAR ME - I -
I HAVE TO TELL YOU - I LOVE YOU, ANNA.
ANNA - ANNA, ARE YOU AWAKE?
NICHOLAS - IS IT REALLY YOU? WHERE AM I?
WE'RE HERE, ANNA... IN YOUR OFFICE AT THE MISKATONIC UNIVERSITY. ARE YOU ALRIGHT?
I FOUND YOU ON THE FLOOR OF THE COTTAGE - DO YOU REMEMBER ANYTHING?
WHAT DID THAT WOMAN DO TO YOU?
I'M NOT SURE, BUT - EVERYTHING'S DIFFERENT NOW - SO MUCH MORE - REAL.
AND YET, IT IS ALSO AS IF I WERE STILL THERE - IN THE COTTAGE... HEARING MARNA VESSELL'S WORD.
TELL ME, WHERE NOW IS THE INFANT'S FATHER?
HE'S BEING BROUGHT BY THE COACH TO THE ASYLUM AS WE SPEAK!

GASP! THE ORDERLY - THE COACHMAN?!
BOTH DEAD!!
AND WHAT OF -
JOSEF VESSELL?
IT'S HAPPENING AGAIN!
I'M IN THAT OTHER PLACE AGAIN - IT'S SO EMPTY - BARREN - DEAD!
WHY AM I HERE? THE MAN IN MY DREAM - HE SAID SOMETHING... ANOTHER WORD! A WORD - BURNING IN MY BRAIN!
WEIRDLING VERMIS!
WHAT NOW?

SLEEP

LIFE!

FROM WHAT WAS DEAD—

SPRINGS LIFE!!

GROAN— WHAT— WHY AM I— OH NO!

BUT YES, ANNA— YES!

NO!

OH NO, NICHOLAS!!

YOU WON'T BE ABLE TO SAVE YOUR LOVER— NOT EVEN WITH ALL YOUR MEDICAL KNOWLEDGE...

ONLY BY USING THE WORDS, ANNA MANDRETTA! THE WORDS WE, THE SERVANTS OF AZAG-THOTH, HAVE GIVEN YOU!

NICHOLAS - NICHOLAS - DID YOU SAY -
YOU - LOVE ME?
WEIRDLING VERMIS!
HNN...
HUH - ANNA!?
ANNA!
OH, NICHOLAS! IT WORKED! IT WORKED!!

ANNA- THE ORDERLY, THE COACHMAN - ALIVE!?
HOW?!
WHAT HAPPENED HERE?
ANNA - WHAT DID YOU DO?
WHAT DID I DO?
WAH
WAAH
WA
ANNA! WHAT HAVE YOU DONE?!
WAH
THAT SOUND-
WAH
WAW

THAT SOUND— WHAT IS THAT—
SOUND?!?
WAAH AA AAH

Ship time 0530. Anna Mandretta, arise and report to Dr. Ripard Schreck.
YES, YES, ACKNOWLEDGED, COMPUTER.
THAT WASN'T MY LUCIDREAM - THE NIGHTMARE CAME BACK! AND THE VISION WITH THE DREAM...
AND THE WORD - WEIRDLING! THAT'S WHAT DISABLED THE XAX! BUT HOW CAN THAT BE?
WHAT DOES IT MEAN?
SIR? DO YOU HAVE MORE QUESTIONS ABOUT THE INCIDENT WITH THE XAX?
ANNA, DO YOU KNOW WHY YOU'RE HERE?
DOES HE KNOW? DOES HE KNOW ABOUT THE WORD?
MMM - I DO BELIEVE YOU HAVE BEEN WITHHOLDING INFORMATION.
SIR?
WE'VE RETRACED YOUR MOVEMENTS IN THE HOURS BEFORE THE ENCOUNTER - YOU EXERCISED YOUR HEMP PRIVILEGES, AS YOU DO QUITE FREQUENTLY -
HE DOESN'T KNOW ABOUT THE WORD, AH MAN, HE DOESN'T KNOW...
I'D LIKE TO STATE FOR THE RECORD, SIR, THAT I HAVE NOT DEVELOPED AN ADDICTION TO SMOKING.
OF COURSE NOT. BUT YOU HAVE BEEN CARRYING AROUND A...
DARKER SECRET FOR A WHILE NOW, HAVEN'T YOU?

OH CRAP, HE DOES KNOW! HE KNOWS ABOUT WEIR-
ANNA, IT'S NOTHING TO BE ASHAMED OF. MANY FROM YOUR GEN BECOME HOOKED ON VIRT.
CYBER-ADDICTION CAN BE TREATED.
HE THINKS I'M A CYBERJUNKY! HE'S NOT GONNA ASK ABOUT THE XAX. OH, BUT SPIT, WAIT, IF HE THINKS I'M A-
SIR...?
BUT NO, SIR, WAIT, I'M NOT!
DO YOU RECOGNIZE THIS CHIP?
NO, SIR, THAT'S NOT - I MEAN, I DIDN'T -
AS YOU KNOW, IT IS A PASSKEY TO A PROHIBITED TYPE OF VIRT ENVIRONMENT. PARTICIPATION IN SUCH AN ENVIRONMENT CONSTITUTES A FORM OF FRATERNIZATION.
HOWEVER, YOU'VE BEEN PLACED UNDER MY DIRECT AUTHORITY, AND BASED ON WHAT I'VE FOUND OUT ABOUT YOU, BASED ON YOUR PROBLEM, I AM PLACING THAT CHARGE ASIDE - FOR NOW.
YOU HAVE BEEN ACCESSING THE VIRTMATRIX WITH SOME FREQUENCY, QUITE OFTEN DURING OFF-DUTY HOURS. WHILE WE ENCOURAGE SOME USE OF DESKTOP DISTRACTIONS DURING ONE'S DATA-PROCESSING DUTIES, BASED ON THE SHEER NUMBER OF HOURS YOU'VE BEEN SPENDING IN VIRTUAL ENVIRONMENTS - I HAVE TO CONCLUDE YOU ARE AN ADDICT-
ANNA, I MUST WARN YOU. I AM GOING TO SUSPEND YOUR VIRT PRIVILEGES, BUT I FEAR THAT WON'T BE ENOUGH. THIS IS A VERY LARGE SHIP AND I FEAR YOU MAY FIND SOME WAY TO INDULGE YOURSELF. IF CYBERADDICTION IS ALLOWED TO PROGRESS, THE ADDICT WILL BEGIN TO LOSE THE ABILITY TO DISTINGUISH REALITY FROM VIRTUAL REALITY. YOU MAY BEGIN TO SEE ELEMENTS OF VIRTUAL REALITY IN THE REAL WORLD, OR YOU MAY BEGIN TO BELIEVE THAT POWERS OR ABILITIES YOU HAVE IN CYBERSPACE WILL CARRY INTO REALITY.

YOU MUST BE CERTAIN TO ACTIVATE YOUR REGULATION LUCIDREAM EVERY NIGHT - TO WARD OFF SHIP-BOUND NEUROSIS - SPACE DEMENTIA - AS WELL AS SUPPLYING THE IMPORTANT SUBLIMINAL INFORMATION THAT WE NEED YOU TO KNOW. IT WILL BOND YOU, IN SHARED EXPERIENCE AND PURPOSE, WITH YOUR CREWMATES.
WE ARE OUT HERE TOGETHER, DEFENDING THE FUTURE OF THE HUMAN RACE!
REPORT TO ME ONCE IN EVERY THIRTY-SIX-HOUR PERIOD. AND ANNA - I'M CUTTING OFF YOUR HEMP PRIVILEGES ANYWAY - I WANT YOU FIRMLY GROUNDED IN REALITY.

NO HEMPS- NO VIRT!?! I'M GOING TO GO CRAZY.

COMPUTER, DO YOU HAVE ANY NON-VIRT DESKTOP DISTRACTIONS? MUSIC, SOOTHING VIBRATIONS, CASUAL CONVERSATION MAYBE?

This unit is equipped with a holo-projector for use in tri-d diagrams. There appears to be one program designated as a diversion - an avatar equipped with the casual conversation option you requested. The program is entitled Cat.
COMPUTER, LOAD AND RUN "CAT."

YOU... YOU LOOK JUST LIKE THE CAT FROM MY DREAM.
HEH—
HA HA!
PRR PURR RRR RRR RRR
WELL, I DON'T KNOW ABOUT CASUAL CONVERSATION, BUT YOU ARE A PRETTY THING!

WEIRDLING
continued on page 102

ONE, TWO, FEDE'S

COMING FOR YOU!

BY BRIAN ASMAN

NAME'S CRAVEN. DEX CRAVEN.
*AS A PI WITH A SIDELINE IN THE OCCULT, I'VE HAD SOME TRULY ODD JOBS.
WATCHING A GROWN MAN SLEEP MIGHT BE THE WEIRDEST.*

The client's name is Sherman. Few years younger than me, late 20s. Earlier, over slices at the pizza joint that serves as my office, he explained why he wants somebody to watch him sleep and wake him if he looks *distressed*:

A year ago, at the Larchbark retirement home, he and some other visitors caught a nurse named—I'm not joking—*Fede Crocker* smothering somebody's grandma with a pillow. Crocker died while being "subdued" and was later linked to a ton of suspicious deaths.

With his last breath, he swore to return from the grave and kill his assailants in their sleep.

The whole thing sounded like a practical joke, a sick riff on my last name, until I saw the news articles. All the "Senior Samaritans" have died mysteriously over the last year.

Except Sherman.

So now I'm sipping coffee and watching him sleep, snug in his pajamas.

A soft creak comes from the living room. I stare into the shadows. The hairs on my arm stand up. Feels like someone's playing a prank on me.

I don't like it.

"Sweet, it worked!" Sherman cries.

I whirl around to find Sherman sitting up in bed. "What's going on?"

"Look, this guy's trying to kill me. But then I realized, what if I had help? A…dream warrior?"

"Oh, fuck off. I don't know what you're trying to pull—"

"I'm not pulling anything. Or, uh—" he glances at my coffee, "—I already did."

"You poisoned me?"

"No! Just an Ambien."

"Why?"

"So you'd fall asleep. And when—" he stage-whispers, "*he* comes, you can kick his ass!"

"Okay, I'm done. Good luck with…all this. I better make it home before the Ambien kicks in." I turn to leave.

That's when the pillows rise off the bed and slam into Sherman's face, then rise, hauling him up until he's hovering above the bed, kicking his legs wildly.

What. The. Fuck.

I yank Sherman down and rip the pillows from his face.

He gasps, eyes glistening with fear.

I toss the pillows into the corner, turning in a slow circle, fists clenched.

"One, two, Fede's coming for you!" unseen voices cry. The pillows swirl off the ground like plastic bags in a Sam Mendes movie.

A shadow detaches from the wall, and suddenly there's a man standing there. Middle-aged, plump, wearing a kitten sweater and a pillow on either hand. His face is gruesomely battered.

"Ever hear of Edward Scissorhands?" he says, flashing a mouthful of broken teeth. "Well, meet Fede Pillowhands!"

You've got to be kidding me.

Fede leaps across the room and slams into me. I hit the floor. He straddles me, pushing pillow-hands into my face.

"Revenge is mine!" Fede shrieks.

The pillows clamp down hard. I'm trying to hit Fede but my fists glance ineffectually off his bulk.

My lungs burn. I'm going to die here, in Sherman's dream or wherever we are. I grab a pillow, trying to muscle it away long enough to take a breath.

No use, I can't breathe—

Wait.

I don't need to.

This is a dream. You don't need to *breathe* in dreams.

The pillows burst, filling the room with hundreds of goose feathers. I shove Fede off easily.

Through a swirling hurricane of feathers, Fede glares at me. "You think you can stop me?"

"Sure. But I don't need to."

Fede blinks. "Why not?"

From behind, Sherman clocks him with a chair, dropping him. "Back for seconds, asshole?"

"Hey," I say. "Don't gloat. Just finish it."

"Yeah." Sherman cocks back the chair.

I join in. Together, we punch and stomp and chair-bash Fede fucking Crocker until he's nothing but a stain on Sherman's dream-carpet. Then we keep going, until we've torn through the carpet and we're cracking the floorboards and then—

Morning. I wake up in the chair in Sherman's room. There's no sign of a struggle. No bloodstains, no busted up floor. Not even an errant goose feather stuck to the ceiling fan.

"Crazy night, huh?" Sherman says, yawning.

I tell him to lose my number, then head home.

I'm driving down the 710 when something tickles my ear. I feel around until I find it.

It's a goose feather.

"Nope," I say, flicking it out the window. The wind takes it. I take the next exit, looking for any bar that's open at this ungodly hour.

Your boy needs a nightcap.

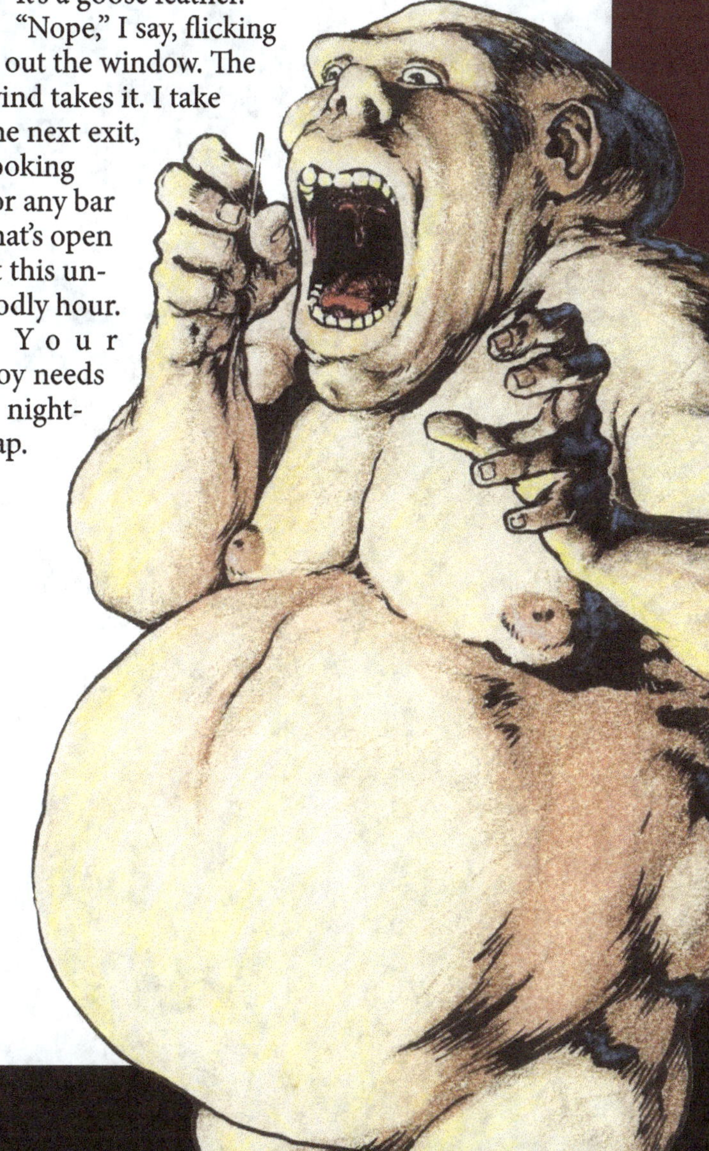

THE DREAM SIEVE

BY ANTHONY TREVINO

FREE FROM THE EXPECTANT EYES OF THE ELITE CROWD IMPATIENTLY TAPPING THEIR SHINY WINGTIPS AND DESIGNER SANDALS ON THE POLISHED CEDARWOOD FLOORS OF THE UPSTAIRS PERFORMANCE SPACE, REINHARDT LUCZAK LIFTED HIS GOLDEN BOY FROM THE SALTWATER TANK'S CAVERNOUS DEPTHS WITH A CARE USUALLY RESERVED FOR NEWBORNS.

However, unlike those joyfully entering motherhood, Rein's kindness for Arlo wasn't driven by altruism or parental instinct. Just necessary maintenance. Vitals needed monitoring. Teeth scrubbing. Occasionally, the body rejected the dream sieves crudely installed at the temples, leading to infection which was why Rein kept a hearty stock of antibiotics on hand. "Home," Arlo mumbled, groggy.

"Yes, you're home."

"Dreamt about the fish again."

Rein lowered him to the tank's edge. "Hold yourself up. We're trying something new tonight."

"Can't tell if I'm dreaming them, or if they're dreaming me."

Their paths had crossed a month prior when Rein was skulking the halls of an obscure labyrinthian art gallery nestled under a dead mall. Gory anime-inspired paintings showcasing big-eyed women devouring miniature businessmen and photorealistic pencil sketches of extreme body modifications decorated the walls. None of the untethered fantasies on display stood out to Rein, which was why finding Arlo at the end of the ghoulish tapestry was a welcome surprise.

Rein knew he'd stumbled upon the rare intersection of beauty and the unknown in this sullen pale creature, quietly drawing at a small table where you could purchase any of his prints for a modest price. He looked tired. Hungry. It didn't take much to get him into the car, and later to the basement. Just the promise of a real shower, soft bed, and a bat to the cranium.

Arlo had a way of painting southern California that Rein had never seen among the droves of forgettable watercolor sunsets that cropped up at every art walk along the west coast. Through his eyes, the state was a glowing alien planet. Violet oceans buzzed with otherworldly sea life. Black sand beaches backdropped by gargantuan palm trees cocooned in writhing vines, and the multi-limbed creatures that benefitted from their shade inhabited every inch of space.

Which was what Rein wanted to curate for those expectant assholes. Instead, though, all Arlo had given him was fish. Gorgeous aquatic life unseen even in the deepest ocean trench, but he needed more. The dream sieve promised full access to the host's imagination, and after the fourth week of glimmering schools of mutant tiger barbs, Rein felt doomed to the one-and-done bin—the reviews from the few critics he'd invited had even said as much.

So, he escalated.

The books his father left behind when his brazen expedition to North Sentinel Island never returned were in languages Rein could barely make sense of, but when you had money, it was easy to find translators. Even easier when their specialty is niche occultism and they're your father's former teaching assistant. Modest in her navy blue pinstripe suit, grey eyes searching Rein's sun worn face for traces of the man she learned from, Darlene Roache explained that possession is merely being a conduit for unruly energy that has no place to go.

"It isn't good or bad. It just *is*," she said, searching the extensive library until she found the right book.

"And if I can't say this perfectly?"

"You won't need to. They'll hear you. Just be prepared to host longer than you're planning."

Rein eased the needle into the pruned crook of Arlo's arm, letting the morphine sink in before setting him back inside.

"Will you tell me if I'm their dream?"

"Sleep, Arlo."

The door to the pod slid shut. Rein peeled the lid off a can of black paint, drew jagged lines that vaguely resembled a shattered window onto the front, and recited the words from the mildewed tome as best he could.

Before heading upstairs, he tapped the node installed above his own sieve, slipped the purple silk hood on. Anonymity was comforting. If anyone with a keen eye made the connection between the paintings he produced and Arlo's unique style, at least he'd be free from getting lambasted in the street for plagiarism.

Most of the patrons sat unamused and impatient, twirling empty champagne flutes, ready to see what they paid a premium entry fee for. Without acknowledging them, Rein dragged a rusty cart of art supplies to the middle of the raised stage. Music trickling in from the ceiling speakers transitioned from elevator jazz to an industrial drone.

His body flushed with heat as Arlo's sieve synced with his. Blank spaces terrified him. White canvas. Empty paper. Even existence felt like one massive hole Rein could never fill. Always surrounded by more imaginative folks, his jealousy of creative types was born from an inability to think in the abstract and only deepened with age. He found brief solace in shitposting on message boards about indie bands, leaving snark-laden reviews for art house films, and any other outlet where he could knock down those pursuing their passions. When that got old, he'd show up at conventions, positioning himself as a challenger, and grilling the panelists about their work.

He lifted his paint brush, paused. Brain buzzing, Rein found himself staring into snowy static until multiple pasty eyelids opened across the white expanse. Ebony orbs with red, fist-sized pupils watched him curiously. He knew this time would be different, but even with that knowledge tremors seized his legs, and he gripped the rickety cart to steady himself. Blue tendrils of smoke slithered into his vision, solidified into cobalt branches. Leaves the color of limestone and studded with teeth sprouted along their slimy trunks. Heavy mist filled the room.

High-pitched laughter needled his ears before the ceiling tore away. Chunks of wood fell upward, making way for the harsh orange searchlight of a black-spotted sun. Beneath him the wood groaned, split like dehydrated skin to allow a burbling red sea to seep in. Screams competed with raucous applause from those in the audience that had been waiting their whole lives to experience something truly remarkable, and he let that sound crash over him.

Elation overpowered the terror manifesting in Rein's bladder. This was *his* moment. He'd been the one to harness Arlo's creativity beyond what the artist's hands were capable of. All it had taken was dedication, risking it all to capture and hone that raw vision no matter the method.

He needed them to know who he was.

Rein whipped around, pulling his mask off as theatrically as he could without falling face first into the scarlet pool at his feet. "My name is—"

They were gone. Every one of his carefully vetted and selected patrons had vanished. Not even the folding chairs were left, swallowed by the shimmering seaside jungle before him.

Before he could call out to them, the door to the basement exploded inward. With more alertness than Rein had ever seen, Arlo stood in the shattered frame. Rings of iridescent electricity enveloped him, and on the crackling currents rode multi-limbed crabs, blind eels striped with undulating rainbow stripes, and fish that dazzled like glossy fireworks. His flesh had become a landscape of torn and drooping meat from where these dream-sea monstrosities had burst forth to join the quivering frenzy that encircled him. That once pretty face had become a cycle of tormented masks, as if whatever hijacked Arlo's body reveled in the shifting personas.

"Do you know the answer to his question," asked a miasma of voices.

Rein backed away, lost his footing. Where he expected a wall to be there was nothing. Warm water enveloped him. Brine flooded his sinuses. Gagging and gasping, he tried to push himself up, find the logic in the situation. The sieve had malfunctioned. That's all. The conjuring spell wasn't real. This was simply broken code.

But all the forced logic and wishing in the world didn't strip away Rein's fantasy turned nightmare.

"It doesn't matter."

Rein looked up, grateful that no one would know he'd finally pissed himself. Snot and seawater dribbled down his nose. "What doesn't?"

"Whether the beasts that came before are dreaming us or we're dreaming them. Those awakenings when the physical body relinquishes control are what keep us going. Without that yearning for more, there's only stagnation. Death."

"Are you going to kill me? For what I've done?"

The Arlo-thing knelt down to be eye level with Rein. It's shifting face a patchwork of dancing muscles. It pressed a bony finger into Rein's forehead, parting the thin web of skin and skull like rice paper, turning Rein's mind into a supernova. "No. I'm going to show you what it's like to finally dream."

THE SPIDER'S DREAM
BY JAN STRNAD

It was an easy shot, no more than fifty yards. According to Slocum, the Judge stepped out onto the back deck every night, a Scotch in one hand and a cigar in the other, and stood at the railing and smoked and drank and looked up at the stars and out toward the woods where, this night, Elliot crouched in the scrub, watching, waiting for the perfect moment to pull the trigger.

One problem was nailing down the time, and time made all the difference. Later was always better, when most people were asleep or drunk. He didn't need the Judge's grown boys racing out to the woods to see who'd shot their dad. Late enough, maybe they wouldn't notice until Elliot was long gone, might never even hear the shot that ended the Judge's life. Elliot knew the boys and what hotheads they were. If they weren't the Judge's sons, they'd have done more time than Elliot had. They were animals.

But he couldn't show up late because the Judge might've come out for his smoke earlier in the evening and Elliot would spend half the night in the damp woods, chilled to the bone, before he realized that he'd missed his chance before he ever got there.

It wouldn't do to take a hasty shot and miss. The Judge's house was full of family and he entertained a steady stream of visitors. There would be hell to pay with Slocum if Elliot capped an innocent bystander. Two nights ago, the Police Chief had spent the evening and stayed late and the Judge skipped his nightly smoke entirely. The night before that, something was on the Judge's mind, causing him to pace anxiously, then to mash the half-smoked cigar underfoot and march inside before Elliot could take his shot. The first night was purely surveillance, selecting his spot, planning his approach and getaway, getting a feel for the rhythm of the place.

He'd come close the night before. It seemed the time was right. The Judge appeared on the deck after the house had gone dark, stogie in hand, and struck a match. But then the Judge's wife joined him, entering tentatively from the house. Elliot had heard them arguing before. Now it looked as if she wanted to make up. She touched the Judge on the back which he'd turned to her upon her arrival. The Judge, rigid at first, softened. He shook out the match, pocketed his unlit cigar, took her in his arms, and bent to kiss her. Then they'd gone inside. The Judge got lucky that night, in more ways than one.

Maybe tonight it was Elliot's turn to get lucky.

Elliot and Buckley lay in a wadi in Kandahar Province, Afghanistan, waiting for a reported Taliban IED team to come into sight. Elliot and Buckley would engage at around seven hundred meters, a distance the Taliban thought safe, out of range of the old 62-grain rounds. But Elliot and Buckley were packing the new 175-grain ammo. The T-men had a surprise coming.

Elliot shifted his weight, stretched his legs. He took out a maintenance rag and wiped at the dust on his sweating neck.

"Spiders sleep," Buckley said.

"What?" Elliot said.

Buckley was a reader. He would come out with some random fact without preamble, just spit it out like a bug that had landed on his tongue.

"Yeah," Buckley said. "They sleep. Their eyes don't close, but they're asleep. Same as you and me, you know, when you're staring into the distance for so long your mind sort of checks out? You've done that, right? I've seen it. But you wake up when you see something. Same with spiders. Their eyes are open but they're asleep, and they wake up when something hits the web."

"How do you know they're asleep," Elliot said, "if their eyes don't close?"

"They twitch. Like when your body does that jerk. Or their legs work like a dog chasing rabbits in its sleep."

"So spiders sleep."

"Yeah, but here's the crazy part. They dream, too."

Elliot laughed.

"What the hell does a spider have to dream about?" he said.

"You tell me," Buckley said. "But they do. Science says."

Elliot didn't need a military round or an M-24 to drop the Judge. His hunting rifle and scope were plenty good enough, given the close range.

In his career as a sniper, he'd often seen himself as a spider, patiently lying in wait for his wrong-time/wrong-place prey to appear. Did the spider's victim deserve its fate? Usually not. No more than the Judge deserved his, unless enforcing the law against men like Slocum was a Darwin-level lapse of common sense. Crossing Slocum was a mistake Elliot was careful to avoid.

Left jobless with the pullout, with no skills but a sharp eye and a steady hand and a willingness to take a stranger's life without compunction, what choice did Elliot have but to fall in with men like Slocum's bunch of grifters and extortionists? Anything resembling a "normal life" was an illusion, like Brigadoon, a footstep away but vanishing each time he approached. How do you capture the mist?

So he did all the crappy things Slocum commanded him to do, leading to the inevitable culmination of a life such as his—cold-blooded murder. If he refused, Slocum could put him away for years with just a phone call. Yes, Elliot was a spider, but it was Slocum's web, and Elliot was trapped as any fly.

What the hell does a spider have to dream about?

What did Elliot have to dream about?

The Spider Goddess sits in her celestial web; her eyes are the countless stars, her consciousness is the universe itself. She waits and watches. She is aware on a cosmic scale. To her, there is no infinite and no infinitesimal; for her, the grand and the minute and all in between are one and the same.

Omnipotent? No. All-wise? All-caring? No, and no. Kind? Cruel? Capricious? Yes, yes, oh yes.

Sometimes she sleeps. She sleeps for eons. When she sleeps, she dreams, and when she dreams, stars explode and planets coalesce, galaxies collide, storms rage and rivers change their course, sparrows fall, flowers bloom, caterpillars morph, and nebulae collapse into suns. It's all the same to her.

At this particular instant of endless time, she dreams of a man. His name is "Elliot," and he fancies himself a spider. It's a comical notion made tragic by hubris. The man's prideful insignificance amuses her. For a second or a thousand years, the Spider Goddess feels sorry for this Elliot, though not so sorry that she will refrain from destroying him. But first, she will give him a gift.

Elliot knew what Buckley meant about sleeping with his eyes open. It was a state he entered sometimes while waiting for his victim to come into view. Almost a fugue state it was, where Elliot ceased to be Elliot, where memory fled, where his mind freed itself to dream who he might be if he weren't constrained by chance of birth and character and history.

He enters that state now, dreaming while awake.

In his dream, he feels a prickling on his skin. He looks to the sky to check for an approaching storm but sees only the crescent moon and high, thin clouds too insubstantial to promise rain. The hairs on his arms and neck seem drawn to this moon. Diaphanous threads, all but invisible in the dim moonlight, appear from nowhere to wrap around his arms and legs. The weight drains from his body like water from a spigot. The threads reach into the night sky, quivering in harmony with a universe-spanning vibration. He feels himself rising, floating effervescently upwards.

(The Judge stands on the back deck. He sets his glass on the railing, strikes a match. His face glows yellow as he lights his cigar, then is obscured by smoke as he exhales. The smoke dissipates, revealing the Judge limned in the light from a window as he raises the glass to his lips. There is the crack of a rifle and the glass in the Judge's hand and the glass of the window shatter simultaneously. The bullet embeds itself in an interior wall with a dull *thump*. The cigar drops from the Judge's mouth. Elliot, dreaming, registers these events as frozen instants but they hold no meaning for him, like a dream within a dream.)

Elliot floats, light as a thought, up and up, skirting the branches of the trees, then above the treetops, ever higher. He flies, a human kite skating on the wind. Here the air is cold and fresh. Here, he can see for miles even in the feeble light of the stars.

Electricity crackles around and through him as he sails over the forest, the lake, the hills, the incandescent town below. Elliot is in his element at last, swimming among the clouds, above all worldly concerns, out of the reach of Man, even men like Slocum and his tenacious webs. Here, Elliot is free, and at last Elliot knows of what the spider dreams.

It dreams of flying.

Then even the Earth itself falls away as Elliot's consciousness expands to fill the spaces between the galaxies, larger than the largest nebula, grander than anything he could ever imagine. Time loses all meaning as beginning and ending blur into a perpetual Now.

The Spider Goddess grants Elliot these moments (for that is all they are to her, mere moments) of unbounded joy, though to Elliot they seem as lifetimes. She grants him this godlike status, and briefly—because, to the Spider Goddess, eons are but narrow interstices between waking and sleeping—Elliot is the Spider God, infinite in his being, at one with the universe. He sees that there is no life too small to matter and no life too large to matter more, and for once, Elliot is at peace.

The Spider Goddess melds her being with his. For the briefest sliver of time, no more time than it takes a civilization to rise and fall, they are one. Then, as is the way of her kind, she begins to consume her mate.

The brothers' first impulse when they found Elliot in the woods was to beat the living daylights out of him. The elder son grabbed Elliot by the shirt and lifted him off the ground where he lay beside his rifle. He raised his fist and looked Elliot in the eye. The sight gave him pause.

What he saw through Elliot's dilated pupils was a void black and deep as the night, endless, infinite, abysmal. What the brother held was not a man, but a husk. There was nothing there. Nothing to intimidate. Nothing to hurt. Nothing at all.

He let the body drop. Elliot lay on the ground like a mannequin, arms and legs bent at ungainly angles, eyes open but unseeing. He might have been mistaken for a corpse, but Elliot was not dead, only sleeping. He would sleep as long as his physical body endured, and perhaps a few star-lives longer, and he would dream the spider's dream.

JAN STRNAD

JAN'S career began in the late 1960s with underground comix and fanzines. He published his own zine, Anomaly, that featured early collaborations with Richard Corben and helped launch both their careers. He wrote for influential horror magazines such as Creepy, Eerie, Vampirella, Heavy Metal, and Epic Illustrated.

His collaboration with Corben produced genre-defining stories that blended post-apocalyptic psychedelic grit and humor in such classics as Mutant World, Son of Mutant World, and Jeremy Brood. Strnad also co-created the seminal indie sci-fi comic Dalgoda with Dennis Fujitake and the DC cyberpunk tale Sword of the Atom.

Throughout the 1990s and 2000s, Strnad expanded into animation and mainstream comics with such projects as Star Wars: X-Wing Rogue Squadron for Dark Horse and scripted episodes for animation shows such as Darkwing Duck and Skeleton Warriors, as well as numerous superhero series. His prose work includes The Summer We Lost Alice and The Murmuring Field and Other Stories.

Jan's influence echoes through the generations of creators he inspired. His deft blend of horror, sci-fi, and satire makes for innovative storytelling. Jan Strnad remains one of the great, underappreciated voices in speculative fiction and comics.

Now, to sink deep into the mind of Jan Strnad, whose imagination had us roaming radioactive wastelands, battling sword-wielding mutants, and exploring haunted castles... his killer tales linger long after the last panel.

1. We've got to start with the source: What kind of stuff fueled your imagination early on? Were you flipping through EC Comics, dog-earing Ray Bradbury paperbacks, catching The Day the Earth Stood Still on late-night TV, or glued to The Outer Limits and Twilight Zone? What stuck with you and still shapes how you see the world?

Comic books, first. I missed the EC era but grew up on the comic books of the mid-1950s through early 60s. I read nearly everything except the romance books. Casper and Hot Stuff, the Little Devil; the Archie books; DC super-heroes; Charlton titles like Captain Atom and Gorgo by Steve Ditko; Gold Key supernatural and s-f titles—Magnus, Robot Fighter by Russ Manning was a big favorite—ACG titles such as Forbidden Worlds and Herbie; the Marvel monster books; and with Fantastic Four #1 I became a Marvel Maniac with special emphasis on Steve Ditko and Jack Kirby.

The neighborhood drugstore, Tompkins Sundries, shelved the comic books next to the paperback books. The cover of Fletcher Pratt's Alien Planet caught my eye and that became my first s-f novel. The first of many. I loved the Ace Doubles and the short story anthologies, especially the Year's Best S-F series edited by Judith Merril. I loved the old masters such as Isaac Asimov, Ray Bradbury, Richard Matheson, etc., and when I read Harlan Ellison's Paingod and Other Delusions in high school, my brain practically exploded.

I went to every s-f movie I could, but my main source for the s-f films I loved was television. King Kong (1933) totally blew me away. I watched it whenever it came on TV and I'm sure it was one of the first VHS tapes and laser discs and DVDs I purchased. I'm a sucker for stop motion animation of all sorts, so of course I'm a huge Ray Harryhausen fan, but I like it all, from Willis O'Brien and Jim Danforth to Brett Piper.

The Universal monsters, of course, have a special place in my heart, but my favorite era has to be the 1950s. Aside from classics such as The Day the Earth Stood Still (1951) and Forbidden Planet and Invasion of the Body Snatchers (both 1956), I also enjoyed—and still do—the B-pictures like Creature with the Atom Brain (1955) and The Monster that Challenged the World (1957) and many others. I especially love seeing what filmmakers can do with super-low budgets.

Later, Corman came along with the Poe adaptations and other low-budget, drive-in fare, and Hammer cranked out a lot of Dracula and other vampire films. I'll watch (again and again) anything with Karloff or Vincent Price. Famous Monsters of Filmland was a must-buy magazine.

Star Trek and Star Wars both made huge impressions on me, though as an influence on my writing, I'd have to say that Star Trek was the bigger influence, though I've never written anything in the Star Trek universe but have dipped my toe into the universe of Star Wars. Life likes to play these little jokes on us.

Then there's The Twilight Zone, the best television show ever. Not every episode is a gem and there are some genuine clunkers, but overall, the quality of writing and imagination remains unparalleled. I dug The Outer Limits, naturally, but nothing, not even Serling's own Night Gallery or the Twilight Zone reboot, ever nailed the form like the original TZ. The show's effect on me is enduring.

Aside from gorging myself on popular fiction, I majored in English Literature in college and took creative writing from two mainstream authors, Jack Matthews and Richard Yates. Yates was particularly influential as he was one of the advisors on my project to earn Honors in Creative Writing. I remember his supporting my decision not to pursue a master's or PhD. Part of my project was a short story based on my experiences as a ride operator at an amusement park (ages 14-16) titled "Fun Park." Yates said that working places such as Fun Park would be as valuable to me as a writer as further time spent in academia. In hindsight, I'm absolutely certain he was right.

Nobody writes a short story like Ernest Hemingway, and I believe that John Steinbeck's The Winter of Our Discontent should be read by everyone for its exploration of moral dilemma in everyday life. Joseph Heller's Catch-22 is another must-read; once you make your peace with the absurd human universe of Catch-22, you're well prepared for the real world. The same goes for the marvelous work of Kurt Vonnegut, Jr., another unique wordsmith whose view of the world is simultaneously skewed yet truthful, superficially cynical but deeply optimistic.

2. Let's rewind to Anomaly. What inspired that zine in the first place? What drove you to start publishing your own material, and how did it evolve once Bud Plant got involved?

I've been fascinated with the printing process since I received a present, as a young kid, of a set of rubber letters and numbers that you painstakingly inserted into a wooden holder to make a rubber stamp. It frustrated the hell out of me that the letters were never perfectly aligned. I'm more than a bit OCD about things like that. But I loved the concept.

When my father died while I was in college, I inherited the princely sum of $1000. I spent it publishing my fanzine, Anomaly, for three issues, after which the money had played out. (I am a terrible businessman.) A local fan, Jerry Weist, was publishing his fanzine, Squa Tront, and he linked me up with a terrific artist he hadn't found appropriate for Squa Tront named Robert Kline. Bob Kline was in the Air Force, working as an artist, but he loved the same fantasy/s-f stuff that I did. His artwork set the standard for Anomaly.

Maybe there was a market for the science fiction and fantasy comics and prose stories that I wanted to write, but maybe I was too impatient to go the "submit-and-wait-get-rejected-and-submit-elsewhere-until-it-sells" route. By self-publishing in Anomaly I got to write what I wanted and see it in print. What I didn't know was how Anomaly would

set my career on the trajectory it ultimately took. More on that topic later.

Anyway, after I'd blown through my inheritance money, I approached Bud Plant about publishing one more issue of Anomaly as an underground comic book, he did, and that was that.

3. Your collaborations with Richard Corben are the stuff of legend (Den, Mutant World, Son of Mutant World, The Last Voyage of Sindbad, and Ragemoor). How did you two first connect, and what was it about that creative bond that let you both cut loose in such unforgettable ways?

We met through Anomaly. I'd discovered and loved his work from another fanzine, Voice of Comicdom. My co-publisher, Don "Saj" Bain, and I attended a World Science Fiction Convention in St. Louis, Missouri, in 1969. We had a table where we sold copies of Anomaly. While I was away from the table, Corb came by and subscribed. I didn't discover this until I got back home to Wichita, Kansas, and my jaw dropped! I wrote to him and asked for a contribution, and he kindly contributed covers, a painting, and our first collaboration, an s-f tale called "A Brief Encounter at War."

Somehow Corb and I just clicked. We were both experimenting with non-super-hero material. Working in the underground comix doing horror and fantasy was very heady (so to speak).

Corb was actually a very mild fellow who loved to laugh, which you might not guess from all of the martial arts in his work. He introduced me to Monty Python's Flying Circus during one of my overnight visits. (I lived in Wichita and he lived just outside Kansas City, about a four-hour drive away.) His wife Dona was really sweet to me, getting a foam pad out of storage for me to sleep on, feeding everybody… just being a great hostess. She's now in charge of preserving his legacy with reprints of his work domestically through Dark Horse and other publishers internationally.

4. Mutant World still feels like it wandered in from another dimension. I can still taste the leaded fumes of the apocalypse in those tales. What sparked the creation of Mutant World, and when you revisited it all those years later, did it feel like the same place or something entirely new?

Mutant World did wander in, from my point of view. I'd been writing some horror comics for Warren Publishing, and one day Corb sent me the first chapter of Mutant World, a series he'd committed to doing for Warren. He also sent the artwork for the second chapter, which he hadn't dialogued or captioned yet. He wasn't sure where it was going and asked if I'd take over the writing. I jumped at the chance.

The project was tainted by unwanted changes inflicted on it by editor Bill DuBay. One sequence of panels was reversed right-to-left for some inexplicable reason, and DuBay changed the dialogue to include juvenile expressions that I guess he thought were edgy. After the series had run, Warren wanted to issue a graphic novel and we both said "Nyet" to that. The graphic novel wouldn't come out for some time afterward with the original artwork and dialogue restored.

DuBay pissed off a lot of creators (Wally Wood being notable among them) with his changes. DC came to L.A. once to recruit talent and I spoke with Dick Giordano. His closing question to me was "Is there anybody you'd definitely NOT want to work with?" and the only name I came up with was "Bill DuBay." He said he'd heard that from a number of other people.

When Corb suggested a sequel to Mutant World, I came up with Son of Mutant World. I wanted to do a story that followed the original but went in a different direction. For one thing, Corb was really, really tired of drawing piles of bricks! So we left the city behind and headed out to the wilderness where civilization was being rebuilt.

Unfortunately, the color printing of the underground comic was terrible and sales weren't great and we ended up printing the last chapters in black-and-white. It would be years before Corb's daughter, Beth, would recolor Son of Mutant World under his guidance for the book Mutant World/Son of Mutant World which we sold as a Kickstarter project. I was delighted to see SoMW finally get the respect it deserved. Corb said he actually liked that story better than the original.

5. MEAD brought your early story To Meet the Faces You Meet to life in animated form. What was it like seeing it adapted after so many years?

It was a shock! Corb had emailed me that "a fan" wanted to make an amateur movie based on "To Meet the Faces You Meet" and asked my permission. I said "Sure" because, why not? Then I saw the work Jeffery Allen Williams was doing and it totally blew me away! At that point I volunteered to tweak Jeff's screenplay which expanded greatly on the original sixteen-page comix story, and I even flew from L.A. out to Missouri where MEAD was being filmed in the garage of a friend of Jeff's to help out for a week. It was fun seeing it on the big screen at the premiere and meeting Robert Picardo and getting his autograph on my DVD of The Howling in which he played a werewolf.

6. You've written for Star Wars, Amazing Spider-Man, Stalkers—some of the biggest franchises around. But let's say in a perfect world, you could pick the gig, any comic series you want, past or present… what do you jump on?

I'd love to have written Adam Strange stories, and I actually did pitch a Space Ranger mini-series to DC once (they passed). I'd still like to do a Space Ranger comic but Star Wars has pretty well taken over that territory.

I'm drawn to the second-banana characters because you have more freedom with them. I wrote "secret origins" of the Silent Knight and gave him

a stutter, and Man-Bat, illustrated by the incomparable Kevin Nowlan, with very little editorial guidance. Even Sword of the Atom with Gil Kane only came about because DC needed to do something with the Atom to maintain the trademark, and they let us go wild with the little guy in a barbarian/s-f mini-series. SotA ended up reviving the character.

It was great writing for Star Wars. Lucasfilm laid down a few easy-to-follow rules and then let us alone, which was quite a surprise. Also, after attending signings at comic book shops where, literally, NO ONE showed up, it was fun having fans lined up down the sidewalk to get an autograph. The experience really drove home to me how unimportant the writer is in comics compared to the artist and, especially, to the property.

7. You've written for Aladdin, Darkwing Duck, and Goof Troop (stories that still hit decades later). Are you an animation fan, and what shows do you enjoy watching today?

After I moved to L.A., I went to visit my Anomaly pal, Bob Kline, who was then working at Disney Television Animation. I wasn't planning to hit him up for a job, but when I saw the show he was working on, TaleSpin, I thought, "I could write this!" Bob set me up with Jymn Magon who was a former Anomaly subscriber. Jymn hired me to write a couple of freelance scripts, Disney liked them, and they hired me as a staff writer. So there's that three-issue fanzine still working for me!

After three-and-a-half years on staff with Disney, they fired most of their staff writers but continued to hire me as a freelancer. I was free to work elsewhere, too, and wrote cartoons for a number of studios, from small ones doing shows like Skeleton Warriors and Ace Ventura, Pet Detective to Saban, writing X-Men, HBO for Harold and the Purple Crayon, from Biker Mice from Mars to Trollz. The first shows I worked on for Disney—TaleSpin, Darkwing Duck, and Aladdin—were right in my wheelhouse of adventure stories with humor, for an older audience. As my fifteen-year career in animation progressed, I found myself working on shows for younger and younger audiences, which was harder for me because I didn't relate as well to the audience. Finally, I hit Harold and the Purple Crayon which was a preschool-level show. Hardest show I ever worked on.

I'm a fan of the early Disney animated films, but it's really the Warner Bros. Looney Tunes that grabbed me as a kid. Oddly, that's one studio I never managed to work for. I used to watch The Simpsons and King of the Hill religiously but I can't say there's any animation today that I follow regularly.

8. From the gritty sci-fi of Jeremy Brood to the Lovecraftian shadow of Ragemoor, to the pulpy fantasy of New Tales of the Arabian Nights… The Summer We Lost Alice shows an entirely different side. What inspired that story?

Hard to say. The Summer We Lost Alice was my second novel, after Risen and before Visitations (formerly titled One Last Time) and Trib: Murder

in the End Time. Risen had been published by a New York publisher, and then it did even better as a self-published ebook once the rights reverted to me. I figured that if I retired with a few novels out there, they'd be a nice revenue stream. I was wrong about that, as Risen had come out when ebooks were relatively new and pretty soon the field was crowded with crap and sales disappeared.

I love writing prose because there's no one between me and the audience. On the other hand, there's no Richard Corben or Kevin Nowlan or Gil Kane or Disney or Star Wars coattails to ride. I wish more people would give the novels a try since those few who read them seem to like them, but I'm not up for any of the marketing techniques that sell novels these days, like developing a video presence. I'm too old and unattractive for that stuff, and not much of a performer. I'd have to hire someone to play Jan Strnad to make that work.

9. You've been in the game long enough to see it all. What's the weirdest fan encounter or piece of mail you've ever gotten? (No judgment)

Very little weirdness has come my way, actually! I remember one kid at a convention telling me that I was his fifth favorite writer. I took it as a compliment and may have promised to try harder. Another kid struck up a conversation with me at the snack bar at a convention because his therapist told him he should try to talk to people he didn't know.

10. Say you had to live inside one of your own stories for a day—mutants, mechs, monsters, and all. Which world would you pick… and how long do you honestly think you'd make it?

Dalgoda, definitely. Dal is the purest expression of what I've wanted to write in comics. The Dalgoda Omnibus collecting the series that was published by Fantagraphics just came out this year. I read it from cover to cover. I hadn't visited the story in nearly forty years and I was pleasantly surprised at how well it held up. The artist, Dennis Fujitake, was the perfect artist for that story. That was a world I could live in.

11. You've created stories across decades, across genres. If someone was cracking open your work for the first time, what's the one story you'd hand them that says, "This is me, right here," and why?

Again, Dalgoda. Adventure, humor, dogs, science fiction. That's me.

12. You've worked with some absolute legends. But if you could build a dream team (any artists, alive or dead) to draw an epic comic to save the world… who's on the squad?

I don't know that I can answer that, but I'll tell you one guy I wish I'd been able to work with: Steve Ditko. He was just so off-center and weird. As long as we stayed away from politics, I think we'd have

made a great team. Doctor Strange would be fun to write, or some monster-based comic. A Ditko-illustrated Fin Fang Foom mini-series would be a hoot. (I know that's a Jack Kirby character, but Ditko's version would also kick ass!)

13. And here's your "choose your own adventure" moment: What's something you wish more people would ask you about, or something you've worked on that never got the spotlight it deserved? Or what is your favorite book?

Some of my favorite books are, in no particular order, a) Richard Matheson's I Am Legend, b) Daniel Keyes' Flowers for Algernon, c) Kurt Vonnegut, Jr.'s Cat's Cradle, and d) Nathanael West's Miss Lonelyhearts, because they are, respectively, a) terrifying, b) edifying and heart-breaking, c) so damn clever, and d) so damn bleak.

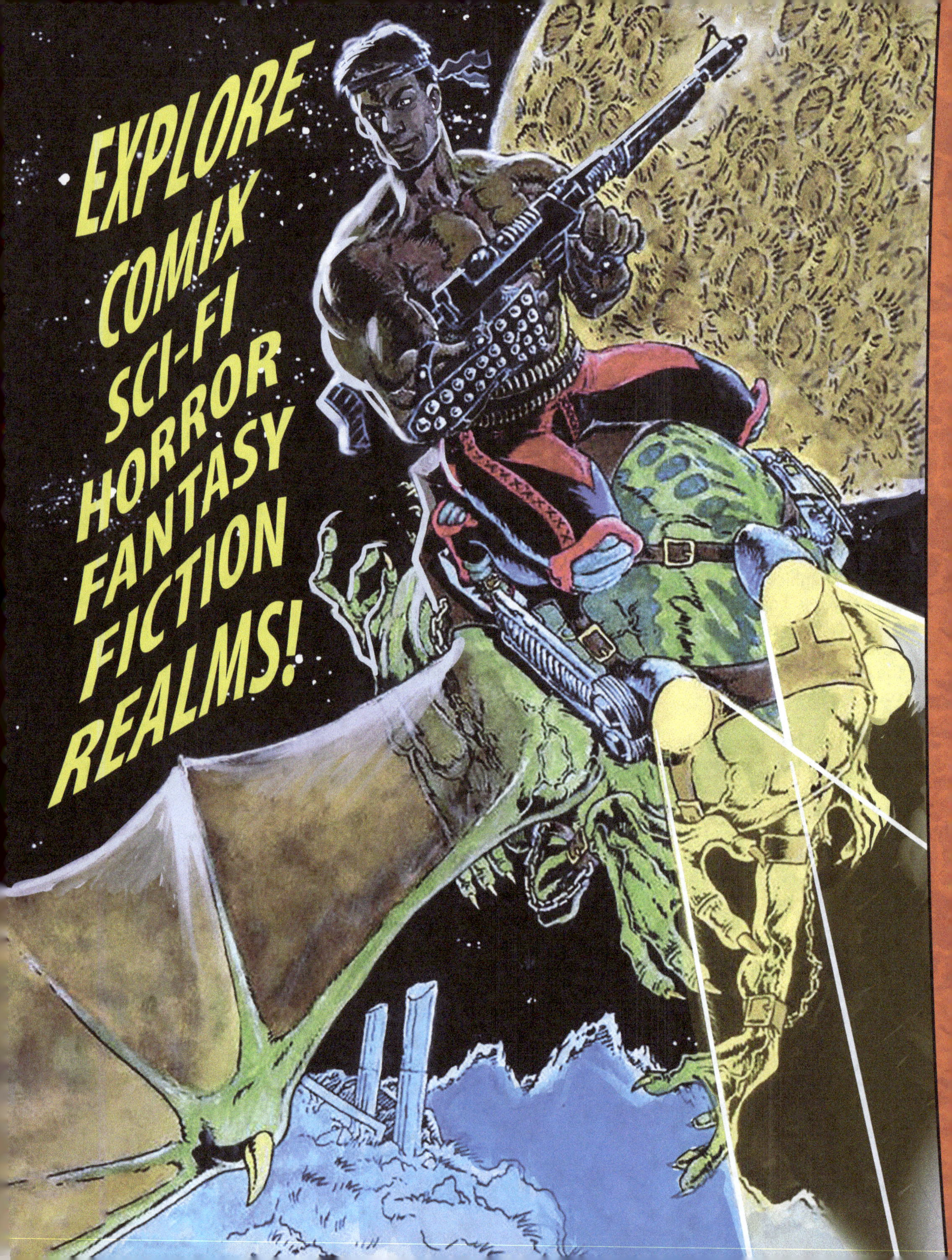

EXPLORE
COMIX
SCI-FI
HORROR
FANTASY
FICTION
REALMS!

JOIN THE ADVENTURE!

A fiendish tech-mage hacked our reality into fractured regions—each one a strange pocket realm stitched together from dream logic, lost futures, and pulp weirdness into the following sectors available to visit:

STARFALL STATION
A crumbling outpost at the edge of space.

THE LONELY TOWER
A curse tower returns from the dark void.

DARK ALLEYS
Lost nightmares lurk in liminal corridors!

CHOOSE YOUR DESTINATION*
WWW.ODDNESS.US

AGE RATING:

R

FOR
NUDITY
VIOLENCE
HORROR

DESTINATIONS™ produced by ©**ODDNESS**

*No gurantee given that any literature will transport you to alien lands. That's on you or really good drugs.

PART III: NIGHTMARES

In Noah Webster's 1828 Dictionary, "nightmare" is defined as "the state of being oppressed or frightened in sleep; a distressing dream

I was trapped in half a dream. My body was cast in stone, like the marble lids of sarcophagi carved in the images of kings and queens eternally sleeping in the catacombs of some forsaken castle. I only could neither breathe or move in the clammy stillness. Every second was both fleeting and eternal. When I willed myself to scream, the screams caught in my throat. Hordes of demons were encroaching.

I prayed through bloodless lips—Holy Mary, Mother of God, pray for us sinners now and to the hour of our death—my eyelids flew open, and I gasped.

This is the actual sleep paralysis experience of a fifteen-year-old girl. I was that girl. Between the ages of ten and eighteen, I would relive this hellscape again and again, lucid but petrified, as if my final breath had been snatched from my throat by a demonic hand. Raised by Eastern European immigrants who believed in changelings, vampires, and the evil eye, I was born into

superstition. Charms to ward off curses and protect me from demons were pinned to my white eyelet baptismal dress. My episodes of sleep paralysis were something I feared to speak of.

Sleep paralysis is haunted by superstitious beliefs across cultures. Entities such as incubi, succubi, and night hags are thought to be the culprits in folklore, but there is a non-paranormal explanation. This phenomenon is actually an interruption in REM sleep, the phase of sleep when most dreams occur, known as atonia. It throws the sleeper into a quasi-dream state with

THE INCUBUS: DEMON TYPE I

In Webster's Dictionary (1828), "Incubus" is defined as the nightmare; an oppression of the breast in sleep, or sense of weight, with an almost total loss of the power of moving the body, while the imagination is frightened or astonished.

some awareness but an inability to breathe or move otherwise. Panic disorder, post-traumatic stress, and narcolepsy are some of the conditions associated with sleep paralysis, during which there can be a phantasmagoria of visual and auditory hallucinations.

Superstition can still have a powerful grasp on the human mind. While sleep paralysis demons have often been memed as anything that is remotely unsettling, their origins may cause insomnia. In the darkest vaults of Judeo-Christian belief is Lilith, the mother of nightmares. There are mentions of her as a demoness in ancient Sumerian scripts. In the Talmud, she was Adam's first wife, who refused to be subdued. Chased by angels who heard her utter the forbidden name of God, she fled from Eden to the Red Sea as the angels demanded she either crawl back to Adam or drown. Then she morphed into a sea dragon and hissed:

"Let me be, for I was created to weaken the babes."

Lilith swore she would have power over any newborn who had not yet been blessed, though she swore that if she saw amulets bearing holy names or images, she would leave the child unharmed. Many Jewish women in the Middle East wear protective amulets when giving birth, but fear of Lilith reaches beyond the maternity ward. She is said to have returned to Adam after Eve's fateful temptation from the serpent. Through forced sexual encounters with him, she spawned demon offspring, which were unleashed on humans wandering at night or sleeping alone. While Lilith became the succubus of legend, she is not the only embodiment of a nightmare.

Nightmares themselves are often seen as visitations from evil things. Hmong culture has its own version of Lilith, the *dab tsog* or night hag, whose hollow eyes and dagger teeth are the last thing men see as she slinks up to their chests and suffocates them. Men are supposed to be the keepers of ancestral spirits and make offerings of incense, food, or paper money to guard

against what belongs in hell. A Hmong man who neglects his duty could be killed by attacks known as *tsog tsuam*. Thousands of miles away in Newfoundland, folklore beliefs in the Old Hag evoke a female figure with long, stringy hair who strangles her victims in their sleep. There is a reason Old Hag is supposedly linked to the word "haggard."

Some cultures believe more than one entity can cause sleep paralysis. The Japanese see *kanashibari* as sleep paralysis that is the doing of a yōkai, a supernatural creature or spirit. Yōkai can range from nuisances to actual demons. The makura-gaeshi, which appears as the ghost of a small child like Sadaku from Ringu and smothers sleepers with their own pillows, is straight out of a horror VHS but not lethal. *Tsukimono* are the "possessing things" that may need an exorcism. These can be something like the kitsune, the temperamental nine-tailed fox spirit, or *kappa*, an anthropomorphic reptilian species that is capable of drowning its human prey and might even gorge on their flesh.

Other literal sleep paralysis demons go by many names and faces. *Zmory* are Slavic spirits of those who died unnaturally, shapeshifting, and may manifest as animals, zombies, vampires, or an impenetrable void. They are said to suck the strength or blood from their victims while sitting on their chests. Even worse is **Kikimora**, also known as *Mora* or *Zmora*, the swamp crone that kidnaps both children and adults and is known for disturbances in the dark. Similar to zmory are the Turkish *karabasan*, or "dark pressers," which also crush the ribcages of their victims by sitting on their chests.

Could it be that sleep paralysis is (at least sometimes) more than parasomnia? Lurking in the backs of libraries and every dusty corner of the internet are firsthand accounts of demonic intervention that cannot be explained any other way. There are believers among the crowds who dismiss them as hallucinations. My teenage ghost self is still trembling, still superstitious.

MIKE DUBISCH
WEIRDLING 3

From the journal of Dr. Nicholas Van Hise, Miskatonic University hospital - I don't know how the cat got in here. It had gotten into some medical tale and was tracking it about. Somehow I found its small presence comforting.

Anna Mandretta, my mentor and friend, the greatest doctor in the history of the Miskatonic, remains in the strange fugue state in which I found her after her most recent encounter with the sinister family of Josef Vessell, his wife Marna and the child Adar.

In desperation I have hooked her up into the Neural Cryptometer, an experimental device that Anna and I had been developing - Its intended purpose was to stimulate the pineal lobe, the alleged "third eye," to allow travel between the different worlds that Anna theorized existed at different vibrations of the cosmic ether.

Now I hoped only for the return to this world of the mind that I'd fallen in love with - the woman who'd brought me back from death with terrible consequences.

If only she'd heeded my cries of warning. Marna held up her wailing infant in triumph - reborn from death, wailing - as others still crawled from their tombs around us. If only I could have reached her, but the walking dead blocked my way -

WAAH! WHAAAAAAAAH!! WAAAHGH!!

ANNA!

ANNA, STOP!

MANDRETTA - SEE HERE THE CHILD TO WHOM YOU HAVE GIVEN NEW LIFE - TRUE LIFE, NOT THE WALKING UNDEATH!

FOR THIS IS HIS TRUE BIRTH - BIRTH INTO POWER - THE POWER HE SHARES WITH YOU!

WHAT DO YOU MEAN – HOW CAN THIS BE?
TAKE THE CHILD – HOLD ADAR AND HEAR HIS WYRD, AND ALL YOUR QUESTIONS SHALL BE ANSWERED.
NO, ANNA, DON'T DO IT!
WOULD YOU DEPRIVE YOURSELF OF THIS KNOWLEDGE?
KNOWING THE CONSEQUENCES OF THE WORD YOU HAVE JUST VOICED – WOULD YOU NOT INVOKE IT AGAIN TO SAVE YOUR LOVER?
I WILL TAKE THE CHILD... FOR A MEDICAL EXAMINATION.
THOUGH THE TUMOR HAS IN FACT GROWN WHILE HE WAS IN THE EARTH, HE SEEMS NO LONGER UNDER ITS SPELL – HE IS FUNCTIONING AS A NORMAL CHILD– OH!
OWW!

WHAT... WHERE AM I?
WAIT-THIS PLACE-I KNOW IT- IT'S MY DREAMSCAPE! BUT NOW IT'S NO LONGER BARREN, IT'S FULL OF GROWTH AND LIFE...
AND YET- THIS GROWTH- IT IS DARK, STRANGE-
DO NOT FEAR IT, ANNA!
WHAT- WHO?
IT GROWS AS YOU GROW-MERGING, BECOMING SOMETHING WONDERFUL! SOMETHING AWESOME TO BEHOLD!
IN THIS PLACE THAT IS TIMELESS I MAY BE AS I WILL BE-SOON EVEN AS THE MAN I WILL BE-THE MAN WHO WILL TAKE YOU AS HIS BRIDE AND WILL RULE THIS WORLD-
REMAKE IT IN HIS IMAGE, AS I AND MY FAMILY ARE BEING REMADE-
IN MY TRUE FATHER'S NAME!

AZAG-THOTH!

WE SHALL MAKE ALL THE WORLDS HIS!

SPILL THE BLOOD OF AN ANNOINTED ONE AND HIS REACH WILL EXTEND AS FAR AS NEED BE TO YOUR CALL.

I HAVE BEEN WITH HIM IN THE PLACE BEYOND DEATH — I KNOW SOMETHING OF THE ART THAT IS HIS TO COMMAND — POWER OVER REALITY ITSELF! THE WYRDLING — CONTROL OVER FATE, DESTINY, LIFE, DEATH AND BEYOND!

SLEEPLESS, HE CANNOT SEE, MINDLESS, HE CANNOT ACT—

BUT HIS WILL AND HIS POWER OVER ALL THE MAGICS AND SCIENCES IS OURS TO USE AND FULFILL!

THE CEREMONIAL BLADE! FIND IT, SPILL THE BLOOD OF AN ANOINTED ONE AND SUMMON HIM FROM THE PLACE BEYOND DEATH! SO THAT WE SHALL RULE!

HEAR MY WYRD!

WEIRDLING TROMORT AZAGTHOTH!

MY TRUE
FATHER
AWAKES!

ANNA?
THANK HEAVENS! I GOT THE FREQUENCIES RIGHT! YOU'RE COMING OUT OF IT...
CAN YOU STAND? SLOWLY NOW - HOW DO YOU FEEL?
I'M ALL RIGHT, NICOLAS. THE INFANT - ADAR?
THE WITCH-WOMAN TOOK HIM FROM YOU IN YOUR THRALL.
DO YOU REMEMBER ANYTHING FROM WITHIN THAT UNCONSCIOUS STATE?
ER - NO... NO, NOTHING.
I DID NOT WISH TO REVEAL TO MY ASSISTANT THE CURIOUS, APPALLING OFFER THAT HAD BEEN MADE TO ME BY THE BOY ADAR.
I ONLY ASK BECAUSE YOU BEGAN TO SPEAK OF A STRANGE OTHER WORLD FOR JUST A FEW MOMENTS BEFORE YOU WOKE -
YOU WERE ON SOME GREAT SHIP - A VESSEL CAPABLE OF TRAVELING THE STARS - YET IT SLUNK AROUND THE DEPTHS OF AN ALIEN OCEAN AND WAS STALKED BY CREATURES BEYOND MY CAPACITY TO DESCRIBE.
YOUR MEDICAL SKILLS WERE OF VITAL IMPORTANCE THERE AS WELL - YET YOUR POSITION ONBOARD WAS ONE OF LOW STATURE AND YOUR ACCOMPLISHMENTS WENT UNREWARDED, UNACKNOWLEDGED.
IT WAS A DISMAL WORLD, HORRIBLE AND FRIGHTENING, YET -
IN THE MOMENTS THAT YOUR VOICE CAME FROM THAT WORLD, IT WAS AS IF IT, AND YOU, WERE MORE - REAL - THAN I'D EVER SEEN YOU.
? ...

WE HAD WALKED FROM THE COLD OPERATING ROOM WHERE THE N.C.M. DEVICE WAS SET UP INTO THE DOCTOR'S PRIVATE STUDY. FORLORNLY HE CONTINUED.
I'M SORRY, ANNA - IT DOESN'T MAKE SENSE, I KNOW -
NOTHING MAKES SENSE ANYMORE -
NOT SINCE THE EVE THAT YOU HEALED THE INJURY I SUFFERED AT THE HANDS OF JOSEF VESSELL.
ANY FOR WHOM THE HALLS AND CHAMBERS OF THE HOSPITAL HAD BECOME HOME.
LOOK! THE DEAD CROWD UP TO THE DOORWAY - THEY ARE FORMER DOCTORS, NURSES, STUDENTS - EVEN LONG-TERM PATIENTS -
THAT'S ALL THEY WANT - TO GO HOME, TO RETURN TO THEIR ROUTINES OF LIFE. THEY ARE HARMLESS - UNLESS YOU TRY TO IMPEDE THEM - THEN...
THE VILLAGE HAS BEEN - IT'S HORRIBLE - A TRAVESTY. THE PEOPLE HAVE ALL BEEN DRIVEN AWAY - OR - BECOME LIKE THEM!
NICHOLAS...
YOU SHOULD NOT HAVE DONE WHAT YOU DID, ANNA!
I'M SURE THAT JOSEF WAS WRONG - KNOWING THE CONSEQUENCES, YOU WOULD NEVER HAVE SAVED MY LIFE...
JOSEF, IT'S PASSING STRANGE, I KNOW, BUT - SOMEHOW I BELIEVE THERE IS A KEY TO THIS MADNESS - WHAT YOU SAID ABOUT THAT OTHER WORLD. I DON'T KNOW WHY, BUT I THINK THAT ANSWERS MAY LIE THERE...
I WANT YOU TO HOOK ME UP AGAIN TO THE NEURAL CRYPTOMETER!

THE DEVICE IS SET UP IN MY OWN OFFICE, WHERE NICHOLAS CAN BETTER MONITOR ME. I DO NOT ANSWER HIS STATEMENT UNTIL PREPARATIONS ARE NEAR COMPLETE.
NICHOLAS -
YOU'RE MY TRUSTED FRIEND -
I VALUE YOUR LIFE ABOVE ANY OTHER IN THIS WORLD - I DON'T REGRET WHAT I DID.
I WILL RETURN TO YOU SHORTLY, MY LOVE.
ENGAGE THE DEVICE!
HMMMM...

MY SURROUNDINGS ARE BOTH FAMILIAR AND STRANGE.
THE CLOCK ON THE ODD DEVICE SEEMS TO INDICATE THAT IT IS THE WEE HOURS OF THE MORNING. TIME MUST PASS DIFFERENTLY HERE.

I CATCH SIGHT OF MY VISAGE IN A SMALL LOOKING GLASS.
I, ANNA MANDRETTA, HAD CROSSED OVER TO THE OTHER SIDE.

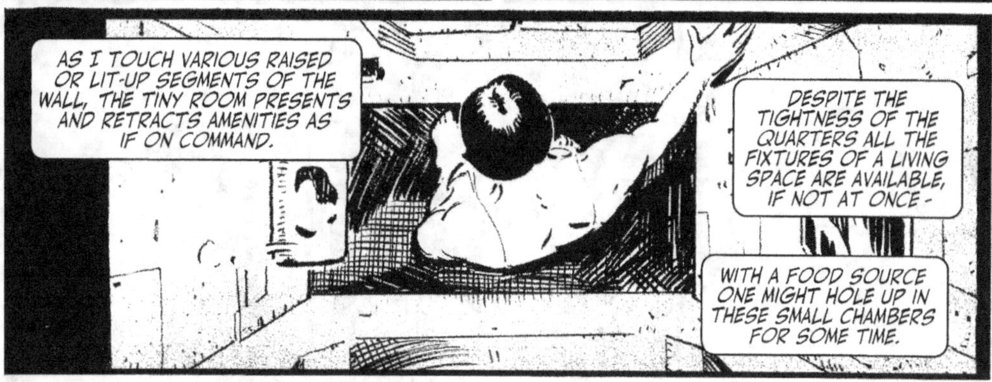

AS I TOUCH VARIOUS RAISED OR LIT-UP SEGMENTS OF THE WALL, THE TINY ROOM PRESENTS AND RETRACTS AMENITIES AS IF ON COMMAND.
DESPITE THE TIGHTNESS OF THE QUARTERS ALL THE FIXTURES OF A LIVING SPACE ARE AVAILABLE, IF NOT AT ONCE –
WITH A FOOD SOURCE ONE MIGHT HOLE UP IN THESE SMALL CHAMBERS FOR SOME TIME.

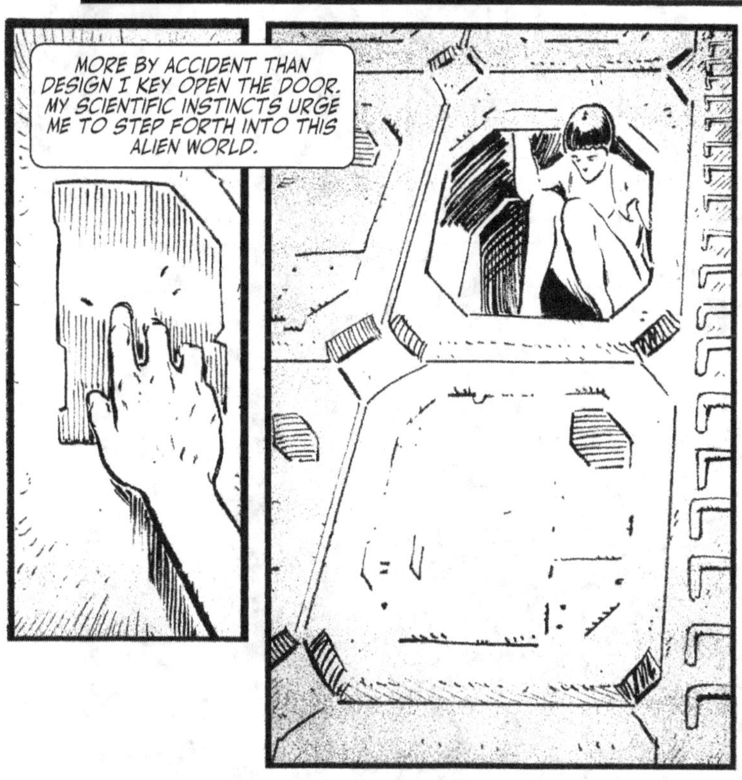

MORE BY ACCIDENT THAN DESIGN I KEY OPEN THE DOOR. MY SCIENTIFIC INSTINCTS URGE ME TO STEP FORTH INTO THIS ALIEN WORLD.

I'M PLEASED TO REPORT I SEEM TO HAVE RETAINED COMPLETE LUCIDITY.

I HAVE NOT GONE FAR WHEN I REALIZE...
I'M LOST.
PERHAPS DUE TO THE HOUR, THE DENIZENS OF THIS PLACE ARE FEW AND FAR BETWEEN. THOSE WHO NOTICE ME GIVE ME CURIOUS LOOKS BUT DO NOT STOP OR QUESTION ME.

DETERMINED TO EXPERIENCE AS MUCH OF THIS STRANGE WORLD AS I CAN WHILE IN THIS LUCID STATE, I LET MY FEET GUIDE ME.

HELLO?

IS THAT A PERSON? I CAN'T QUITE MAKE IT OUT - HELLO? I'M A DOCTOR - ARE YOU HURT?
HELLU - OH! OH GOD -
THE XAX! I'M IN HERE WITH THE XAX!!
YEEAAHHGH!!!

Subject: Mandretta, Anna. Under the supervision of Doctor Ripard Schreck.

The prisoner had activated some sort of self-destruct, or perhaps ingested some Xax equivalent of a suicide pill. It is not known whether the subject was present during the creature's death or was placed there after the event.

Subject has been diagnosed with cyber-addiction. Subject is also under suspicion of cyber-fraternization. Following the events of last night and subsequent discovery in a disuniformed state, subject has been upgraded to a suspicion of fraternization. Accomplice unknown.

...NNNNG... WH - DR. SCHRECK?
YOU'RE IN MY OFFICE, ANNA. HAVE YOU ANY MEMORY OF THE EVENTS OF LAST NIGHT?

THE LAST THING I REMEMBER - I WAS IN THE ROOM WITH - THE XAX!

DO YOU RECALL HOW YOU CAME TO BE THERE - OUT OF UNIFORM?

I - MUST HAVE SLEEPWALKED?
SOMNAMBULISM?

WHILE UNDER THE INFLUENCE OF THE LUCIDREAM EMITTER?
ER - I BELIEVE MY EMITTER IS - MALFUNCTIONING.
MALFUNCTIONING? BY THAT YOU MEAN - WHAT EXACTLY?

It is the subject's claim that her lucidream experience is gone awry - beyond that she has not been entirely forthcoming.

Her status as a cyber-addict might normally make such a claim less than credible. However, computer records indicate that indeed the device was active well into the hours she was seen wandering the halls.

Therefore I have once again put aside the charge of fraternization. While it would be logical to assume that such infractions might have been pursued in order to obtain contraband V.R. access, the entire picture of events, including her coincidental presence during the capture and subsequent death of the Xax prisoner, indicate that I am not in possession of all the facts.

In pursuit of the truth, I have sought out the virt-tech so that he might examine the lucidream emitter to determine if it is indeed malfunctioning.

As I step into the inner door of the virtech's work area my senses are assailed with a noxious odor of the solders and chemicals used in the upkeep of the V.R. equipment.

EXCUSE ME? TECHNICIAN?

ARE YOU FINDING ANYTHING?
FOR YOUR PATIENT TO BE EXPERIENCING SUCH A DRAMATIC SHIFT IN TONE AND CONTENT IN HER DREAM, THE REGULATION DREAM FEED WOULD HAVE TO BE INTERSECTED AND REPLACED BY A SEPARATE EMISSION.
JUST A MOMENT, DOCTOR-
THE PATIENT HINTED THAT AT SOME POINT SHE MAY HAVE TAMPERED WITH THE DEVICE IN AN ATTEMPT TO SHUT IT OFF OR POSSIBLY ADJUST THE FREQUENCY IN ORDER TO EXPERIENCE THE PRESCRIBED LUCIDREAM OF AN OFFICER OR DOCTOR.
THERE WE ARE - AND THE DISK -
WHAT ELSE CAN WE FIND AROUND HERE?
AH HA.
NOPE, NOT POSSIBLE. IT'S A COMMON MISCONCEPTION THAT THE DEVICES CAN BE ALTERED IN THAT WAY, BUT IN FACT TO AFFECT DREAM CHANGES OF THAT NATURE WOULD REQUIRE A SEPARATE DISK PLAYER INSTALLED INSIDE HER EMITTER, ENTIRELY REPLACING THE REGULATION LUCIDREAM.
SO - WHAT IS YOUR ASSESSMENT, TECHNICIAN?
NO UNUSUAL DEVICES, OR WIRING. EMITTER IS IN PERFECT WORKING ORDER.
I DID FIND THIS UNUSUAL OBJECT.

AN ANTIQUE JOURNAL?
THIS PATIENT OF YOURS - SHE'S THAT VIRT ADDICT, RIGHT?
I WOULDN'T GIVE HER STORY TOO MUCH CREDIT...
DON'T EVER BELIEVE NOTHING AN EFFIN' CYBER-JUNKY TELLS YOU!
HEMP 2 UNITS
MY LAST HEMP....

IT'S SWEET. WHY DOES HEMP FROM RECOMBINED MATTER TASTE SO EFFIN' GREAT, BUT THE MERKED FOOD TASTES LIKE DUNG?
COULD BE BECAUSE THE BASIC MATTER MOLECULES ARE ACTUALLY HEMP - THE HIGHEST-YIELD CROP NATIVE TO TERRA.
MOST NON-METALLIC SUBSTANCES ON BOARD, INCLUDING OUR UNIFORMS, THE FOOD TRAYS, THE SHIP'S CLEAN BURNING FUEL, AND OF COURSE THE HYPER-THIN PAPER THE SMOKES ARE WRAPPED IN ARE MADE OF HEMP.
I'M NO CYBERJUNKIE, DESPITE WHAT THEY'RE SAYING, BUT -
THERE'S NOTHING I ENJOY LIKE INHALING A HEMP AND SLIDING INTO ANOTHER REALITY.
IF I CLOSE MY EYES, I CAN ALMOST IMAGINE IT - THE FEEL OF BEING ON SOME OTHER WORLD.
THAT'S IT, NOW YOU'RE DOING IT.

HUH? WHAT? OH, IT'S YOU.
WHAT A PRETTY CAT - THAT'S FUNNY I THOUGHT I HEARD YOU SAY SOMETHING AGAIN.

THAT'S WHAT I'VE BEEN TRYING TO TELL YOU, ANNA.
WE HAVE TO TALK.
YOU SEE, I AM AN EXTRA-DIMENSIONAL BEING.

YOU TOO ARE BECOMING SUCH A BEING!

YOU ARE SO BEAUTIFUL AND TALENTED I WANTED TO MEET YOU IN YOUR WAKING WORLD.

UM, OKAY.

DON'T WORRY, ANNA, NOTHING CAN HARM YOU NOW.

MMM, THAT'S GOOD.

I'M STARTING TO REMEMBER.

I'M EATING WITH MY SHIPMATES - DOCTOR'S ORDERS. HE CAN'T MAKE ME TALK TO THEM, THOUGH. GOT LUCKY - FOUND A SEAT BETWEEN A PREOCCUPIED CARTOGRAPHER SIPPING MERKED JAVA AND AN ANIMATED CONVERSATION ALREADY IN PROGRESS. I DON'T JOIN IN.

I DON'T UNDERSTAND WHAT'S GOING ON. I'M NOT SURE I WANT TO. I'M TRYING NOT TO THINK, REALLY, WHICH MAKES IT EASIER TO SPORK THIS CHUM INTO MY MOUTH - BUT I CAN'T DENY IT.

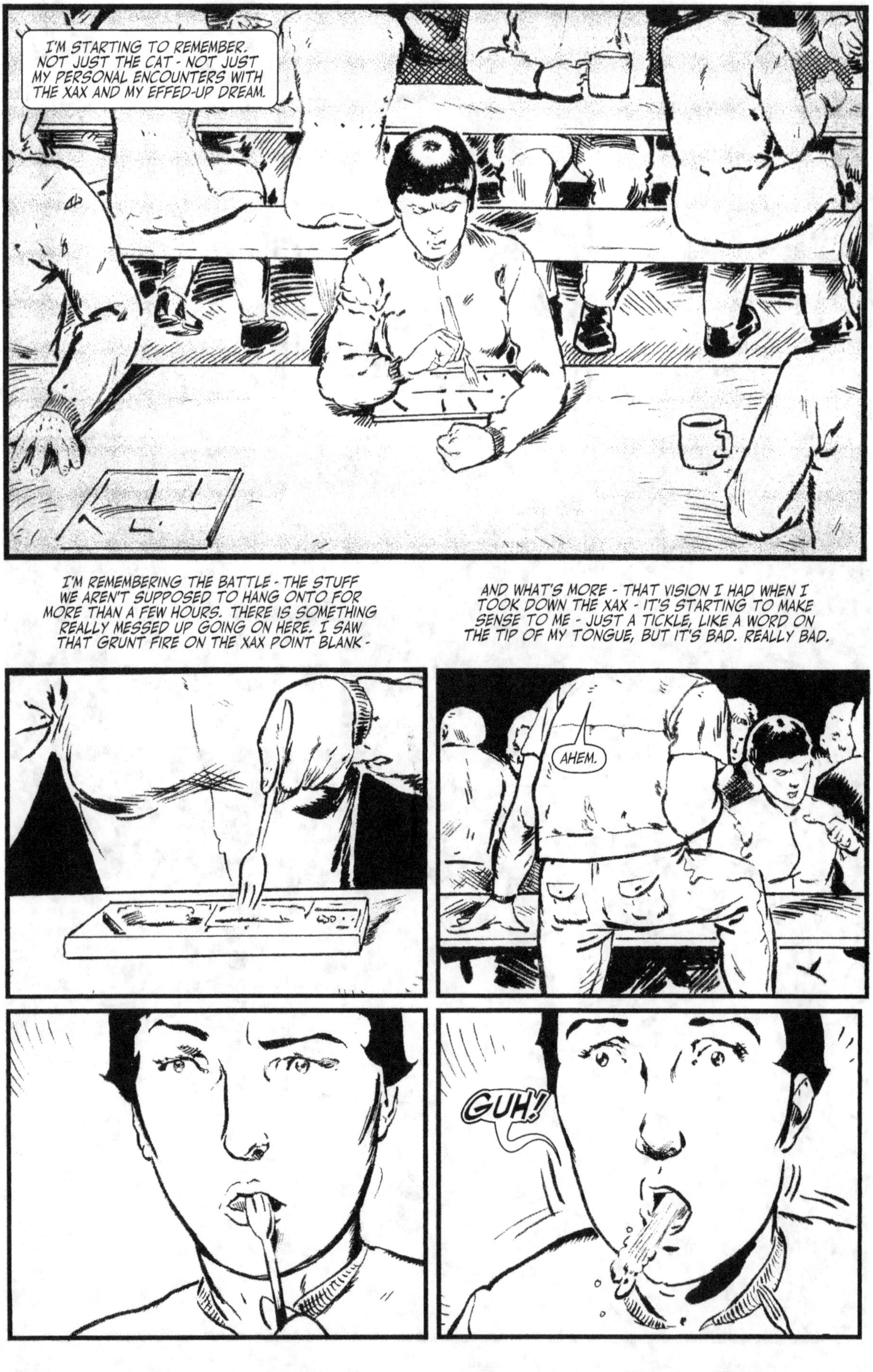

I'M REMEMBERING THE BATTLE - THE STUFF WE AREN'T SUPPOSED TO HANG ONTO FOR MORE THAN A FEW HOURS. THERE IS SOMETHING REALLY MESSED UP GOING ON HERE. I SAW THAT GRUNT FIRE ON THE XAX POINT BLANK -

AND WHAT'S MORE - THAT VISION I HAD WHEN I TOOK DOWN THE XAX - IT'S STARTING TO MAKE SENSE TO ME - JUST A TICKLE, LIKE A WORD ON THE TIP OF MY TONGUE, BUT IT'S BAD. REALLY BAD.

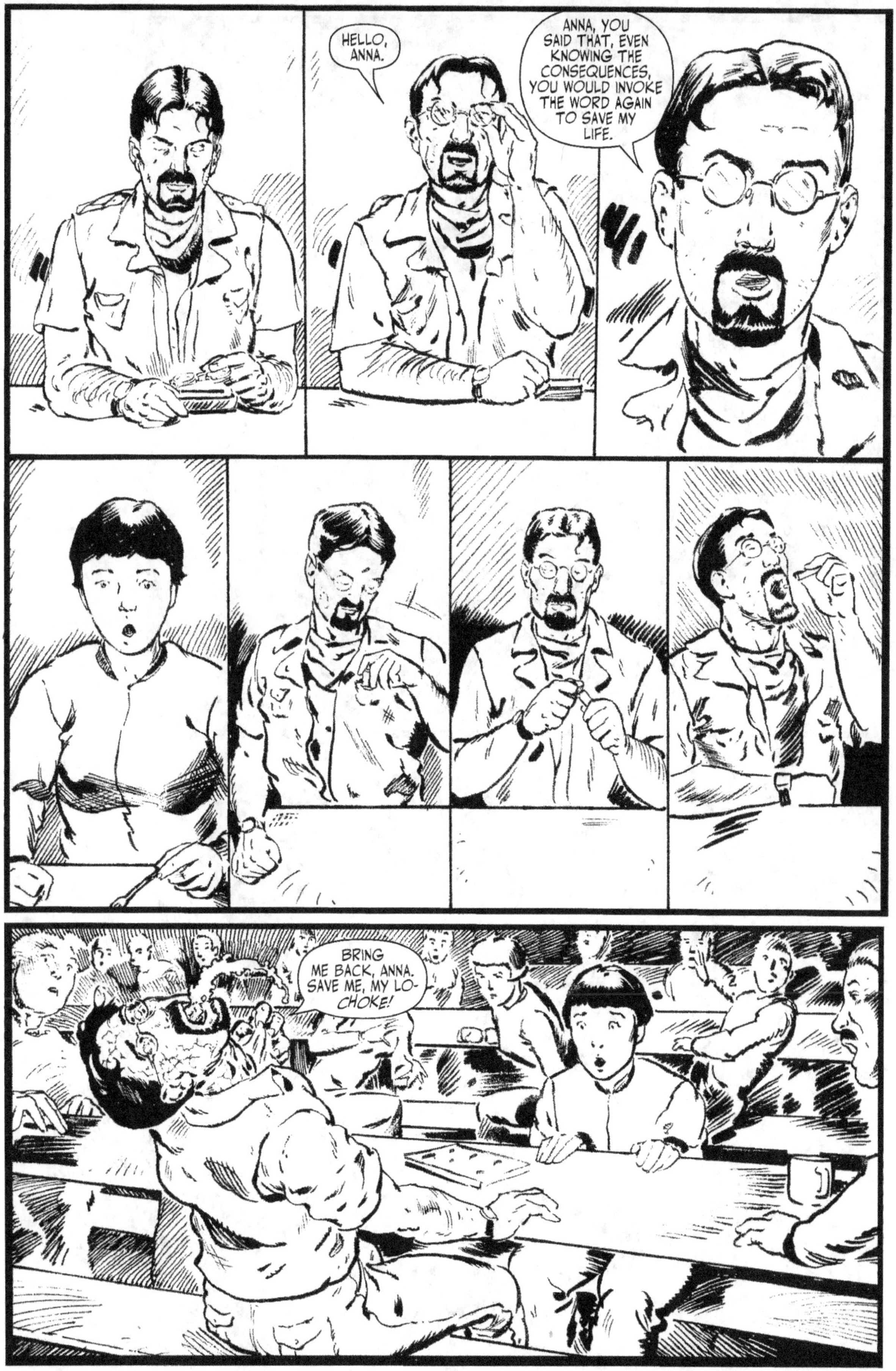

HELLO, ANNA.

ANNA, YOU SAID THAT, EVEN KNOWING THE CONSEQUENCES, YOU WOULD INVOKE THE WORD AGAIN TO SAVE MY LIFE.

BRING ME BACK, ANNA. SAVE ME, MY LO-CHOKE!

WHA-!
WHAT DO I DO?
WHAT IS GOING ON!?!
HE'S DEAD!
HE TOLD ME TO SAY THE WORD-

BUT ALL THESE PEOPLE HERE TO SEE-
WHAT SHOULD I DO?
WEIRDLING VERMIS!

HUUUUAAAHG...

Subject: Obliv Shivean, virtech. Examining doctors conclude the subject had ingested lethal dose of the suicide toxin Kersylla. Inexplicably, subject's vital signs appear normal.

Unusual detail- animal blood found under subject's fingernails. No reliable witnesses to the event. Despite inexplicable bio readings, subject remains in stable condition.

INEXPLICABLE? HIS BLOOD HAS BEEN TURNED TO FORMALDEHYDE!
I'M BEGINNING THE TRANSFUSION PROCESS NOW.
LEAVE HIM! IT WILL MAKE MY JOB EASIER WHEN HE FINALLY REALIZES HE'S SUPPOSED TO BE DEAD!
MORTICIAN? MAY I SPEAK TO YOU? I AM THE MEDIC WHO REVIVED THAT MAN.
REVIVED HIM? HOW? WALK WITH ME, I AM A BUSY MAN.
ANOTHER MAN DIED TODAY?
YOU HADN'T HEARD?
A DEAD XAX, AND TWO DEAD MEN - IF YOU COUNT THE CORPSE IN THERE THAT'S STILL BREATHING.
OLD MCCREEGY, THE ENGINEER. DIED IN HIS SLEEP CHAMBER. HEART FAILURE. MONITORED THE AUTO-DOC'S AUTOPSY MYSELF.

BUT THAT STIFF IN THERE - YOU SAY YOU REVIVED HIM -
HOW? WHAT TECHNIQUE DID YOU USE?
I CAN'T QUITE EXPLAIN THE TECHNIQUE.
I THINK IT WAS SOMETHING I KNEW SUBLIMINALLY, FROM THE LUCIDREAM.
UM, I WAS WONDERING - WHAT WAS IT THAT-
KILLED HIM? IT WAS A POISON USED BY UNDERCOVER AGENTS.
TURNS ONE'S BLOOD INTO EMBALMING FLUID, INSTANTLY.
IT LEAVES A DISTINCTIVE MARK ON THE EPIDERMIS. THAT'S THE SKIN, MY DEAR.
THERE CAN BE NO MISTAKING IT. IT TAKES EFFECT SO QUICKLY, THERE IS NO CURE. EXCEPT THE ONE YOU HAVE, OF COURSE.
I, I MEAN, WHAT I MEANT WAS...
I KNOW WHO YOU ARE.
THE CRYO-COFFINS BEAR A DISTURBING RESEMBLANCE TO OUR OWN SLEEP CHAMBERS, DON'T YOU AGREE?

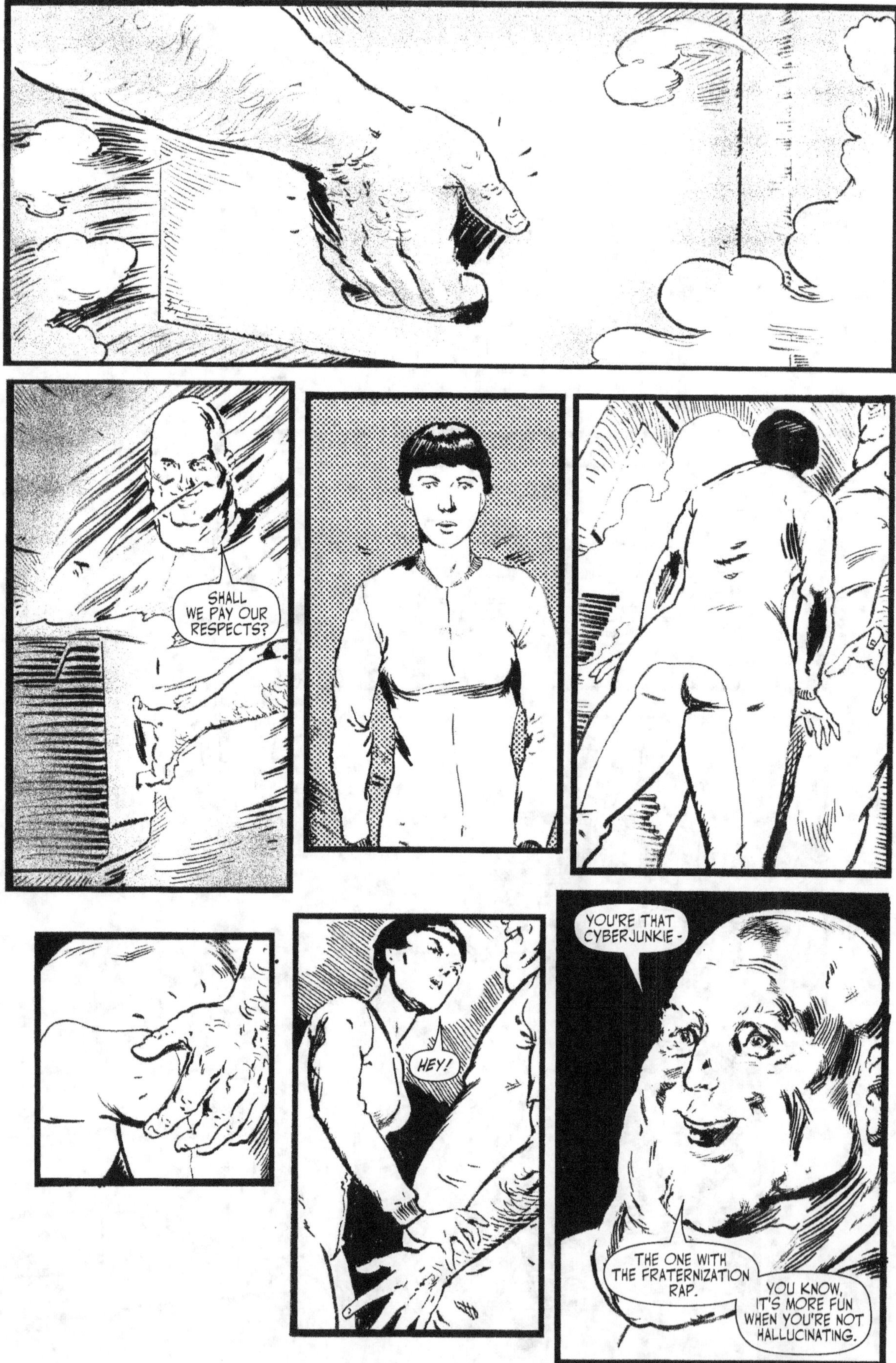
SHALL WE PAY OUR RESPECTS?
HEY!
YOU'RE THAT CYBERJUNKIE -
THE ONE WITH THE FRATERNIZATION RAP.
YOU KNOW, IT'S MORE FUN WHEN YOU'RE NOT HALLUCINATING.

DON'T BELIEVE ME? JUST ASK OLD MCCREEGY - NOW THERE WAS A LADIES' MAN!
YEP, A REAL LIVE ONE!
THUMP!
HOLY SNOT!
SKWK!
WHAT THE-?!!

ЦUHHHЦUHHHA HHHUUH...
GREAT UNIVERSE!
AAAAAAAAAIIIEEEEEEE!
GARGGL...

IT'S GOTTA BE SPACE DEMENTIA.
YEAH, THAT'S IT.
NOTHING I SAW WAS REAL. THAT CORPSE WASN'T REAL.
THERE WAS NO MAN THAT LOOKED LIKE NICHOLAS VAN HISE. THERE WAS NO MAN, AND I DID NOT BRING HIM BACK TO LIFE.
I DID NOT HAVE ANY CONVERSATIONS WITH A CAT. THERE ARE NO CATS ON DEEP SPACE VESSELS LIKE THIS ONE.

NONE OF IT WAS REAL. I SHOULD ACTIVATE MY LUCIDREAM EMITTER AND GO TO SLEEP, AND I WON'T REMEMBER ANY OF THIS TOMORROW. IT WASN'T REAL.
UNLESS...
COMPUTER, DEHUMIDIFY.
ALL OF IT WAS REAL.

From the journal of Dr. Nicholas Van Hise: The doctor has said nothing since she reactivated the NCM.
I am beginning to grow concerned that she has been drawn deeper into that other world.
Were I never to get my friend back, I do not know how I would live with myself—
NO. NO, I'M NOT.
I'M ANNA MANDRETTA, FIELD MEDIC ON THE DREADNOUGHT XII ALL-TERRAIN WARSHIP.
ANNA, THANK GOODNESS YOU'RE ALRIGHT!
HUH! I'M IN THE MISKATONIK HOSPITAL—THIS IS MY OFFICE.
YOU— YOU ARE DOCTOR NICHOLAS VAN HISE. I REMEMBER.
THAT'S RIGHT. AND YOU ARE DOCTOR ANNA MANDRETTA.
I HAD AWAKENED INTO THE DREAM WITH FULL LUCIDITY.

continued on page 166

THREE DREAMS OF MY ALMOST-FAVORITE WITCH
BY DANIEL BRAUM

1 Somehow there is another woman drunkenly hanging on my arm when *she* walks into the apartment Christmas party.

I watch my host see her in. "Did someone say astrology?" I hear her say, miraculously despite the music and miasma of the shoulder-to-shoulder crowd. We are two points. There is an invisible line between us. I can hear her speak. She beelines for me and me to her and the rest of what would have been an insufferable time was lost in blissful conversation.

She raises a staff to the sky and the train to take her home arrives in the night. She is fishing with the right kind of bait and lures me to a summer day. Union Square bustles all around us. Our world is still as we traverse the past. Secret gardens can still be found in New York, at least then. That is how love goes. It is found and lost. Three hours of forever. What we swear will be endless is revealed as finite. Yet we come alive for the chance to know beautiful ways to spend time once more. We are served delights fit for royalty and I believe the world can be ours. I'm looking to the future and maybe so is she.

2 The binding line, the ethereal connection is an arm in the constellation that is us. If this keeps up she very well could wind up as my all-time favorite witch. Her mother is *her* favorite witch. The line that is *her* life crosses with the railroad tracks just up the block from the Botanica in her home town where she has taken me. Where last month she had taken her mother for a ritual. I use restraint and do not purchase the statue of Santa Muerte. She does not realize it but she has shown me the two swords she is choosing between. One of them is me. She describes the other blade with the names of things about myself I have not told her. At first I thought otherwise but this test is not for me. This is the way we dream our lives into being. Blindly. Sometimes holding on for dear life. Sometimes holding hands. Sometimes standing outside the house of Edgar Allan Poe, a dream house that the world has seen fit to preserve. We're making decisions together only no one is telling us what the choices are. I decided I could trust myself with either blade.

3 Christmas time comes again. All the lives at the party, all the lines of those lives shooting off in a million directions into space, spiral around us. Some disappear into the astral. Some descend into the nether. Some come together in unions meant to be followed in the here and now. I was right that I saw the necklace around her neck in a dream only it was not a dream of me. The vinyl, the bliss, the music, the new life and purity and green—all things not meant for me. Not for *this* me. Maybe not for *this* her. She wonders what it is like. She wonders if she can grasp before letting go. She wonders if she will ask if she will see me there and does speak the words aloud and the spell is done.

The subway tunnel is almost unbearably hot but I stay. I watch the necklace curve with her hair. Follow the lines of her contour. And for the first time she realizes she is seen. You are looking at my arms. At my veins, she says. But I am not. I am seeing the train coming. This time not from the night but from the dark of the underground.

This time it takes her away and despite the few times after- when I checked the lines for signal—I never see her again in all my days.

CONJURED SLEEP

BY KARINA COURTWAY

Sweat began to pour, and the screams echoed. The chaos of slain men is vivid in my dreams.

Friend and foe turned into beasts, ending the lives of those who stood at the behest of war, armed with shields and swords. Never had my eyes seen the innards of a man scattered in daylight. The flesh's glistening texture, spurts of blood, mangled muscles, and shattered bones all haunt me. Gouged eyes, amputated limbs, and heads visit me in my sleep. My body tosses violently, unable to shake away the carnage. I begin to sob.

"Wake up, you're dreaming. Everything is alright," I hear her soothing voice.

I feel a gentle shake. My wife comforts my torment and nurtures me like a child. I feel relief that I have awaken and in the darkness, I am not alone.

"You must go to her," she whispers.

"There is no honor in forgetting war," I respond.

"The hell with honor, I want my husband back."

My wife squeezes me tightly pleading with her embrace. I give some thought to what my wife desires and feel shame for wanting the same. Urshla, the wizard who lives in a cavern just beyond our village, can conjure the spell of forgetfulness. Warriors who've been discovered going to her are ostracized. They are tormented by their former comrades, whose rage becomes a mystery as oblivion takes hold. Many leave their homes behind, while others commit with their hand what the battlefield could not.

Dare I go to her? The question frays my thoughts. By now, my wife is asleep. I slip away from our bed. I clothe myself and use my hands to guide myself through our darkened home. I approach the entry door, and before reaching it, I kneel. The moonlight draws my hand to a secret floorboard. I pry it open.

My palm feels the cool dirt below, but then touches the satchel of gold and silver.

"What is the price for such alchemy?" I whisper to myself.

Before wandering out into the darkness, I take a deep breath and grab my sword. The wolves howl in the night. Their cries do not stop me. I venture forward ignoring my reluctance. I am lucky that there is a clear sky, allowing the moon to shine its silvery illumination upon the path. I veer off the trail into the dense forest. The canopy of the trees casts shadows that play with the mind. The dark entrance of the cave swallows me. I tread slowly, until finally I see a green light. I creep slowly, hiding behind boulders. To my surprise, she has already begun a ritual with two patrons. She hums and sings words I do not understand. I feel relieved I am not the only one who seeks magical consolation. But as I look closer, I notice their complexion and shaven heads.

They belong to the enemy army. Anger fills my soul. They are the reason for my suffering and sleepless nights. They are the reason my comrades lie beneath the ground. They look pathetic, filled with cowardice, as they allow Urshlas's trance to wash away their woes. Urshla's magic levitates their disconnected heads above their bodies. Quickly, I make way for them. The sword falls heavily, striking the first soldier in the shoulder, rending its way down to the heart. He slumps forward, hitting the floor.

His head went thumping into the darkness. Urshla screams and falls backwards.

"You brute! How dare you taint my ritual of conjured sleep!" Urshla yells.

The second soldier remained kneeling when Urshla's spell was broken, it sent his living head tumbling to my feet. His milky, cloudy eyes sickens me. I step on his forehead. The eyes stare back at me, and I cleave his mouth, severing his lower jaw. His extended tongue slumped on the cave's floor.

Urshla is petrified.

"Let the wolves feast and take away this mess," I tell her. I gaze at the sorceress for a brief moment and rapidly the guilt stifles my belligerence. I toss my satchel of coins at her feet and walk away. Tonight I return home as a warrior with all its wretchedness and all its pain.

FORBIDDEN FUTURES 14

SPECTER

BY PHILIP FRACASSI

1

THE LAST PRESENT.

It's wrapped in black paper embossed in silver cycles of the moon, crisscrossed with a glittery string tied in a loose bow. Holding the box in her small hands, Jenna looks up at her nana, who sits stoically among a few straggling parents clutching plastic cups of cheap wine. A smattering of young girls grow restless and bored watching Jenna open gifts. Jenna's mother stands to the side, arms folded, a tight smile on her face, as if nervous.

"That one's from me," Nana says, sucking on a cigarette and ignoring the side-glance grimaces of some parents, each of them surely debating whether to discuss the effects of secondhand smoke with the old woman.

Jenna, sitting cross-legged on the living room carpet, gives her nana a smile. "Thank you, Nana," she says.

The old woman nods, frowning. "It's not another dress; I can tell you that."

Jenna's eyes flick instinctively to her mother in time to see her face harden, her eyes shift momentarily downward. Jenna has opened three new dresses, all of which she adored. She was eleven years old now. Next year, she'd leave her middle school for junior high, which was practically high school.

Clothes were essential.

In addition to the dresses, she's been given absolutely *perfect* gold-colored ballerina flats and a gorgeous pair of cherry-red Mary Jane's with a matching red leather belt. She doesn't like that Nana makes her mother feel bad about giving her new clothes, especially since it's what—frankly, *all*—she'd asked for.

Her friends have mainly given her jewelry—a pair of earrings, a charm bracelet, a set of pretty hairclips decorated with fake pearls. Her best friend, Esther, always eager to surprise, gave her a mahogany jewelry case that, when opened, played music and revealed a twirling ballerina. Esther's mother, gushing with pride at having delivered the knockout punch of 'best gift,' announces the tune to be "March of Wooden Soldiers" by a Russian composer whose name she couldn't remember.

"Tchaikovsky," Nana says through a haze of smoke, "killed himself with poison, but wrote beautiful music."

"Mom, please," Jenna's mother says nervously, avoiding eye contact with any of the other parents.

Some of the girls giggle into their palms.

Nana simply shrugs, like she always does when chided.

Despite her nana's age (Jenna didn't know it exactly but had a shaky memory of an 80th birthday being mentioned when she was a few years younger), she was an intimidating woman. Small, thin, and bony, but with a spine straight as a yardstick and hard gray eyes to match shiny silver hair (which was always perfectly coiffed in a backswept style that made Jenna think of Disney villains, although she'd never admit such a thing).

Jenna studies the package a moment longer, then gently frees the hand-tied bow at its center. She runs the tips of her fingers lightly over the embossed moons, knowing full well her nana's love of the stars, which she once told Jenna: "revealed all the secrets of the universe, if you only knew to read them." In addition to studying the stars (which she'd repeatedly informed Jenna was called *astrology,* a word Jenna could never quite remember), Nana also enjoyed telling fortunes using a deck of special cards. Jenna's favorite of these was one called *The Empress*—the woman in the image seeming so powerful with her revealing clothes, her horns of hair, her golden scepter. But Jenna also thought her beautiful. The kind of woman she'd like to be when she was older—sexy, sure. But *strong.*

Flipping the box over (*too thin for shoes, too heavy for a belt*) she pulls the paper apart at the neatly taped seam to reveal a black cardboard box. She turns it back over, right-side-up. Another half-moon—this one stamped gold into the box's lid—stares back at her. Intrigued, Jenna pulls off the top… and, at first, her heart sinks.

A book?

Momentarily thinking she might have said the word aloud, she quickly glances up at her nana, who studies her with cold, indifferent eyes, her black turtleneck and halo of cigarette smoke giving her pale head an al-most detached look. Jenna has a flash memory of the bulbous floating head that was the Great and Powerful Oz. *All she needs is flames shooting from her ears.* Jenna feels a wash of shame and drops her eyes once more to examine the gift.

"What is it?" Esther asks, with all the giddy coyness of someone knowing the event has finished, the last challenger falling short of competing with this year's winner: she who brought the musical jewelry box with the twirling ballerina.

"A book," Jenna replies, doing her best to shovel a modicum of enthusiasm into her response.

"What kind of book, hon?"

Jenna looks up at her mother, whose seemingly innocuous question sounds rife with tension. Worry.

"It's a dream journal," Nana announces before Jenna even has it out of the box. "You put it next to your bed when you're sleeping. When you wake up, you write down your dreams before you forget them. There's a guide in there, as well, at the back, that tells you what they mean."

"Cool," Jenna says excitedly, meaning it this time. She lifts aside a fold of black tissue paper and studies the cover.

The book is large, almost like a dictionary. The cover is black leather, and there's no title. No words at all. There are designs, however, carved into the leather. Intricate, beautiful designs: a pair of large hands holding sand that spills between cupped fingers; a snake eating its own tail; a large, closed eye in the center; stars, moons, planets…

Jenna lifts the cover to reveal a neat inscription written in the center of the first, blank, page.

For Jenna,
When you dream, dream of me.
Nana

"It's beautiful," Jenna says, part of her wanting to leaf through the book then and there, feel the thick pages within, read the different meanings of dream symbols…

But her friends are already standing, antsy and ready for the cake and ice cream portion of the event. The final meal before the party is officially over and they can go home to daydream about their own childhood birthday parties, the wonderful gifts they'll hope to receive.

Jenna carefully sets the book back into the sturdy black box, her eyes unable to leave the cover.

"Jenna?" her mother says. "Come on, let's blow out the candles."

"Okay," she replies, and begins to fold the thin tissue paper back over the book's cover, when she pauses.

The embossed eye in the center—the one she would have sworn was closed only a moment ago—is now open wide. As if watching her.

As if seeing her for the very first time.

Realizing she must have seen it wrong the first time, Jenna dismisses the chill that climbs up her spine at the sight of the open eye. She dutifully covers it with the paper, replaces the cardboard lid, then heads for the kitchen to have cake and ice cream with her friends.

She doesn't notice Nana watching her as she passes by the table, a rare smile curling the old woman's lips.

Later that night, Jenna is settled in bed, turning the interior pages of her new journal, when her nana comes to say goodbye.

"I'm not good at gifts for little girls," she says, sitting primly as a perched crow on the edge of the bed. "My Thomas always hated getting clothes on his birthday."

Jenna smiles, having grown used to the old woman referring to him in those words: *My Thomas.*

Never *your father* or *my son*. Almost always—and especially when speaking to Jenna's mother—it was simply: *My Thomas.*

"You like the book?" she asks.

Jenna nods. "I've been reading the descriptions. Did you know, in dreams, a horse symbolizes strength? And losing your teeth means you're anxious."

"That's right," Nana says, sniffing. "But it's more than that, Jenna. You must put things in context."

Jenna studies her for a moment, brow furrowed. "What do you mean?"

"For instance," Nana says, with a small sigh, "a horse in a blizzard can mean perseverance, which could represent finding the strength to meet your goals in life. But a horse that's kicking you in the face, smashing all those little bones," she says, running a cold finger down the bridge of Jenna's nose, "well, that might mean something completely different."

Jenna scowls at the idea of her broken face, annoyed at Nana for saying such a horrible thing, but curiosity forces her to continue. "Like what?"

The old woman shrugs. "Like you don't have the strength to go on," she says, gray eyes intent on her granddaughter.

Jenna closes the book, runs her fingers over the grooved designs that decorate the leather cover.

"I almost forgot," Nana says. "One more gift before I go."

She reaches into her clutch and brings out an ornate pen, the casing dark wood, the trim silver and bright. "It's a nice one, the kind you refill the ink when it runs out instead of throwing it away. It's a good pen for your journal."

Jenna takes the offering, loving the heavy feel of it. She pops off the top, studies the glistening ink coating the tip. "Cool. I'm going to write my name in it now. There's a page for it."

The corners of Nana's lips twitch, and Jenna doesn't know if she's genuinely pleased, or just trying to hold in a mean-spirited smirk. "You do that. Now give Nana a hug. It's past time we all go to sleep."

Jenna wakes the next morning, eager for school, excited to show off one of her new dresses. It isn't until she's out of bed that her eye catches the dream journal on the nightstand. "Oh, shoot," she says, realizing that in her haste she hadn't given herself time to recall any dreams she may have had. Taking a moment (and forcing herself to forget about school and which dress she might wear), Jenna sits on the edge of her bed, curls her fingers into fists, squeezes her eyes shut tight, and tries to remember.

Seconds later, her eyelids shoot open and she snatches the journal, and the wonderful new pen, from her nightstand. She quickly flips past the opening pages (including the one where she'd written her name, the precise handwriting encircled by the image of celestial, dancing figures she thinks of as angels) until she reaches the first blank journal page. At the top, it says DATE, followed by a thin line. She writes the date then, just below, she writes what she remembers of her dream.

I'm standing on a seashore watching giant waves coming in from a huge, gray ocean. I hear a noise and turn around to see a tall, rocky cliff. At the bottom of the cliff is the opening of a large cave. I walk closer to the cave, then stop when I see what's making the noise.

A bear.

He's huge and black as night. He's also very fat, as if he'd just eaten a family of campers. I watch him walk slowly into the cave, and I know he's going there to sleep.

Jenna takes a moment to think of the right word.

To hibernate. Like for the winter.

I keep watching until he disappears inside the cave. I'm about to follow when I hear a scream from behind me. I spin around fast, frightened, but see nothing except the crashing waves of the ocean.

I think now that I must have heard a bird. Like a seagull.

At this point I notice that my feet are itchy. I look down and see they're covered in tiny spiders. Thousands of them! The wet, dirty sand is moving because there's so many of them. It was like I'd stepped on their eggs and they'd hatched beneath me. I see a hand coming out of the sand, fingers clawing through the mass of spiders.

I start to scream.

And then I wake up.

It sounds weird but, thinking back, I wonder if the scream I heard was me. Dreams are weird like that, aren't they?

Jenna stops writing, solemnly puts the cap back onto the pen. She makes a mental note to look up "bear" and "spiders" after school. She doesn't like the dream, and she's curious what it all means.

She closes the journal, sets it on the sheets of her unmade bed, and all but runs for the bathroom and a hot shower.

While she's getting cleaned up, she decides to wear the yellow dress.

Her mother watches from the porch as Jenna walks to the corner. This was the first school year Jenna had been allowed to walk alone to the bus. A rung on the ladder of independence climbed with being a year older, combined with the facts it was only a block from her front door and there were always a few other kids from the neighborhood waiting there, including Esther, who gawked like a fool when she saw Jenna in her new dress.

"Looking good, baby!" Esther says, loudly enough that a couple of the other tired-looking kids momentarily glance up from their phones.

Jenna laughs, then shivers. She hadn't wanted to wear a coat over her dress, and the day would warm up soon enough, but at seven o'clock in the morning it's still chilly, even for early fall.

"Thanks," she says. "And thanks again for the jewelry box. I love it."

Esther nods and loops her arm through Jenna's as the bus pulls up, followed quickly by the sharp stink of exhaust and the high-pitched rumble of the chatting children already aboard. "I knew you'd love it. Better than a stupid book, anyway," she says as the girls climb aboard, navigate the narrow walkway before reaching their usual bench.

The vinyl seat is icy on the back of Jenna's legs, forcing her to suppress another shiver.

Jenna thinks Esther's remark is more a test than a statement, as if making sure the dream journal hadn't somehow trumped her own gift now that the dust of the party had settled. "I actually wrote in it this morning," she says, amused at Esther's grimace. "I dreamed about a bear, and spiders. Isn't that weird?"

"I don't like spiders, and I really don't like bears," Esther says, looking out the window as their familiar neighborhood drifts away like a mirage. "They eat people."

2

When Jenna arrives home that afternoon, she's in a foul mood.

For starters, a rotten boy named Steven Duane Allison Junior, who was rumored to be the neighborhood serial killer of stray cats and squirrels, knocked over his fucking chocolate milk during lunch and some of it leaked over the table and spilled onto her dress. She'd spent ten minutes in the bath-room crying and trying to clean it out with water and paper towels, which *then* made her late for fifth period, and snotty Mr. Jensen gave her a tardy slip even though she'd told him what happened, and it was *obvious* she'd been crying about it. To make the day a total disaster, Esther's mom picked her up at school to go shopping. They invited Jenna to come with them, but she was so embarrassed about her dumb dress (complete with the stupid brown stain from Steven Duane Allison Junior's goddamn chocolate milk) that she'd said 'no,' and then nearly cried again on the bus ride home. *Alone.*

"Mom!" she yells as she walks through the front door, glancing into the kitchen, then the living room, but not seeing her mother. Because *of course* she's not there, waiting for her (or waiting on the porch, like she usually was).

Instead, Jenna finds her mother in her bedroom, sitting on her bed.

Reading her dream journal.

"Mom?"

Her mother audibly *squeaks* in surprise, almost dropping the oversized book to the floor as one hand clutches the fabric in front of her heart. "Jesus, honey, you scared me."

Jenna's eyes narrow. "What are you doing?"

Looking embarrassed, her mother closes the book and sets it gently on the nightstand. "I was curious about your book. I wanted… Well, I wanted to read about some of the meanings, you know? For dreams."

"Why? Also, look at my dress."

Her mom glances at the small stain (*because it is,* Jenna realizes in the aftermath of her day from hell, *small*) and gives a tired nod. "That'll come out in the wash, honey."

Feeling suddenly foolish, Jenna goes to her dresser and pulls out a pair of jeans and a T-shirt. She pulls off the yellow dress and hands it to her mother, who glances once more at the stain, then clutches the dress to her breasts, as if it needed comforting. "And to be honest, I had a very strange dream myself last night. It was…upsetting. So, I don't know, I wanted to see if there was something about it…"

Jenna pulls on her jeans, tugs the shirt down over her head (mildly annoyed at how much more comfortable she feels out of the dress), then sits on the bed with her mother, crossing her legs beneath her. "What was the dream?"

She wants to ask: *Was there a bear? Were there spiders?*

But her mom only sighs, absently runs her fingers down the arm of her blouse. "It was about your father. He was talking to me…but I couldn't understand what he was saying. It was like he was behind glass, or something…but he kept talking, and gesturing in a crazy way, like he was upset, or in pain."

"Whoa," Jenna says quietly. Her mother didn't mention her father often, and Jenna herself has no memory of him, since he died when she was just a baby. But she knows her mom had loved him very much, and that he had been Nana's only child.

Jenna thinks part of the reason her mom doesn't talk about her father is because Nana had helped them after he died. Gave them money for the house, to live. It was as if they'd made an agreement, her mother and her nana: money for silence. A pact she thinks quietly, slowly, broke her mother's heart. Like a hand pressed against cracked glass, each splintering *snap* a beat closer to shattering it completely.

The other reason, Jenna knew, was because Nana blamed her mother for his death. As if it had been her mother's fault her dad had…done what he did. Jenna only knows the details because Esther once overheard their mothers talking late one night, an empty bottle of wine between them. Jenny remembers the flushed cheeks of Esther's excitement when she relayed the information.

That her father had hung himself in the bedroom of their old home.

"Anyway, when I woke up," her mother continues. "I could have sworn he was trying to tell me something important." She looks over at Jenna then, almost expectant, a half-smile appears on her face. "Stupid, huh?"

"Let me see the book," Jenna says, and her mom hands it over.

"What are you doing?"

Jenna opens the book on her lap, begins flipping pages until she gets to the back portion that contains the dictionary of meanings. "Looking up ghost. Why, what did you look up?"

Her mother looks confused for a moment, then sighs. "Husband."

"Here!" Jenna says, finding the entry. "Ghosts can often symbolize fear," she recites. "Or a strong paranoia about death."

Jenna glances up at her mom, who stares at the far wall, her expression blank.

She shrugs, continues. "It can also symbolize loss. As of a loved one through divorce, or death."

"That's enough, hon…"

"Maybe you were dreaming about Dad because you're afraid of something."

Jenna's mother stands up, brushes down the front of her wool skirt, then kisses her daughter's head before turning away. "I'm always afraid," she says.

Five days after Jenna's eleventh birthday, Nana is found dead in her kitchen.

Firemen, responding to a neighbor reporting the smell of gas, find her on her knees, wearing a formal black dress, head bowed into the open door of an antique oven, the pilot light purposely extinguished.

She'd done herself the courtesy of laying a blanket beneath her head.

At the funeral, Jenna overhears a cousin saying, "The fussy old bird probably didn't want rack lines on her cheek." The person he's talking to laughs.

3

The day after her grandmother's funeral, Jenna wakes up crying. Her bedroom window is a hazy gray, the sun having not yet fully risen. She takes deep breaths in the dusky light of her room, recalling a most vivid dream.

She clicks on her bedside lamp and plucks up the journal along with the ornately engraved pen.

Just had the most horrible dream EVER.

I was at Nana's funeral, and at some point I walked out of the room and into the lobby. There was a man there with his back to me. He was staring at the large photo of Nana that the funeral people had put out front on an easel. I said, "Hello?" but he didn't turn around or anything. He just stood there, wearing a dirty brown suit. He was breathing heavily, his shoulders lifting up and down. I could hear his breathing getting louder, like he was getting angry. Then he turned around and his face was blacked-out like a shadow. Like his head was empty.

I ran back into the room where Nana's coffin was but there was nobody there. All the pretty flowers around the coffin had turned black. I started to cry and yell for Mother. I didn't want to leave the room because the man was out there. Then I heard my name.

"Jenna."

I spun around to where the chairs were and Nana was sitting there, smiling at me. She held out her arms and I ran to her and hugged her. She was stroking my hair and calming me down. Then I realized she couldn't *be there because she was dead.*

I said, "Nana, why aren't you in the coffin?"

She smiled even wider, and it was creepy because Nana hardly ever smiled, and she said, "That's not me in the coffin, honey. That's your mother."

Then she took my hand and stood up, walking towards the coffin, which was open like it had been for Nana. She was dragging me toward it.

"You should join her," she said.

I started to pull back and scream. I didn't want to be anywhere near that coffin so I yelled, "Stop! Stop!"

But then I heard the man behind me, breathing like a horse, and he smelled bad, like rotten but also like dirt. And Nana pulled me right up next to the coffin and my mom was in there, but she wasn't dead. She was alive! She was alive and she turned to look at me, and her eyes were wide and scared and she wanted to open her mouth but the stitches inside kept her from talking. The stitches inside her mouth stretched. Unable to open her mouth, she moaned horribly. Tears ran from her eyes.

And then I woke up, and now I'm crying and I hate this stupid journal.

Jenna slams the journal closed and tosses it onto the nightstand. She's been recording dreams every morning since her birthday, and mostly it's been fun remembering the crazy, fantastic things that happen in her mind while she sleeps. The ominous bear hadn't returned (*or the spiders,* her inner voice reminds her, *the ones that were crawling all over your feet*) and, until this morning, hadn't recorded a single nightmare.

She climbs out of bed to use the restroom, then debates whether to put a sweatshirt over her pajamas and go watch television, preferably curled beneath a blanket (it was chilly in the house), or just go back to sleep, since it was Sunday and not quite 6 a.m.

Yawning, she decides on sleep versus television, and crawls back into bed.

When she wakes for the second time that morning, her window glows with warm yellow sunlight. She tilts the face of her charging phone toward her and is shocked to see it's past 10 a.m., both pleased and surprised her mother hasn't come in to wake her for breakfast. She stretches and folds back the covers, feeling more alert and relaxed than when she'd woken earlier, and is excited for a free day of doing whatever she wants.

She didn't dream in the short window of her second sleep and has a hard time remembering the details of her initial nightmare, the one so awful she'd woken in tears. Curious, she opens the dream journal to reread her entry.

As the details come back, she feels her mood dampen, mad at herself for rehashing the stupid dream in the first place.

But it's not until she reaches the end of the entry that a chill of pure terror fills her chest like ice water, freezing her lungs and causing her heart to beat faster, faster…

Below the neatly printed words of her nightmare are two lines of flowing cursive.

That wasn't a dream, my sweet.

Your mother is dead.

Wide-eyed, Jenna reads the second line again.

Your mother is dead.

The handwriting is easy to recognize. She'd seen it on birthday and holiday cards, once on a postcard sent to her from Italy.

It was Nana's.

Jenna throws the book aside and leaps from the bed. She pulls open her bedroom door and runs into the house screaming, "Mom! Mommy!"

When she sees her mother sitting at the kitchen table, reading the newspaper and having coffee—the mug caught midway between the table and her mouth, her face a mask of surprise at her daughter's distress—Jenna runs to her and throws her arms around her, crying her heart out.

"My God, Jenna, what's wrong?"

Jenna shakes her head, rubbing tears into the shoulder of her mother's soft robe. "Had a nightmare," she says, and decides it's best to leave it at that.

During the rest of that Sunday, Jenna avoids going to her room.

She calls Esther from the living room couch and they talk about nothing and everything. She watches a movie while her mother makes dinner, then reads a book at the dining room table once the dishes are stacked away, the kitchen cleaned. As nine o'clock rolls around, she knows she can't stay out of there forever, and—with a heavy heart—goes into her room to get ready for bed.

Everything seems the same. The bed is still unmade, and there's nothing hiding beneath it (she checked). The lone window is closed and locked. The lights aren't flickering, and there's nothing in the closet other than clothes (also checked).

The journal is on the nightstand, closed and harmless.

She takes her bath, puts on her pajamas, kisses her mother goodnight, and climbs into bed, offering a silent prayer to the darkness that she won't dream.

Before she has the chance to fall fully asleep, or to dream, something—*someone*—walks into her room.

The floors of their house are old, bare hardwood, and she plainly hears the creaking of every step as they move around at the foot of her bed.

Jenna's face is turned away from the door, toward the far wall, but she doesn't open her eyes. She doesn't want to know. Doesn't want to see.

The footsteps are beside the bed now.

Moving from her feet to her head.

Jenna hears soft breathing, followed by the faint rustle of pages, the light scratching of pen on paper. The almost inaudible *thump* as the book is placed back on the nightstand, the *click* of the pen cap being secured.

There's a pause which—to Jenna's terrified mind—lasts an eternity. She waits, shivering with fear, to feel a cool hand on her head, or shoulder; for the sheets to be pulled

slowly off her body, down past her hips, her feet. Exposing her to whatever stands beside the bed.

But then the footsteps are retreating across the floor, back toward the door, which gives a creak of protest as it's opened, then softly shut.

Jenna doesn't know how long she lies there, shaking, breathing fast, her mind numb with fear. She doesn't know because at some point—somehow—she falls asleep, and doesn't wake again until morning, the tweeting birds of her phone's alarm telling her it's time to wake up for school.

Bright daylight fills her room through the window, as if the sun itself was hunched low in the backyard, one eye brought down just far enough to peek in at Jenna's sleeping form. In the sobering daylight, she decides the nighttime visitor was a dream.

Because it *had* to be a dream.

A dream Jenna has no wish to write about. Or remember.

Instead, she has breakfast with her mom, then puts on white stockings, a pink dress, and her new cherry-red Mary Jane shoes. She puts her hair in a ponytail and clips it with a pink bow that matches her dress *exactly*.

It's only when she's at her bedroom door that she turns back, sees the dream journal on her nightstand, recalls the sound of rustling paper, the click of the pen cap, the scratching of someone writing inside of it.

She lets out a breath and, without allowing herself time to overthink it, walks briskly to the nightstand, lifts the book, and opens it—somewhat roughly—to the point of her last dream, marked with the black ribbon bookmark.

And sees…nothing. Just her last entry. Something about swimming in a big pool with a bunch of other kids. How it started sunny but then got dark and began to rain. How cold it was and how she was afraid of lightning striking the water, but she couldn't get out, couldn't swim to the sides or to a ladder, so she kept swimming and swimming and praying she wouldn't be electrocuted by a white blast of high voltage.

On a whim, she turns the page, expecting to see the blank page that follows.

But it's there she sees the writing.

I know you're not asleep.

It's in that same spidery hand she recognizes immediately, and as she reads the message, something in Jenna's mind snaps like a broken power line. She can almost hear the *fizz* of the loose end buzzing behind her ears.

She reads the line once, twice, then (*gently*) closes the book and sets it down on her bedspread. She knows she must hurry to make the bus, so she runs out of the room and heads for the hallway where she hangs her backpack, yells 'goodbye' to her mother as she bursts out the front door.

Walking to the corner, and seeing her best friend wave cheerfully as she does so, Jenna forces herself to smile.

She also decides that later, when she gets home, she's going to throw that fucking journal in the trash, and never think about her dreams again.

During seventh-period study hall, it's Esther who changes her mind.

Jenna hadn't planned on telling her best friend about the strange journal, but Esther commented on how tired she looked, and Jenna confessed to having nightmares. When Esther asked if Jenna had been writing the nightmares down in her new journal (and subsequently hinted at wanting to read such entries), Jenna broke down in tears, revealing all that had happened since her nana's funeral.

"I think that's the coolest thing I've ever heard," Esther says, eyes bulging, cheeks flushed red. "Are you sure it's not, I don't know, your mom playing a trick on you?"

Jenna, wiping away tears, shakes her head. "She'd never. Never ever."

Esther nods, as if in agreement. "Well, I think it's kind of spooky, for sure. But it's also pretty neat, don't you think? I mean, come on Jen, your grandma is sending you messages from the beyond. Do you know how awesome that is?"

Admittedly, Jenna hadn't thought of it as cool, neat, or in any way positive in the slightest. She'd thought it terrifying.

But now, in the light of day, surrounded by students and the extreme normalcy of school, she thinks maybe, in a way… it *is* a little bit awesome.

"What do you think I should do?" she asks. "Honestly, I was planning on chucking the stupid thing."

"What? No! Jen, you can't do that. You'd be throwing away an incredible gift. I mean, you loved your grandma, right?"

Jenna realizes she doesn't honestly know the answer to that question, but she sniffs, wipes drying tears from her cheeks, and nods.

"And she died in that horrible way, you know?" Esther says, her enthusiasm growing, contagious. "Offing herself like that? Don't you want to know why she did it? Think about it. You could *ask* her, and she'd *tell* you. That's insane!"

Jenna laughs at her friend's enthusiasm, suddenly feeling better than she had in days. She especially likes the idea of the journal not being something bad, per se, or scary. But something incredible. Like a miracle. "You think I should?"

Esther nods madly. "Or whatever. Ask her what the afterlife is like. Is there a Heaven? A Hell? Jenna, this is the chance of a lifetime."

"I'm surprised you even believe me," Jenna says.

"Well, and I hate to tell you this, but you're a terrible liar," Esther says, giggling. "There's no way you're lying about this. You should have seen your face when you finally told me what was going on. Jesus, dude. You were white as a ghost."

When Jenna gets home that afternoon, her mother is sobbing on the couch. Jenna wants to talk to her, to comfort her, but when she tries her mother pulls away, red-faced and ugly. "I'm sorry, honey. I just need to be alone."

She goes into her bedroom and shuts the door. Jenna, confused and concerned, grabs a banana off the counter and goes into her own room, quietly shutting the door behind her, not wanting to hear the hitched, muffled sobs of her mother coming from just down the hall.

She sits at her small oak desk, an antique her nana bought for her when she turned ten, then opens her laptop to watch videos while she eats, part of her mind always thinking about the journal sitting quietly on the opposite side of the room. Just behind her.

When she's done with her snack, she closes the browser and walks around her bed to the nightstand. She plucks up the journal, opens it to the page where Nana had written her last, cryptic message: *I know you're not asleep.*

Beneath it, she writes: *What happened to my dad? Why did he kill himself?*

She closes the journal, sets it on the nightstand, and leaves her room to pull her homework from her backpack, deciding she'll do it at the dining room table. Between sitting in her room with the journal—which feels to Jenna how it might feel to have a loaded gun sitting next to your bed—and listening to her sobbing mother, she chooses the latter.

After pulling her binder from the backpack, she turns on the television and sits at the table to work. She quickly discovers that if she turns the volume up loud enough, she no longer hears her mother crying.

The next morning, Jenna wakes to the soft sound of a tinkling melody.

She sits up, stares past the foot of her bed to her vanity, the smeared reflection of her torso in the oval mirror perched on its top.

In front of the mirror, her jewelry box is open. The ballerina twirls slowly as "March of Wooden Soldiers" plinks gently from deep inside the box. For a moment, she can only stare at the raised lid, the spinning ballerina.

Her mind, her *body,* fills with conflict: excitement mixed with fear.

She turns and quickly, almost absently, checks the screen of her phone. It's not yet 6 a.m., but that's fine. That's okay.

Jenna grabs the leather journal, opens the cover and flips to the page neatly marked by the black ribbon.

She sees her note: *What happened to my dad? Why did he kill himself?*

And, below that, in the unmistakable, spiraling handwriting of her dead nana: *Ask your mother. Tell her he's waiting for you both in Hell.*

For the remainder of that morning, Jenna's mother doesn't come out of her room. Doesn't make her daughter breakfast, or kiss her cheek, or stand on the porch as she walks for the bus. After eating cereal and getting herself dressed, Jenna knocks on her mother's bedroom door.

"Mom? Mom, are you okay?"

There is a *shifting* sound from the bedroom. As if her mother was sliding furniture from one place to another.

"I'm fine, baby," her mother replies. "Go to school."

Jenna thinks about opening the door to see if her mother really is okay or just pretending to be. But something stops her from turning the doorknob. A premonition. A fear. She worries about what she'll see. Will her mother be in bed, under the covers? Or will she be standing atop the bed, the sheets thrown to the corners of the room?

Jenna has the strange thought that she might find her mother huddled in a shadowy corner, naked and dirty. Maybe even bloody. Jenna imagines her mother leering toward the voice at the door, wild-eyed, teeth bared, perhaps hoping her daughter *would* come in…come into the bedroom so she could show her little girl what she'd become, what she'd turned into.

"Okay," Jenna says, and pulls her hand from the cool doorknob as if burned. She runs for the front door, desperate to be away.

When she reaches the corner where the bus stops, Esther notices the distress on her friend's face and pulls her into a hug. A few minutes later, as they climb onto the bus, Jenna tells her friend about the message, about her mother's increasingly strange behavior.

Just as they're pulling into the school parking lot, Esther grips Jenna's hand tight in her own. "Don't worry," she says. "I have an idea."

The next day, Esther comes over to Jen's house to hang out. As they enter the front door, they see Jen's mom at the kitchen table, hair messy, work clothes wrinkled. She gives them a blank-eyed stare as they walk past.

"Hello, Mrs. Crane," Esther says politely. "Anything new at the shop?"

Jenna's mother works the opening six-hour shift at a gift boutique in their small downtown, primarily selling knickknacks and candles, handmade soaps, stationary, and artisan items that came primarily from local residents. She'd been there for as long as Jenna could remember.

"Hello, Esther," she says, ignoring the question. "I'm sorry, hon. I didn't know you were coming by. Are you girls hungry?"

"No, thanks," the girls say in unison, as if fully expecting the question.

Jenna's mother nods and her eyes grow distant once more. "Okay. I'll order pizza later if you want to stay for dinner. I'd cook, but I haven't been sleeping well. I'm very tired lately."

"It's fine, Mom," Jenna says, and tugs Esther away.

In her bedroom, Jenna closes the door and looks at her friend meaningfully. "She says she's been having nightmares. She cries a lot, and sometimes I hear her talking. Like she's having a conversation with someone in her room. Oh, and the other night I heard her scream in her sleep. It was scary."

"Weird," Esther says, walking to the jewelry box she'd given Jen on her birthday. She winds the small brass crank on the side a few times, then lifts the lid. The ballerina dances and the music tinkles softly. "You said this was playing when you woke up the other night?"

Jenna nods. "And don't forget the footsteps. And the messages, of course."

"Speaking of which, did you write down your dream this morning?"

Jenna laughs. "You mean did I bait the hook? Yes, ma'am. It was a very pleasant dream in which my bed slowly submerged into a roomful of black water. According to the book, it means my conscious mind is sinking into my subconscious mind."

Esther dumps her backpack on Jenna's bed and digs inside. "That's some deep shit," she says, then pulls free a small black device about the size of a remote control. "This is what I was telling you about. It's a camera." Esther points to the lens. "It has night vision and a motion sensor. My parents use it when we go on trips because they don't trust the pet sitter. There's software you need to download, and you have to connect it to your network, but I can help with that."

Jenna holds out her hand and Esther hands the small device to her.

"Careful," Esther says, "that thing's worth a couple hundred bucks. If my dad finds out I borrowed it he'll kill me."

"It's so small," Jenna says, impressed.

"Right? So look, once you hook it up, it'll record any movement and save the video to your laptop. You can also access it from your phone, if you want, but I'm not sure how to do that."

"That's okay," Jenna says, handing it back. "Laptop is fine."

Esther closes the music box, snuffing the soft plinking sounds of Tchaikovsky. She looks around the room, then nods her head toward a bookcase next to the window that faces the bedroom door, and Jenna's bed. "That should work. It's a wide lens, so it should see that whole side of the room."

Jenna nods. "This is crazy, huh?"

Esther smiles. "Yeah, but it's also kind of cool, right? I mean, if someone is coming into your room at night, writing stuff in your dream journal, this will catch them red-handed."

"Unless it's a ghost," Jenna says.

Esther's smile grows even wider. "Even cooler," she says. "If it's a ghost, it might catch that, too."

Esther stays for pizza, then calls her mom to pick her up.

Jenna informs her mother she has homework, then locks herself in her room to test the camera.

She turns off the lights, steps carefully to the center of her bedroom—making sure to be in full view of the camera's lens—and begins doing jumping jacks. After ten, breathing heavily from the exertion, she turns the lights back on and goes to the laptop. A folder on the screen reads MICROV22_CAPTURE, and she double-clicks it. There are two video files inside.

One she knows is her and Esther dancing and waving before breaking out into a fit of giggles, their initial test run saved forever. She double-clicks the second file and a window pops up. It shows her standing in the middle of her bedroom, the night vision washing the room in shades of gray, her eyes full white.

"Creepy," she says, and plays the file.

She laughs at the bizarre image of watching her digital twin do jumping jacks in the dark, decides to save the file to show Esther the next time she comes over.

Satisfied everything is in working order, she gets ready for bed.

5

Jenna sleeps soundly that night, and she doesn't dream. She isn't woken until her alarm goes off at 7 a.m. She feels rested, even cheerful. She glances toward the bookcase, sees the nose of the camera sticking out from beneath a stack of books, the laptop closed on her small desk by the window. Excited despite herself, she throws her legs out of bed, ignoring the chill morning air on her skin, and grabs the dream journal off the nightstand.

Flipping to her last entry, she looks for further messages. A response.

But there's nothing.

She turns the page. Then another.

Nothing.

Disappointed, she sets the book down and hurries to the laptop. She opens it, types in a password, and her desktop image—a close-up photograph of a bouquet of roses—appears. The folder containing the camera's captured videos is already open.

There are two new files.

Feeling a surge of jagged nerves, Jenna opens the first file, which is time-stamped as the earlier of the two videos. Her breath catches at the image of her room, the exact same framing from when she was doing her jumping jacks, except now she's nothing but a lump under the covers of her bed.

Her bedroom door, securely closed when she went to bed, is partway open.

She takes a deep breath, needing to pee but willing to hold it (for now). Biting her lip, she glances behind her to make sure the door is (currently) closed, and then plays the video.

On the screen, the door continues opening, the beginning motion of which must have cued the camera to begin recording. The hallway beyond is mostly dark, but there's a ghostly figure standing in the doorway, a shadow in contrast, pale shades of gray instead of black, its head turned toward Jenna's bed.

It's a woman. She's dressed in a pajama top and shorts, her hair wild, her eyes glowing that same, unnerving pure white.

Jenna's mother.

She enters the room slowly, walking in small, shuffling steps, until she's standing at the foot of the bed.

Jenna holds her breath, staring, wide-eyed, at the bizarre (and unsettling) image of her mother looking down at her. Watching her sleep.

Slowly, her mom bends over, puts her hands on the bed, palms resting a few inches from the misshapen lump of Jenna's feet. Moving carefully, as if not wanting to wake her sleeping daughter, she *crawls* onto the bed, pale skin shimmering white in the camera's night vision, her hair a tangle of shadows. She continues upward until her head is even with Jenna's, then she settles down next to the blanket-covered body…and goes still.

"She sleeps with me?" Jenna whispers aloud, not quite knowing how to feel about

M is for Marooned

the strange revelation. Could it have been her mother this whole time? Creeping into her room to write bizarre journal entries, mimicking Nana's handwriting?

The video stops, and Jenna quickly slides the cursor over and clicks open the second file. She has a good idea what she'll see.

The second video plays, an odd reversal of the first. Her mother rolling gingerly off the bed, then standing to face the direction of the camera.

Jenna's eyes flick to the time stamp on the video: 4:35 a.m.

Her mother had only lain with her for an hour, and Jenna feels suddenly ashamed of herself—ashamed of thinking her mother would do something so cruel as to write those things in her journal, ashamed of seeing her mother's vulnerability, her obvious,

desperate need to be comforted. Distraught, she'd come to lay beside her daughter for a bit, find some temporary solace against whatever was inflicting her mind as of late.

Jenna closes the laptop. She needs to get ready for school, and when she sees Esther, she's already decided to lie.

She'll tell her the camera didn't record a thing.

That nothing had happened in the night.

"Well, you'll just have to try again," Esther announces when Jenna tells her about the initial failure of their project.

"I don't know if I want to," Jenna says. The two of them sit in the cafeteria, each picking at school-supplied cheesy pasta and limp green beans. "It's kind of freaking me out."

Esther shrugs. "More than the ghost of your dead grandmother writing notes in your journal? Saying your dad is in hell and shit? That's what would freak me out."

"My mom feels guilty about his suicide, I think," Jenna says, finding herself thinking more about her father than she ever has. "In a way, I think Nana blamed her…blamed both of us, for what he did. They had a fight once, a couple of years ago, and I heard Nana say as much; said he'd still be alive if he'd never married my mom."

"Dude, that's horrible."

Jenna nods, pushes away her tray.

"Well, if that's true," Esther says, chewing thoughtfully on a green bean. "And assuming it's your grandmother writing those messages, I'm beginning to think you shouldn't mess around with it anymore. The journal, I mean."

"Why? You said it was cool."

"That's when I thought old granny was communicating with you because she missed you or something. But, based on the messages? I don't think she misses you," Esther says, swallowing the bean with a grimace. "I think she's pissed."

The following morning, Jenna is eager to write down her dream.

She dreamed about the bear again. But this time he wasn't in a cave, but trapped inside a massive cage. He was roaring in frustration, pawing at the thick metal bars. The cage itself sat deep within a swampy, muddy patch of land, a great sea storming in the distance, just out of her sight. Jenna stood outside the cage, watching the frenzied animal pace, annoyed she couldn't figure out a way to free him. There was no door. No lock. Just thick, black metal bars.

Jenna walked to the cage, reached her hand between the bars.

The bear came to her, sniffed her fingers, pushed his giant head against her palm. Jenna scratched obediently. "Daddy?"

Wanting him free and relying once more on the bizarre nature of dream logic, Jenna realized she *could* help him escape. That she could, just maybe, *dig* him out.

Knowing she had to try, she began clawing furiously into the mud, pulling up giant clumps of wet dirt and weedy grass with impossibly powerful swipes of her hands. She dug deeper, and deeper, until she came to pieces of white rock lodged far below the surface. Knowing she had to go further, she kept on, pulling the white rocks free before tossing them behind her, a growing pile as she tunneled further into the earth, finally digging so deep that she could no longer see the sun overhead. At this point, she didn't know if she was getting closer to the bear, or further away.

Exhausted, she turned around and studied the large pile of white rocks, and realized they weren't rocks at all, but bones. Her dream logic informed her quietly, calmly, that they were *human* bones.

Hastily, without rationalization, she began assembling the bones, like a puzzle, laying them flat on the floor of this tunnel—this cave—she'd created.

Legs. Feet. Ribs. Skull. Arms.

The skull, she noticed, was toothless.

Deep down in her heart, staring at the man-sized skeleton, she knew it was her father. Long dead and buried. Flesh rotted away.

There was a roar from above. Jenna ran back, looked up toward the opening—a pale sky staring back like a sightless eye, and then a face appeared at the jagged hole.

Nana.

She's dressed in black and crawling on all fours, like a spider. There's a roll of distant thunder and a heart-stopping scream from the clouds above, as if the sky itself is tormented by the jagged lightning. The screams continue as the storm above swells, and Jenna watches in horror as Nana scurries around the edges of the tunnel entrance, pushing down rocks and great piles of earth. The dirt began spilling down on Jenna from above, sealing her inside the tunnel, entombing her in the cold dark. Burying her with her father.

As the dirt squeezed in around her, and it became more and more difficult to secure a breath, the pressure on her chest and lungs increasing steadily, Jenna found that she wasn't upset, or scared.

In a way, she was happy.

When she woke, gulping in deep breaths of fresh air, Jenna felt sickened by her dream. She had a terrible headache and her stomach gurgled and burned, as if she were close to throwing up. She wondered if she was coming down with the flu, or a bad cold. Her entire body was achy, her nose stuffy, her eyes burning with exhaustion.

Still, through her exhaustion and discomfort, she slowly reaches out for the journal and pen from her nightstand, uses the ribbon to find the next blank page.

However, once she opens it, she finds someone has already written in the blank space where she'd hoped to record her dream.

I'm coming for both of you.
Nana is waiting.

And then, further down the page, scrawled with haste: *WE'RE ALL WAITING.*

Jenna drops the book to the floor in disgust, as if she'd lifted it to find it crawling with ants, or spiders. Then—remembering her precautions—she turns her head toward the camera set in the bookcase, to the laptop on her desk.

At the computer, Jenna double-clicks the new video file, the one recorded during the night. As with the last video, she's greeted by the frozen image of her bedroom submerged in ghastly shades of gray. A blur of frozen movement at the side of her bed, a finger smear distortion of reality.

She plays the file.

In the video, Jenna sees herself.

She's standing beside her own bed, wearing an oversized T-shirt a shade paler than the exposed flesh of her face, arms, and legs. She picks up the journal, opens it, and begins to write. A few moments pass, and she sets the journal back onto the nightstand. Turning fully around, she walks quickly across the room, past the foot of the bed, toward the dresser. Once there, she pauses a moment, as if thinking. Then she opens the musical jewelry box, watches the ballerina spin.

Then, in the blink of an eye, her head turns.

She looks directly at the camera.

Horrified, Jenna watches herself move toward the camera slowly, step by step. She gets close enough that the entire frame is filled with her head—white eyes glowing around dilated pupils, shimmering pools of silver. Her pale gray skin is sickly, corpse-like, her tussled hair a nest of ink-black snakes. She stares into the lens, as if staring not at the camera but at *herself*, and for a moment Jenna is held breathless as she stares back into her own haunted eyes.

A is for Anchor

Then, the Jenna in the video cocks her head slightly, her white eyes opening wide.

And she smiles.

Jenna cups a hand to her mouth to stifle a scream, and is about to slam the laptop closed when the Jenna in the video steps away from the camera, her movements now spasmodic, as if the video file has been corrupted, split seconds of time gone missing, causing the image of her body to move around the room in jerky, blurred movements.

Taking a breath, fighting back tears, it is only now that Jenna notices the shape in the bed, lying still as the girl in the video staggers across the bedroom floor. It's the shape of someone sleeping.

The face, poking free from the humped blankets, rests atop a blazing white pillow.

Her face.

Before she can begin to rationalize how there are *two* of her, the version of her moving around the room suddenly stops at the foot of the bed. Then, in those same, twitchy motions, it (because Jenna can only think of the girl as an *it*, not a *she*, and certainly not a *me)* crouches low, knees bent like spider legs, her body impossibly close to the floor.

Then it crawls beneath the bed.

The last thing Jenna sees in the video is the image of her own feet disappearing, as if swallowed up.

6

When she leaves her room for breakfast, Jenna's only mildly surprised at not finding her mother already awake and at the table, smiling at her while holding a cup of steaming coffee, asking her if she'd prefer oatmeal or cereal.

She glances at the closed door of her mother's bedroom at the end of the hall, wonders what nightmare vision she'd find if she went inside to look.

A pile of bones? A giant spider? Something else?

Something that would drive her mad?

With a sigh, Jenna sits at the table, forces herself to eat a banana, a cup of yogurt.

As she eats, she sets the small doll she found beneath her bed on top of the table.

The doll had been wedged between the wooden slats of her bedframe and the box spring beneath her mattress. She hadn't found it earlier because she hadn't bothered to look *up* when checking under her bed for ghosts, monsters, whatever.

The doll is made from rough canvas, and it smelled, Jenna thought, of urine. The eyes are tarnished gold studs, earrings Jenna thought she had lost a few months back. The mouth is red cross-stitching, the glued hair wispy and real. The same color as her own.

Jenna had torn the head open at a loose seam, curious what the hard, lumpy things were beneath the cloth. It turned out to be baby teeth. Six of them. She couldn't be positive, of course, but she was almost certain they were hers. She'd had many visits from the tooth fairy when she was younger—a dollar here and there, left under her pillow in the night, no questions asked.

After she finishes breakfast, she takes a large pot from the cupboard and sets it on the kitchen counter. She places the doll inside (keeping the baby teeth in her palm, thinking she'll put them in her jewelry box for safekeeping), then finds the lighter fluid in the pantry; a large plastic, yellow bottle they sometimes use to get the charcoals going for the small grill on the back patio.

In a junk drawer, she finds a pack of matches.

Humming to herself, Jenna douses the doll with lighter fluid, then lights a match and drops it into the pot. She makes sure to turn the stove's overhead fan on to suck away a majority of the smoke, but as the doll begins to burn she opens a kitchen window as well, not wanting to set off the fire alarm.

As she crosses back to the smoking pot, she glances toward the hallway, where she can just make out the open door of her bedroom.

Her Nana stands there, watching her. Hunched and scowling.

Jenna sits down at the kitchen table once more, letting the doll burn, doing her best to ignore the old woman screaming at her from the bedroom.

Later, she'll go check on Mother. She is fairly certain who her mother has been dreaming of, and who she's been talking to. Jenna knows she will find another doll, similar to her own, hidden beneath her mother's bed, and that the head of her mother's doll is not filled with baby teeth, but adult ones, pulled from her father's dead mouth, and left to rot in their house like a cancer, a contagion.

A curse.

JOIN THE
ADVENTURE!

GET THE LATEST ISSUES OF

FORBIDDEN FUTURES

AVAILABLE AT ODDNESS.US

BELIEF SYSTEMS   **SLEEP**

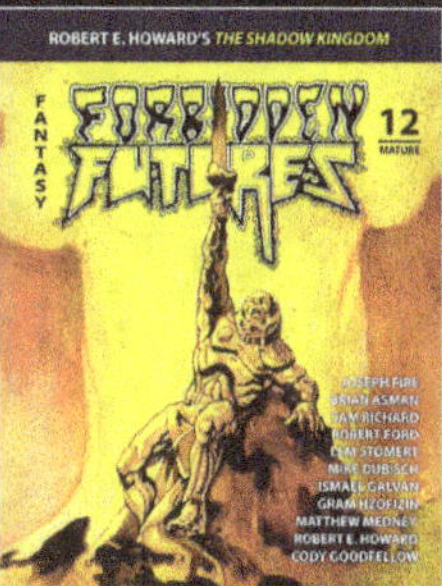

OMNIBUS 3: ISSUES 9-12   **CHAOS MAJICK**   **BEYOND TOMORROW**   **ALL PUNK**   **BACK TO THE STONE AGE**

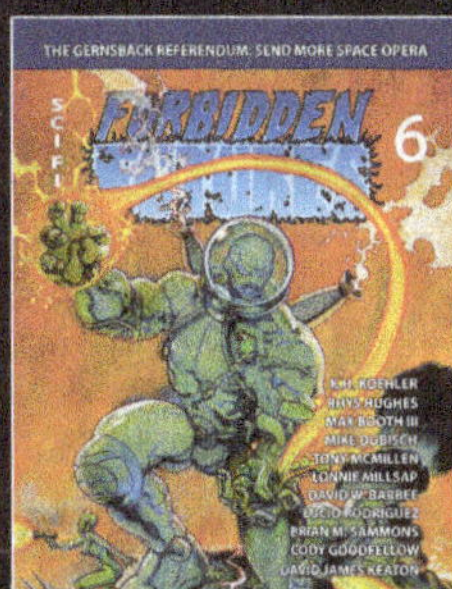

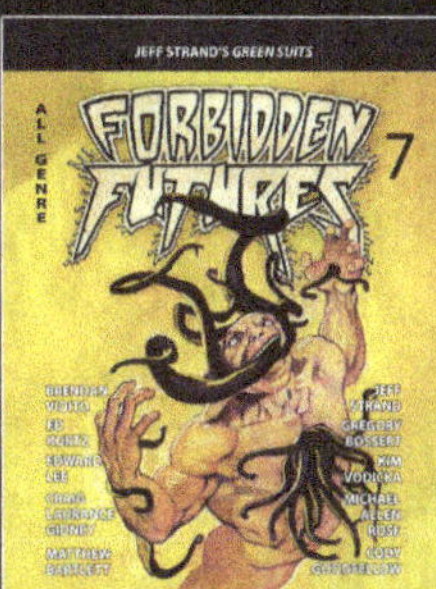

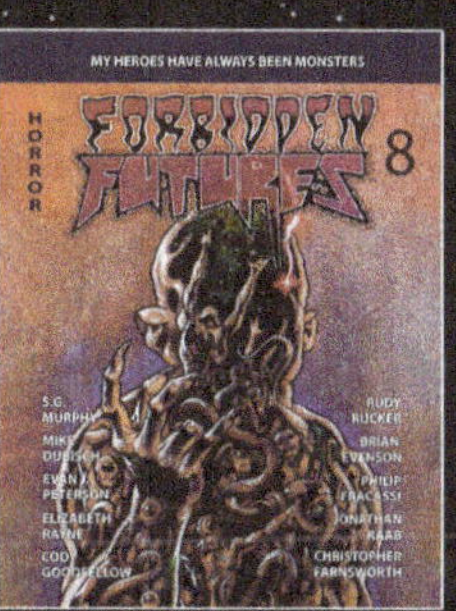

OMNIBUS 2: ISSUES 5-8   **THE CRYPT KID RETURNS**   **RAYGUN FUN**   **SEX & VIOLENCE**   **CREATURE FEATURE**

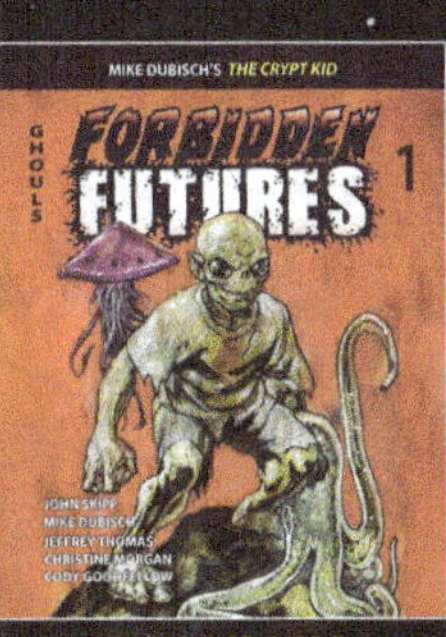

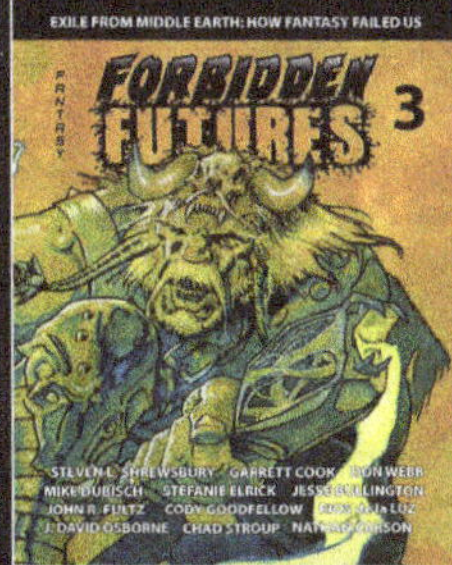

OMNIBUS 1: ISSUES 1-4   **GHOULISH DELIGHT**   **COSMIC HORROR**   **HIGH ADVENTURE**   **ALL-FEMALE ACTION**

PART IV: PANPSYCHISM

the belief that everything, has an element of individual consciousness.

PROJECT STARGATE

During the height of the Cold War, the U.S. government conducted a classified operation called Project Stargate, funded by the CIA, Army Intelligence, and the Defense Intelligence Agency, for the sole purpose of utilizing remote viewing to gather intelligence where satellites and spies couldn't always reach.

ORIGINS OF THE PSYCHIC SPY PROGRAM

Project Stargate dates back to the early 1970s, after reports surfaced that the Soviets were spending millions on psychotronic research (mind reading, ESP, and paranormal weapons). To avoid falling behind the Russians, U.S. intelligence agencies began investigating what they called "anomalous cognition" to counter the Soviets' efforts.

For two decades, researchers investigated "remote viewers" who claimed to be able to describe people, locations, and events at great distances. These "viewers" slid into altered states through deep relaxation, meditative focus, or even dreamlike hypnagogic drift, and then they sketched or described what they saw.

Some sessions produced credible leads such as a crashed Soviet bomber, a hidden submarine, and even a kidnapping.

MENTAL DRIFT & MEDITATION

The viewer could access non-local information, provided the state of consciousness wasn't "awake" in the usual sense, for they entered deeply relaxed, liminal states similar to those experienced during transcendental meditation or the moment before sleep, and compared it to dreaming while awake.

Project Stargate researcher Ingo Swann believed the key wasn't psychic power but the ability to quiet the analytical mind, and that the unconscious had access to a kind of mental map of the world and that, with practice, anyone could learn to tune into it.

Remote viewing isn't too different from lucid dreaming since viewers described the experience as trancelike, where space, time, and identity became flexible in a flow of images, sensations, and symbols that would emerge, not unlike the chaotic but meaningful language of dreams.

WHAT THEY CLAIMED TO SEE

Declassified records reveal hundreds of sessions logged over more than two decades, including details such as one remote viewer's description of the interior of a Soviet weapons facility, down to the layout and machinery. Another saw the location of a downed plane before satellite images confirmed it. Yet another saw a U.S. hostage in Lebanon with accurate details of his clothing and health.

Military officials funded the program until 1995, and even the CIA eventually admitted:

"STATISTICALLY SIGNIFICANT EVIDENCE SUPPORTS THE IDEA THAT REMOTE VIEWING IS REAL."

Approved For Release 2001/04/02 : CIA-RDP96-00789R002600360002-3
SECRET NOFORN LIMDIS

PROJECT STAR GATE

SECRET NOFORN LIMDIS

SECRET NOFORN LIMDIS

01MS419-1/BKK

Approved For Release 2001/04/02 : CIA-RDP96-00789R002600360002-3

Approved For Release 2001/04/02 : CIA-RDP96-00789R002600360002-3
SECRET NOFORN STAR GATE LIMDIS

PURPOSE

To Provide an Overview on Remote Viewing Focusing on Definitions, Operations, Management, Participation, Benefits, Primary and Secondary Methodologies, Categories of Taskings, Types of Targets, and Operational Methodology.

SECRET NOFORN STAR GATE LIMDIS

01MM393-2 DOH

Approved For Release 2001/04/02 : CIA-RDP96-00789R002600360002-3

Approved For Release 2001/04/02 : CIA-RDP96-00789R002600360002-3

BASIC DEFINITION
"Remote Viewing"

- Accessing information without the use of:
  - The normal—five senses
  - Information from other people
  - Logical deductions
  - <u>Direct, connective</u> implementation of electronic or other devices.
- A talent which is inherent to every human to some degree.
  - Probably a vestigal form of self-preservation.
  - Largely ignored in todays's societal setting.
  - Through proper training, can be developed to a person's individual potential.

01MM419-4 DOH

Approved For Release 2001/04/02 : CIA-RDP96-00789R002600360002-3

Approved For Release 2001/04/02 : CIA-RDP96-00789R002600360002-3
SECRET NOFORN LIMDIS

HOSTAGE SEARCH PROJECT, 1988-1989

- TASK: LOCATE LTC HIGGINS
- INFO PROVIDED: BASIC ABDUCTION INFORMATION

LTC HIGGINS

DATA GENERATED	COMMENTS
SOURCES DESCRIBED TRANSIENT HOLDING AREAS, ESCAPE ROUTES	DATA GENERALLY CONSISTENT WITH LATER INTELLIGENCE AND ASSESSMENTS
SPECIFIC VILLAGE (ARAB SALIM) WAS INITIAL HOLDING AREA	CONSISTENT WITH LATER DATA
SPECIFIC BUILDING AND LOCATION IDENTIFIES	SG1D

SECRET NOFORN LIMDIS

5MM421-2-DHL

Approved For Release 2001/04/02 : CIA-RDP96-00789R002600360002-3

DEFINITIONS

- **PSYCHOKINESIS**
  - Physical Actions Performed by Mental Powers that cannot be Explained by known Physical Means.
- **ESP & TELEPATHY**
  - Perceptions which cannot be explained by known Sensory Means.

SECRET NOFORN STAR GATE LIMDIS

EARLY FINDINGS

- REMOTE VIEWING IS A REAL PHENOMENON
- NOT DEGRADED BY DISTANCE OR SHIELDING
- ABILITY CAN BE IMPROVED
- HAS APPLICATION POTENTIAL

SECRET NOFORN STAR GATE LIMDIS

SECRET NOFORN STAR GATE LIMDIS

FOLLOW-ON FINDINGS

- INDIVIDUALS PERFORMANCE CORRELATES WITH PROJECT TYPE
- CERTAIN AREAS HAVE PROMISE
  - COUNTERNARCOTICS
  - COUNTERTERRORISM
  - COUNTERINTELLIGENCE
- LIMITED POTENTIAL FOR
  - PREDICTIVE
  - PARAMETRIC DATA
- GENERAL DESCRIPTIONS MORE RELIABLE THAN SPECIFICS

SECRET NOFORN STAR GATE LIMDIS

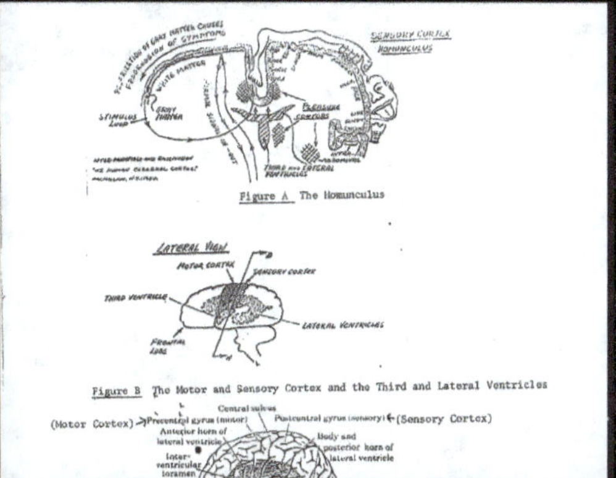

WHY DREAM STATE WORKS

Neuroscience suggests that when we slide into the "default mode network" (imagination, memory, and self-concept), it becomes more active.

At the same time, the prefrontal cortex (home of doubt and critical reasoning) dials down. This combination creates the perfect conditions for non-linear thinking, the kind found in dreams, mystical experiences, and remote viewing, where the brain becomes a receiver of the types of things intelligence officers care deeply about.

This is where panpsychism enters the conversation, since if consciousness is not confined to the brain, if it's a universal field we tap into, then altered states, such as dreams or meditation, may be our best way to access it.

FROM SPYCRAFT TO INNER SPACE

Although Project Stargate was shut down and "officially" debunked in 1995, many of the former officers, scientists, and viewers continued to explore remote viewing privately, convinced that the field had been abandoned too soon.

We may never fully understand what they saw. But it's clear that somewhere, in the space between sleep and thought, lies a door. And for a time, the U.S. military tried to open it.

MIKE DUBISCH
WEIRDLING 4

...my mentor and my friend, the brilliant doctor Anna Mandretta, has succumbed to a delusional state brought on by our experiments with extra-dimensional travel. Though I owe her my very life, I have been powerless to help her and find myself robbed of vitality when she is not by my side - My Love! She does not believe she is herself, or that I and the world around us are even real, merely a dream! Perhaps it would be better if it were so

Though the walking dead have been cleared from the hospital grounds at some great peril, 'tis said the village has been all but abandoned by the living, the villagers chased into the hills. Of the Vessell family, they who claim to be the chosen messengers of Azagthoth, ancient evil of the lake, there has been no sign since they pulled their warped child wailing from the grave dirt...

Third person. The displacement of self, the strange hand, as if indeed the fictional Van Hise had written the entry -

Evidence of a split personality? The threat of space dementia can not be taken lightly -

But Anna is recovering from a disturbing chance encounter with the Xax. These writings - an attempt to deal with that disruption. The encounter with the alien unsettled her in such a way that her mind is resisting the lucidream's memory-soothing function.

She is no threat to the lives of the other crew members and it is my wish to restore ship privileges. But regulations require continued evaluation. I will meet with her shortly. Clearly, in all other ways the lucidream's conditioning is functioning normally, as evidenced by her performance of her duties and her continued progress. I believe she is resocializing normally.

SOMETIMES YOU JUST WANT TO KILL PEOPLE.
I HAVEN'T HAD A HEMP IN OVER A WEEK. THE NEED TO SMOKE IS A LIKE LUMP IN MY THROAT, LIKE MY FLESH CRAWLING, LIKE I WANNA TEAR MY HAIR OUT.
I HAVEN'T ACTIVATED THE LUCIDREAM EMITTER EITHER. BUT I KEEP RETURNING TO THE DREAMWORLD EVERY NIGHT ANYWAY. THE WORLD THE UNDEAD HAVE CLAIMED, WHERE I AWAIT THE NEXT MESSAGE, THE NEXT WORD OF POWER FROM THE DARK GOD.
GREAT GALAXY, HELP ME, SOMETIMES I'M GLAD TO BE THERE. THIS WORLD IS AN ASH-GRAY REFLECTION OF A PILE OF CRAP.
ALL BUT ONE. THE REAL ZOMBIE, THE DEAD MAN, THE MIRROR IMAGE OF MY DREAMWORLD COMPANION—
RAISED FROM THE DEAD JUST AS I RAISED NICHOLAS VAN HISE IN THE CEMETERY OF THE MISKATONIC HOSPITAL.
BUT SHIVEAN HERE ON THIS SHIP, WHERE TWO WORDS WHISPERED IN THE MESS SHOULD NOT, ABSO-EFFIN-LUTELY NOT, HAVE ANY EFFECT ON A CORPSE IN A CRYO-CRYPT IN THE MORGUE—

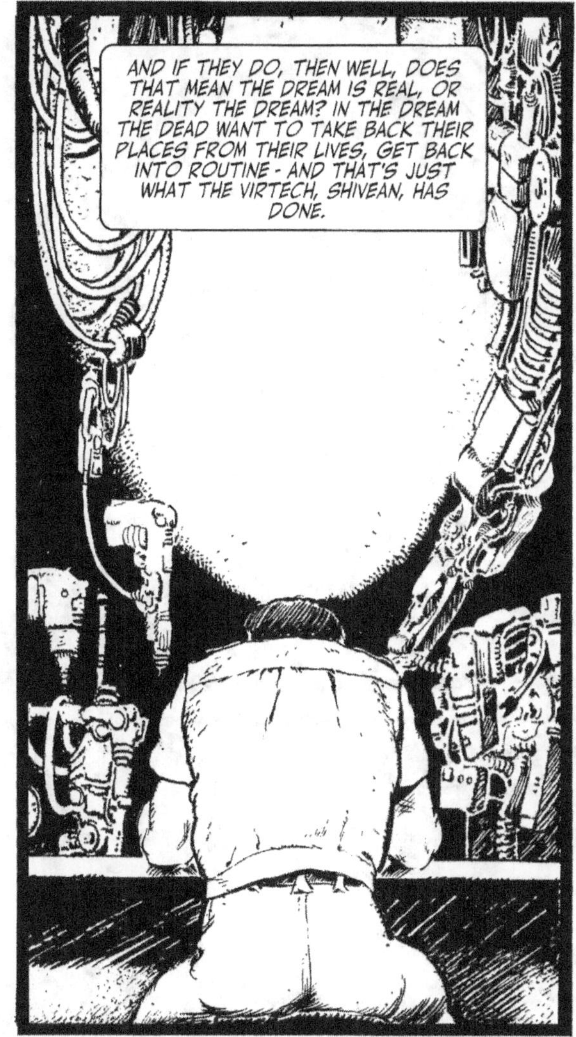

AND IF THEY DO, THEN WELL, DOES THAT MEAN THE DREAM IS REAL, OR REALITY THE DREAM? IN THE DREAM THE DEAD WANT TO TAKE BACK THEIR PLACES FROM THEIR LIVES, GET BACK INTO ROUTINE - AND THAT'S JUST WHAT THE VIRTECH, SHIVEAN, HAS DONE.

SMELLS LIKE SOMETHING DIED IN HERE.
AHH, ANNA MANDRETTA. COME TO CHECK UP ON THE OLD CORPSE, HAVE YOU?
BUT WHERE ARE MY MANNERS?
I'VE BEEN SUCH A ZOMBIE LATELY!
I WISH I COULD SEE THE SUR-VIDS OF OUR FIRST MEETING - ABRA CADAVER!

WON'T YOU COME IN?
DON'T TOUCH ME!
IT MUSTA LOOKED JUST AS AWESOME AS IT FELT!

DON'T YOU EVER EFFIN' TOUCH ME! I MEAN IT YOU UNDEAD SPIT-GOB!

- GASP - BELIEVE ME ANNA!
YOU'RE THE LAST DUDE I'D EVER WANTA EFF AROUND WITH!
YOU EFFIN ROCK!
I MEAN - YOU COULD WASTE ANY OF US IN A HEARTBEAT!

AND, DUDE, LOOK AT YOU!
YOU'RE AWESOME!
I MEAN - HHHH - I REALLY WORSHIP YOU ANNA -

I'M YOUR CTHULU-DAMNED LAP DOG - YOU KNOW WHAT I'M SAYIN'?
THWAK!
QUIT THAT!
I WANT MY INFORMATION IN THE FORM OF ANSWERS! YOU RIGGED MY LUCIDREAM EMITTER - WHY?

ALRIGHT, ANNA... YOU AND I ARE BOTH SPECIAL OPERATIVES IN THE TERRAN INTELLIGENCE. WE'RE ON A MISSION TOGETHER.
I WAS PART OF THE DEVELOPMENT TEAM ON THE PROJECT. THAT'S HOW MY IMAGE WAS PLACED INTO THE SCENARIO, AS A VISUAL CUE - SO YOU'D KNOW YOUR CO-OPERATIVE.
AS YOU OF COURSE MUST HAVE GUESSED BY NOW, YOU'VE BEEN GIVEN SPECIAL LUCIDREAM CONDITIONING - COF, SORRY - CRYPTONIC POWERS TO BE USED AGAINST OUR ENEMY, THE XAX.
I WANT THIS GARBAGE OUT OF MY HEAD - NOW!
I'M NOT INTERESTED IN BEING PART OF THIS PROJECT.
I WANT OUT.
WE BOTH KNOW THAT'S BOVINE CA-CA, ANNA.
KAK-UK
HHHHH - HEY, YOU MIGHT WANT THIS FOR SOME REASON?
YUCK!
WHAT'S YOUR PROBLEM, MAN?
LISTEN, DID YOU PROGRAM SORT OF A WAKING-HOURS TUTOR OR SOMETHING -
IN THE FORM OF A FELINE HOLO-AVATAR?
NO - THERE WAS NOTHING LIKE THAT ON THE DISK. TELL ME -
FORGET ABOUT IT. SO I'M AN EXPERIMENTAL WEAPON. 'SPOSE YOU HAVE THE INSTRUCTION BOOK?
'SPOSE AGAIN, ANNA. YOU DO.
YOUR CASE WORKER, SCHRECK - DON'T TELL HIM ANYTHING.
HELLO? IS SOMEONE THERE?

ANNA!
WHERE HAVE YOU BEEN? I'VE BEEN SCOURING THE SHIP LOOKING FOR YOU!

I SEE YOU'VE CHANGED YOUR HAIR AGAIN.
YOU KNOW, I DON'T BELIEVE I'VE SEEN YOU DO YOUR HAIR THE SAME EXACT WAY TWICE.
I DIDN'T REALIZE I WAS DOING IT.
IT'S STILL A REGULATION BOB, ISN'T IT, SIR?

YES, BUT ONE MIGHT ALMOST BELIEVE YOU WERE TRYING TO BE - MORE INVISIBLE?
ER - NO, SIR. I DON'T THINK THAT WOULD BE POSSIBLE.
HHM. WELL, NEVERTHELESS -
YOU'VE BEEN OUTPRIVELEGED FOR A WEEK AND REGULATION ALLOWS ME TO BEGIN THE REPRIVELEGING PROCESS - PENDING MY CONTINUING INVESTIGATION INTO YOUR CASE.

HUH? THE SMOKING ROOM?
DO YOU MEAN?

WELL - OF COURSE YOU WON'T BE ALLOWED TO ACTUALLY SMOKE A HEMP YOURSELF,
I THOUGHT YOU WOULD APPRECIATE THE ATMOSPHERE.

...AND SINCE THE HEMP HASN'T BEEN FORMULATED TO YOUR DNA—
THE SMOKE MOLECULES WILL NOT LINK TO THE NATURAL THC RECEPTORS IN YOUR BRAIN—
SO YOU SHOULDN'T BECOME INTOXICATED.

I BARELY PAY ATTENTION AS THE DOCTOR INTRODUCES ME. THE WHIFF IS DRIVING ME CRAZY! CHALK THIS ONE UP FOR THE MILITARY TORTURE BOOKS.
HOW CAN THESE PEOPLE BE SO OBLIVIOUS!
DON'T THEY REALIZE HOW THIN THE HULL IS, BUCKLING AGAINST THE EDDIES OF THAT BLACK WATER?
I WILL NOT WIG OUT. I WILL NOT WIG OUT!

HOW CAN THEY JUST BE IN HERE AND IGNORE THE FACT THAT AT ANY MOMENT XAX COULD SLIP RIGHT THROUGH THEM AND JUST TAKE ANY OF US AWAY!
I CAN'T SAVE THEM!
I CAN'T SAVE ALL OF THEM! I—

WELL, ANNA? WHAT DO YOU THINK?
WHA- UH, WHAT? I MEAN, ABOUT WHAT?
OH, I THOUGHT THAT WOULD TICKLE YOU -
STORIES ABOUT PEOPLE RISING FROM THE CRYO-CRYPT -
ZOMBIES, IF YOU WILL, RIGHT ON BOARD THE SHIP!

WELL, YOU TELL HER, DWAYNE!
WELL, NO ONE ELSE'S ACTUALLY SEEN ONE OF THESE, BUT THE MORTICIAN CLAIMS TO HAVE A MORGUE FULL OF THEM!
THE CAPTAIN'S FURIOUS. AFTER HE ACCUSED THE MORT OF LIQUORING -
HE SAID HE WAS GOING TO CONFINE HIM TO QUARTERS -
AS A JOKE, BECAUSE OF HIS GIRTH, YOU KNOW?
BUT HE'D ALREADY GONE AND LOCKED HIMSELF UP, AND HE WON'T COME OUT!

I TOLD THEM, ANNA, YOU MIGHT BE AN EXPERT. WHAT DO YOU THINK?
WELL, ANNA?

OH, THERE WON'T BE ANY TROUBLE FROM THE ZOMBIES.
THEY'LL JUST FALL RIGHT INTO THEIR OLD ROUTINES!

HAH, HAH!
HEH, HEH.
GOOD ONE!
VERY GOOD, ANNA!
INDEED!

FOR A MOMENT THEIR LAUGHTER FEELS REAL, A SWEET MOMENT LINKED TO GROUP PSYCHOLOGY, BEFORE IT CUTS OUT UNDER ME AND I REMEMBER THAT I AM STILL AMONG THE LIVING DEAD.
NIGHT IN, DAY OUT, AMONG THEIR SHAMBLING CORPSES.

NICHOLAS AND I TOURED THE TOWN TO SEE FOR OURSELVES - THE DEAD HAD INDEED TAKEN UP THE ROUTINES OF THE LIVING.
SINCE I WAS A DOCTOR-CERTIFIED MANIAC AND HE WAS MERELY A MISFIRED NEURON WE WERE AVOIDING FRICTION BY NOT SPEAKING.
BUT AS WE PULLED DOWN STREET AFTER STREET CONFRONTED AT EVERY TURN WITH SIGHTS MORE GRISLY AND PATHETIC, THE EMOTION OF HORROR AND PAIN IN HIM WERE VERY REAL.

WHOA—
HEY!
KRAK!
BLAST IT!
BLAST IT ALL!!!!
WE CAN REVERSE THIS! WE CAN RETURN THE WORLD TO WHAT IT WAS BEFORE YOU RESURRECTED ME AND THAT CURSED INFANT!
BUT I CANNOT DO IT WITHOUT YOU, ANNA!

I HAVE BEEN WORKING ON A BRAIN TONIC - I AM GOING TO GIVE YOU A DOSE OF THE ELIXIR - IF YOU DRINK IT, I BELIEVE IT MAY RESTORE YOUR REASON...
NONE OF THIS MATTERS! THIS IS JUST A DREAM!
DON'T YOU UNDERSTAND -
HUH! NO!
A DREAM, A DAMN' DREAM,
AND I WANT TO WAKE UP FROM IT, NOW!
DON'T YOU SEE IT'S ALL POINTLESS?
THE FAULT IS MINE -

I DID THIS TO YOU -
ME AND THAT CURSED DEVICE!
ANNA -
ANNA?!
ANNA, ARE YOU NOT WELL?
HMMM? WHO!
DOCTOR, I -
YOU SEEMED ALMOST ON ANOTHER WORLD FOR A MOMENT THERE -
JUST HAVE A SEAT FOR A WHILE, AND WHEN YOU'RE READY JUST GO ABOUT YOUR DAY AND I'LL TALK TO YOU LATER. YOU'VE DONE WELL TODAY.
HMMM.

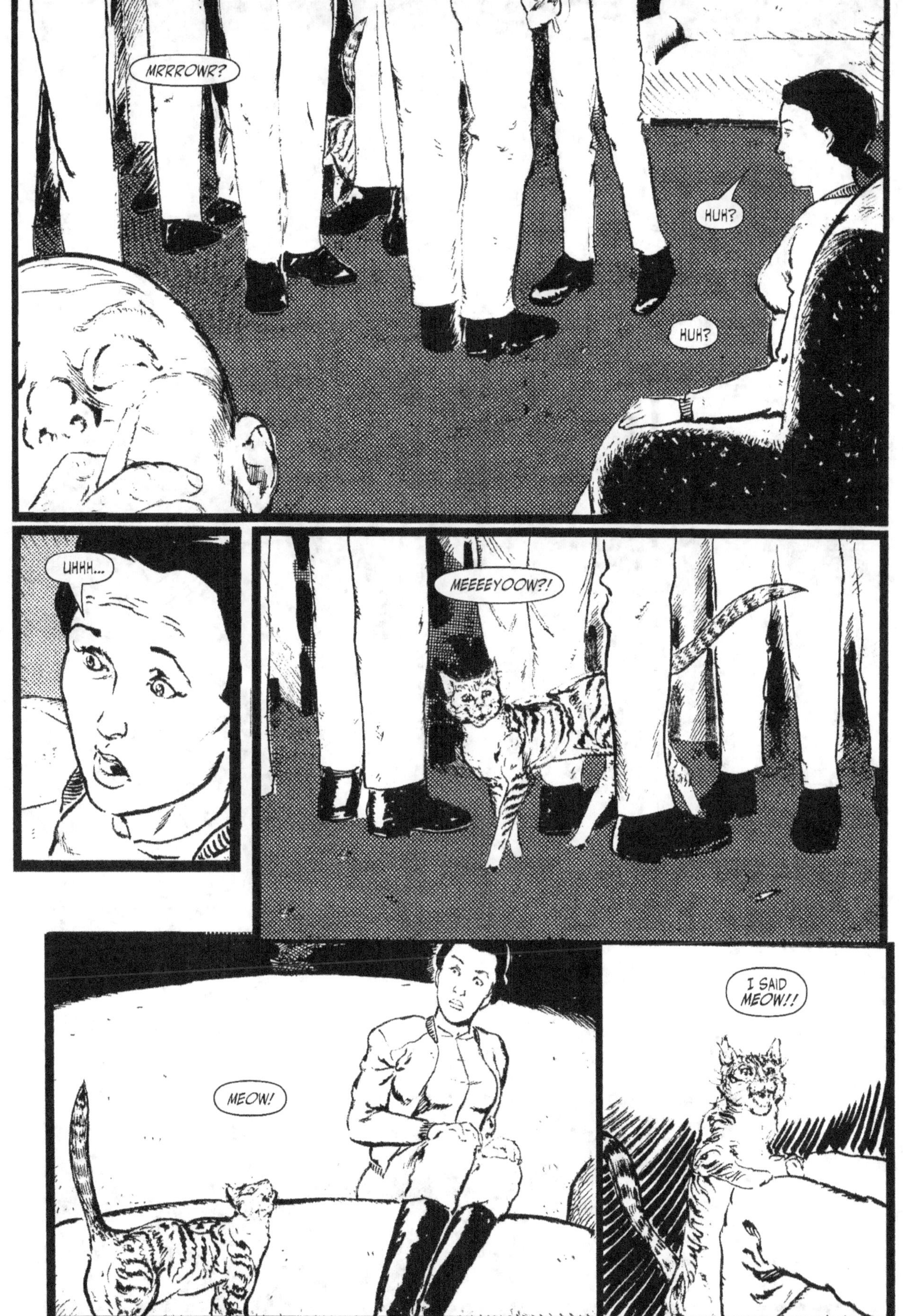
MRRROWR?
HUH?
HUH?
UHHH...
MEEEEYOOW?!
MEOW!
I SAID MEOW!!

HEY, ANNA!
PRRRRR-
HEY -
HEY - PET ME!
TELL ME I'M PRETTY -
RRRRR...
OH I SEE - A
PUBLIC DISPLAY OF
AFFECTION
MRRROWR?
WHY SO
ALOOF?
BETWEEN
WOMAN AND
FELINE -
WOULDN'T
DO, WOULD
IT?
DON'T YOU
KNOW YOU'RE
ALREADY
INVISIBLE?
I THOUGHT
IT WAS THE FIRST
SKILL YOU
MASTERED?
WHO COULD
SEE YOU THROUGH
ALL THIS SMOKE,
ANYWAY?
FOLLOW
ME. I KNOW
A PLACE.

HUH!
WELL, C'MON!
HMM?
UM...?
HMM.

SOME DIMENSIONS ARE LIKE MUSHROOMS, FUNGUS ON THE SIDE OF A LARGER PLANT - THE COSMIC FABRIC ITSELF.
YOUR DREAMWORLD IS ONE SUCH AS THAT, THOUGH YOU ARE THE PLANT.
HOW CAN THAT BE?
PERHAPS BECAUSE AT THE CORE OF SUMMONING IS THE POWER TO LAY HANDS ON REALITY AND EFFECT A CHANGE, THE ABILITY TO MAKE WHAT IS UNREAL REAL.
INTELLIGENCE CRAMMED YOUR MIND WITH EVERY DETAIL CULLED FROM EVERY OCCULT ART ON YOUR PLANET -
DIGITALLY CREATED A PLATFORM WORLD BIO-CYBERNETICALLY, WHERE YOU COULD ENACT THE RITUAL SEQUENCES OF SUMMONING.
SO MY DREAMWORLD IS REAL, BUT THE PEOPLE IN IT AREN'T?

NOT EXACTLY - YOU SEE, THE COSMIC FABRIC INTO WHICH REALITY IS SEWN, LOOPS THAT VIBRATE -
WITHIN EACH VIBRATION A DIFFERENT POSSIBILITY. AT EVERY MOMENT OF EVERY LIVING BEING'S LIFE, THEY REACH OUT AND PICK ONE.
A FREQUENCY ON THE LOOP EXISTS FOR EVERY CHOICE THEY MAKE AND EVERY ONE THAT THEY MIGHT HAVE MADE.
BUT ANNA, WHEN YOU REACH OUT THE FABRIC BENDS AND CLINGS -
STATIC ELECTROPLASM MAY EVEN ERUPT AS YOU LITERALLY SCULPT THE SHAPE OF SPACE-TIME -
AND IT VIBRATES ON THE TIMBRE OF YOUR VOICE.
OF COURSE, ALL YOUR KNOWLEDGE HAS BEEN SO SUBLIMATED YOU'VE BEEN ALTERING REALITY SUBCONSCIOUSLY, AND YOUR MIND, BEING ACCUSTOMED TO REALITY SHIFTS, HAS COMPENSATED.
BUT HE GROWS NEW EYES EVERYWHERE, AND SOMEHOW HE ACTS.
THE REANIMATED ONE - SHIVEAN - HE IS A MEMBER OF THE CULT OF AZAGTHOTH ON TERRA -
THE ONLY THING KEEPING HIM FROM DEVOURING THE ENTIRE CLOTH AND CRAPPING IT OUT IS THAT HE'S BEEN LOBOTOMIZED THROUGH HIS PRIMARY EYE.
ANNA, I DON'T KNOW WHETHER THE BEING CALLED AZAG-THOTH IS REAL BECAUSE YOU MADE HIM REAL OR OTHERWISE, BUT HE IS, AND HE IS A MASTER OF OUR CRAFT.
SLIM AND STRANGE AS THAT POSSIBILITY SOUNDS, IT IS WHAT MOST INTELLIGENT BEINGS BELIEVE.
SURE... I MIGHT HAVE DREAMED YOU REAL OR YOU MIGHT HAVE DREAMED ME REAL - OR SOME OTHER EXTRA-DIMENSIONAL DREAMED US ALL.
UH- I COULD IF I WANTED TO!
AND - YOU CAN DO THIS TOO?
HE INFILTRATED TERRAN INTELLIGENCE'S PSYCHIC RESEARCH DIVISION AND PUSHED THE PROJECT TOWARDS THE OCCULT.
HE WORSHIPS AZAG-THOTH. HIS AGENDA: THE SUMMONING OF THE DARK GOD TO RULE IN THIS UNIVERSE.
WHAT'S HAPPENING NOW?!
WHAT!?
SOMEONE MAY HAVE SUMMONED YOU BACK TO YOUR OWN DIMENSION -
WHILE YOU'RE STILL PROCESSING THE INFORMATION, YOU MAY BE VULNERABLE TO THIS AT THE MERE MENTION OF YOUR NAME.
TAKE CARE NOT TO LET YOUR ASTRAL FORM SEPARATE DURING THE TRANSITION!

WHAT'S HAPPENING?
IT'S THE XAX!
WHERE?

STAND BACK, SHE'S MY RESPONSIBILITY!
SHE'S MY PATIENT - A CYBERJUNKIE -

I THOUGHT SHE WAS GETTING BETTER, BUT IT SEEMS SPACE DEMENTIA MUST HAVE BEEN SETTING IN SLOWLY.
SHE MUST NOT HAVE BEEN USING THE LUCIDREAM EMITTER ALL ALONG.
SHE HAS SEALED HER OWN FATE.

Subject: Mandretta, Anna. Possibility that the subject has colluded or made some sort of exchange with the enemy. Subject has been placed in max-sec until debriefing followed by immediate nullification.
Investigation into prior charges re: fraternization shall continue post-nullification.
Anna Mandretta will never leave the surface of Tallis One.
WHERE AM I?

...AND WHAT IS THAT- WHOAH! I'M TOUCHING IT! ITS A XAX-SHIP BUT IT'S DISINTEGRATING!
WHEN I ENCOUNTERED THE LONE XAX - IT COMMUNICATED WITH ME, TELEPATHICALLY. I JUST DIDN'T UNDERSTAND WHAT IT WAS SAYING!
THE XAX ARE LESS THAN BUG - THEY ARE THE GOO INSIDE OF A BUG - THEY BUILD EXO-SKELETONS OF DIFFERENT SHAPES AND SIZES AND FLOW FREELY IN AND OUT OF THEM -
THEY'RE SICK - OR PERHAPS THEY ARE UNDERGOING A SPECIES-WIDE METAMORPHOSIS - THEY DON'T KNOW! BUT AS SCARED AS THEY ARE OF THIS DARK DESTINY, THE TERRAN CONGRESS IS MORE FRIGHTENED OF WHAT THE XAX MAY BECOME!

SLEEP

THEY DON'T KNOW WHAT THE XAX ARE TURNING INTO, BUT THEY ARE TRYING TO SLOW IT DOWN. THE XAX CAN NO LONGER REPRODUCE, BUT THEIR BIO-NANITES CAN REARRANGE OUR DNA EN MASSE INTO XAX AND INTEGRATE IT INTO THEIR HIVE-BLOB. THEY'RE FEEDING HUMANS TO THE XAX, THAT'S WHY WE'RE OUT HERE!

I MUST BE HERE TO DESTROY THEM! THE ABOMINATION MUST END! THE THREAT MUST BE ERADICATED!

THEY'RE COMING!

THE XAX KNOW ABOUT ME TOO. THEY'RE COMING TO TAKE THIS WHOLE SHIP.

DOCTOR - A XAX MILLIPEDE - BIGGEST WE'VE EVER SEEN -

IT'S ON ITS WAY HERE! WE HAVE TO HURRY!

TELL ME ANNA - WHEN DID YOU FIRST COMMUNICATE WITH THE XAX?
DO YOU EVEN STILL UNDERSTAND THAT IT IS THEY WHO ARE THE ENEMY, NOT US?
NOT I -
I WANTED TO HELP YOU.
YOU DON'T UNDERSTAND, LISTEN -
WE DON'T HAVE TIME, THEY'RE AFTER ME NOW -
THEY'LL TAKE EVERYONE, THE WHOLE SHIP - YOU HAVE TO GET ME OUT OF HERE!
NO, THE SUBJECT IS COMPLETELY DELUSIONAL. FURTHER INTERROGATION IS POINTLESS.
WAIT!
HEY, DON'T GO, LISTEN -
WE'VE ALL BEEN SET UP!
GET ME OUT OF HERE OR YOU'LL ALL BE DEAD!!
I'M SO TIRED.
LIKE I HADN'T SLEPT IN A MONTH.
I FIND MYSELF NOT CARING ANYMORE ABOUT THE FATE OF THIS SHIP. IT SEEMS SO FLAT, LITERALLY TWO-DIMENSIONAL.
AND I AM SO ALONE.

LET GO OF ME —
HELLO, ANNA.
ADAR VESELL, WHOEVER OR WHATEVER YOU ARE.
WE ARE FOREVER LINKED, FOR I AM THE WYRD IN YOUR MIND.
DEATH AND LIFE REVERSED, AND YOUR MIND AS THE BRIDGE.
AS MY TRUE FATHER EMERGES, SO SHALL WE WYRMS GROW WITH YOUR UNDERSTANDING.
REMEMBER, ANNA MANDRETTA, THE WYRMS — THE WYRD ARE YOURS. THE WYRD IS YOUR DESTINY.

SOON NOW THIS PLANE AND THE WORLD OF MY BIRTH SHALL BE ONE,
HE WILL COME FORTH, HIS MINIONS OF UNLIFE RIDING ON HIS BACK -
HE IS THE BLIND IDIOT GOD OF CHAOS -
LOBOTOMIZED THROUGH HIS PRIMARY EYE.
BUT HE GROWS NEW EYES EVERYWHERE, AND SOMEHOW HE ACTS.
AN AMORPHOUS BLIGHT ON THE NETHERMOST CONFUSION WHICH BLASPHEMES AND BUBBLES AT THE CENTER OF INFINITY!

AAAIIIEEE!
WAKING INTO THE DREAM, SCREAMING, AS IF FROM A NIGHTMARE - BUT THE TRUE NIGHTMARE WAS MY WAKING WORLD, THE TRUE HORROR INSIDE MY OWN MIND.
ANNA - I MEAN DOCT - ER - MISS MANDRETTA, I HEARD YOU CRY OUT.
IT'S ALL RIGHT, NICHOLAS-
CALL ME ANNA. I'M OKAY...
WELL, I'D BEST LEAVE YOU BE -
WAIT NICHOLAS -
PLEASE. COME SIT WITH ME.
NICHOLAS, I'M SORRY FOR LASHING OUT AT YOU -
I WAS ANGRY AT SOMEONE FROM THAT OTHER WORLD.
ANNA - THERE'S NO NEED -
YES, THERE IS, NICHOLAS...
THERE IS NEED...

AND IT ALL MELTS AWAY.
IF THIS WAS WHAT LOVE WAS IN THE LUCIDREAM- THE VIVIDNESS OF IT!
NO WONDER IT MADE MY SHIPMATES SO ECSTATIC IT LEFT THEM WALKING ON AIR EVEN INTO THE PALE FLICKERING INCANDESCENT LIGHT OF DAY.
WE WERE AS ONE - AND, I SUDDENLY REALIZED, SO WAS I.
NICHOLAS - MY DEAR FRIEND.
ANNA MY LOVE -
NICHOLAS - YOU MUST FOLLOW MY INSTRUCTIONS - PLEASE TRUST ME -
I DO, MY LOVE, I DO!
IS THE NEURAL CRYPTOMETER STILL SET AT THE FREQUENCY IT WAS WHEN I AWOKE FROM THE FUGUE STATE?
YES, ANNA, BUT -
JUST LISTEN, MY LOVE. I WANT YOU TO ACTIVATE THE DEVICE ON YOURSELF.
WHAT, WHY -
PLEASE, NICHOLAS, YOU'LL KNOW WHEN THE TIME COMES, YOU'LL KNOW THE MOMENT, I KNOW IT. JUST DO IT - FOR ME.

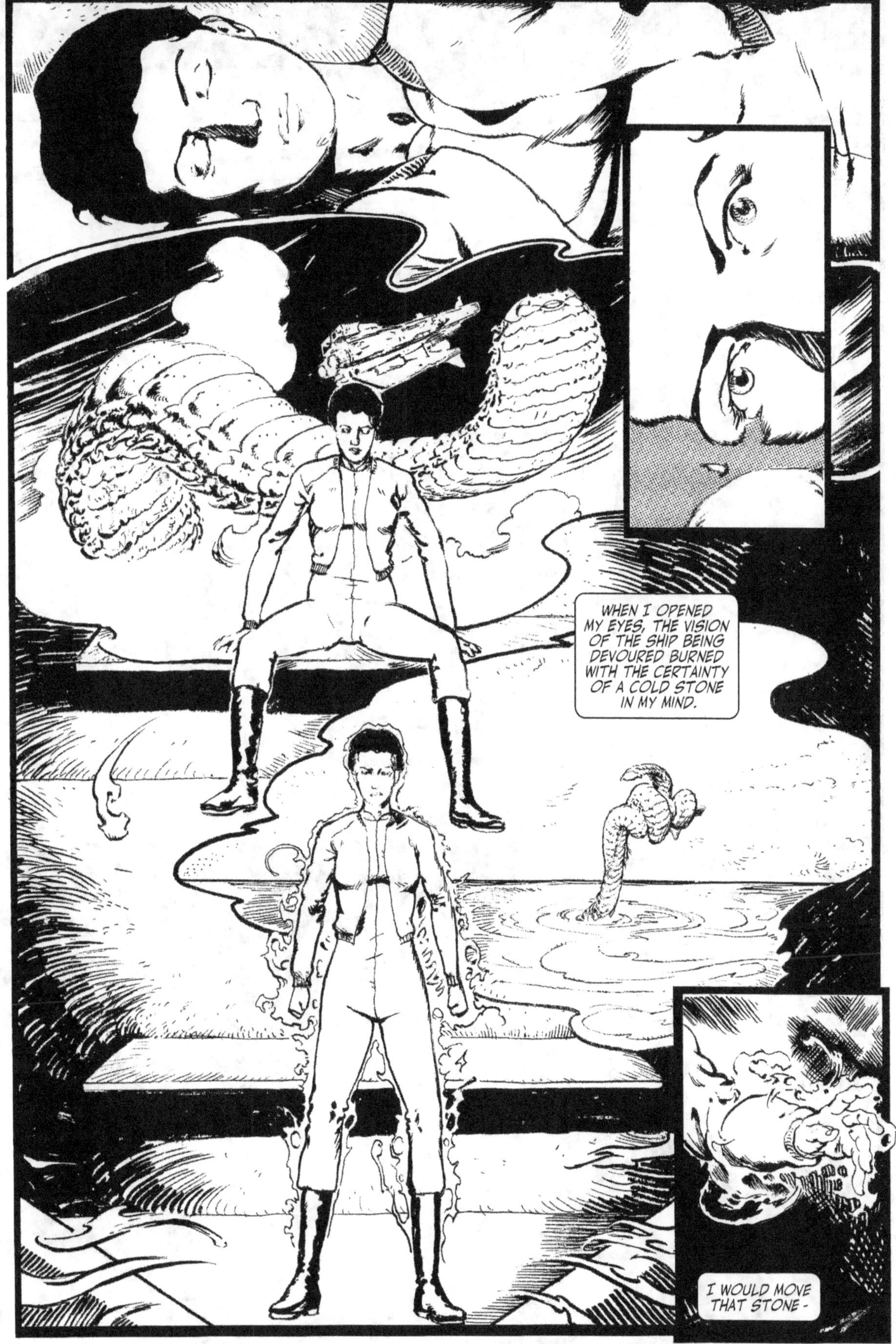
WHEN I OPENED MY EYES, THE VISION OF THE SHIP BEING DEVOURED BURNED WITH THE CERTAINTY OF A COLD STONE IN MY MIND.
I WOULD MOVE THAT STONE -

EVEN AS THE FIRST SANDS SHIFTED ON THE OCEAN FLOOR IN THE WAKE OF THE DREADNOUGHT'S SHADOW, CERTAINTY BECAME PROBABILITY.
AS I WILLED THE DOOR OPEN AND WALKED RIGHT PAST THE GUARDS, PROBABILITY BECAME POSSIBILITY.
EVERY HUMAN ON THIS SHIP COULD BE PULLED DOWN THE TUBES INTO THE BOWELS OF THE CENTIPEDE - AND THERE'S NO LOGICAL REASON WHY I COULD CHANGE THAT.
BUT PERHAPS IF I ENVISION -
FIND MYSELF WHERE I NEED TO BE AND ASCEND -
TILL THINGS GET SO TIGHT I'LL JUST HAVE TO DO WHAT I HAVE TO DO.
BUT THE GROUND HAS JUST OPENED UP BENEATH THIS SHIP!
HOW AM I GONNA DO THIS?
HOW IN COSMIC HELL AM I GONNA DO THIS? THERE JUST WASN'T TIME!
THERE WAS NO WAY I COULD MAKE IT. NO!

GET TO THE HULL AND FIGURE OUT HOW TO FIGHT THEM.
GET TO THE HULL.
AROOGA·AROOGA·ARO
GA·AROOGA·AROOG

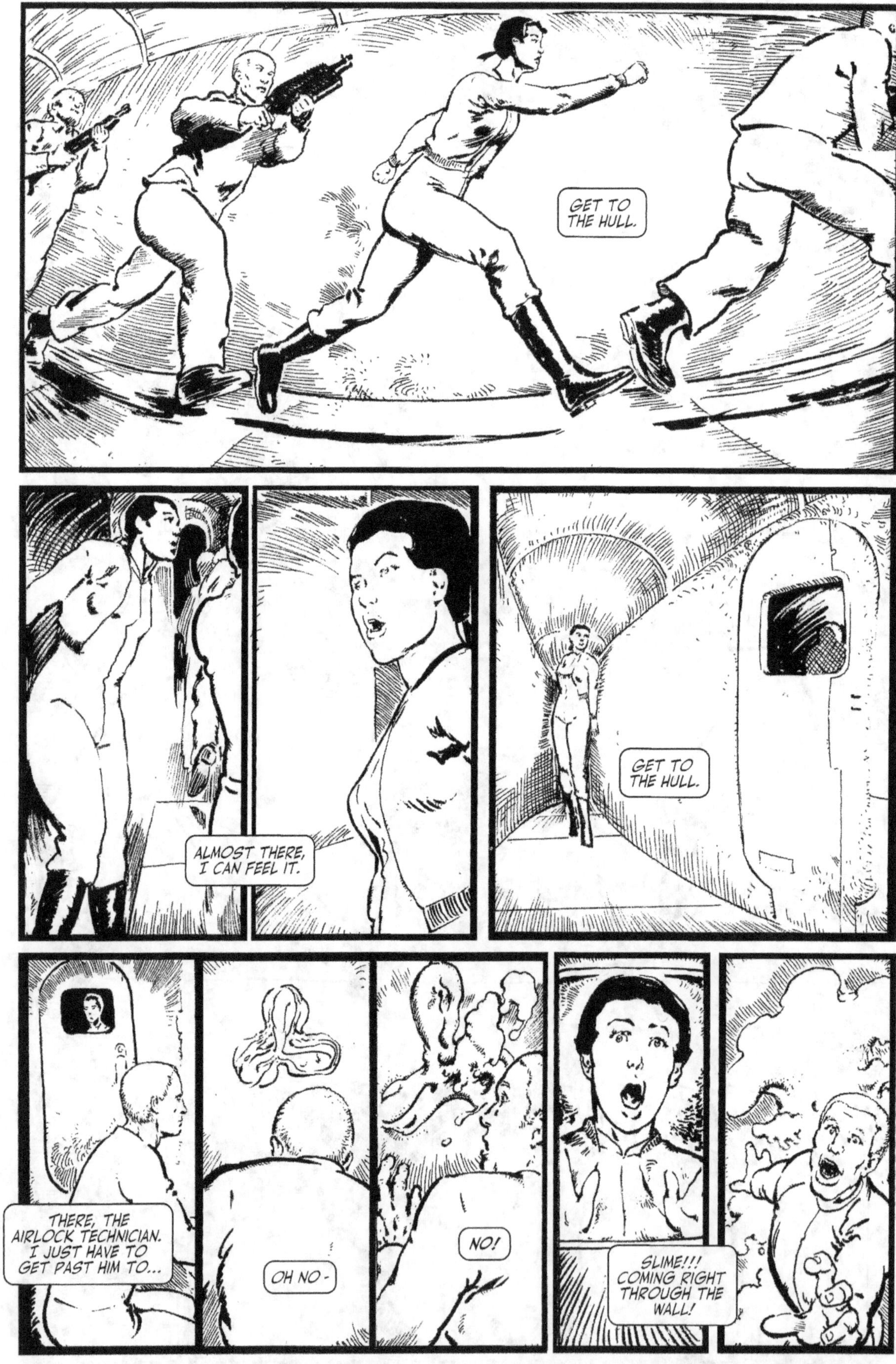

GET TO THE HULL.
ALMOST THERE, I CAN FEEL IT.
GET TO THE HULL.
THERE, THE AIRLOCK TECHNICIAN. I JUST HAVE TO GET PAST HIM TO...
OH NO -
NO!
SLIME!!! COMING RIGHT THROUGH THE WALL!

THEY DIDN'T EVEN HAVE TO INVADE THE SHIP.
THE ROOM WAS PUMPED FULL OF SLIME IN A FEW FROZEN MICROSECONDS. HE WAS XAX BEFORE I COULD EVEN TURN ON MY HEEL AND RUN.
THE SHIP ROCKED AND THE MELODY OF THE BATTLE KLAXON CHANGED TEMPO.
AROOGA·AROOGA·AROOGA·

STEADY AGAIN -
BUT POSSIBILITY WAS SLIPPING AWAY.
TASTED LIKE PROBABILITY. CERTAINTY LOOMED.

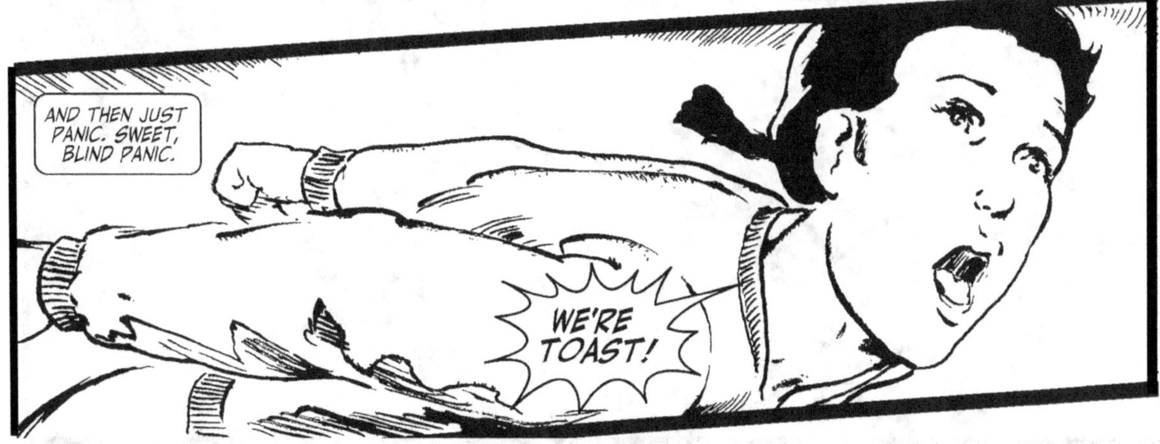
AND THEN JUST PANIC. SWEET, BLIND PANIC.
WE'RE TOAST!

WHY ARE YOU ALL JUST SITTING THERE!
WHY CAN'T YOU HEAR THE ALARM IN HERE?
DON'T YOU KNOW WE'RE BEING INVADED!
ANNA - BUT HOW?!
YOU'VE ALL BEEN SOLD OUT! YOU'RE ALL GONNA BE SLIMED!
DON'T YOU KNOW THE HULL'S BEEN BREACHED?
ALERT! PEOPLE, BE ADVISED, THIS IS PATIENT MANDRETTA! SHE IS EXPERIENCING SPACE DEMENTIA. DO NOT PAY ANY HEED TO WHAT SHE IS SAYING.
I ZIG-ZAG OUT OF THERE AND WAS ABOUT EIGHT MICROSECONDS AHEAD OF THEM.
I DUCKED DOWN INTO A SHADOW.
SOMEHOW ENDED UP IN CREW QUARTERS.

EEEEEEEK!
BAMP BAMP BAMP BAMP
HEGH, ANNA -
AMPS ENOUGH TO REANIMATE!
CAT GOTTA LEARN YOU SOME STEALTH...
C'MON FOLLOW ME.
IF YOU PLEASE M'LO...
ZEDUS SHAT, SHIVEAN, THOSE ARE YOUR QUARTERS?
I CAN SMELL IT FROM HERE!
HERE, ANNA - I FOUND IT-
THE CEREMONIAL BLADE!
WELL, READY WHEN YOU ARE, MASTER.
SPILL THE BLOOD! HHH-HHH

I KILLED HIM JUST BEFORE WE MET IN THE MESS.
SO - WE GONNA DO UP SOME HOMELAND SECURITY OR WHAT?
UNLEASH THE UNFATHOMABLE HORROR!
YOU'VE HAD AN ANIMAL IN YOUR QUARTERS? SINCE TERRA?
HE'S AN ANOINTED ONE NOW - AN UNDEAD ONE - UNLEASH YOUR POWER ON THE XAX!
HIS BLOOD AND YOUR WORDS WILL ACTIVATE THE SUMMONING SEQUENCE.
HIS BLOOD OR YOURS?
SPARE ME, OH POWERFUL QUEEN OF THE UNDEAD!
LET ME BE YOUR LIEUTENANT AND LIVE TO WITNESS THE GLORY OF THE DARK GOD'S REIGN!
THERE SHE IS, THE CYBERADDICT! SEIZE HER!

WEIRDLING TROMORT AZAGTHOTH!

TIME FROZEN INTO COLD SLIVERS OF ICE.
INHALE.
HUH!
ANNA'S SIGNAL!

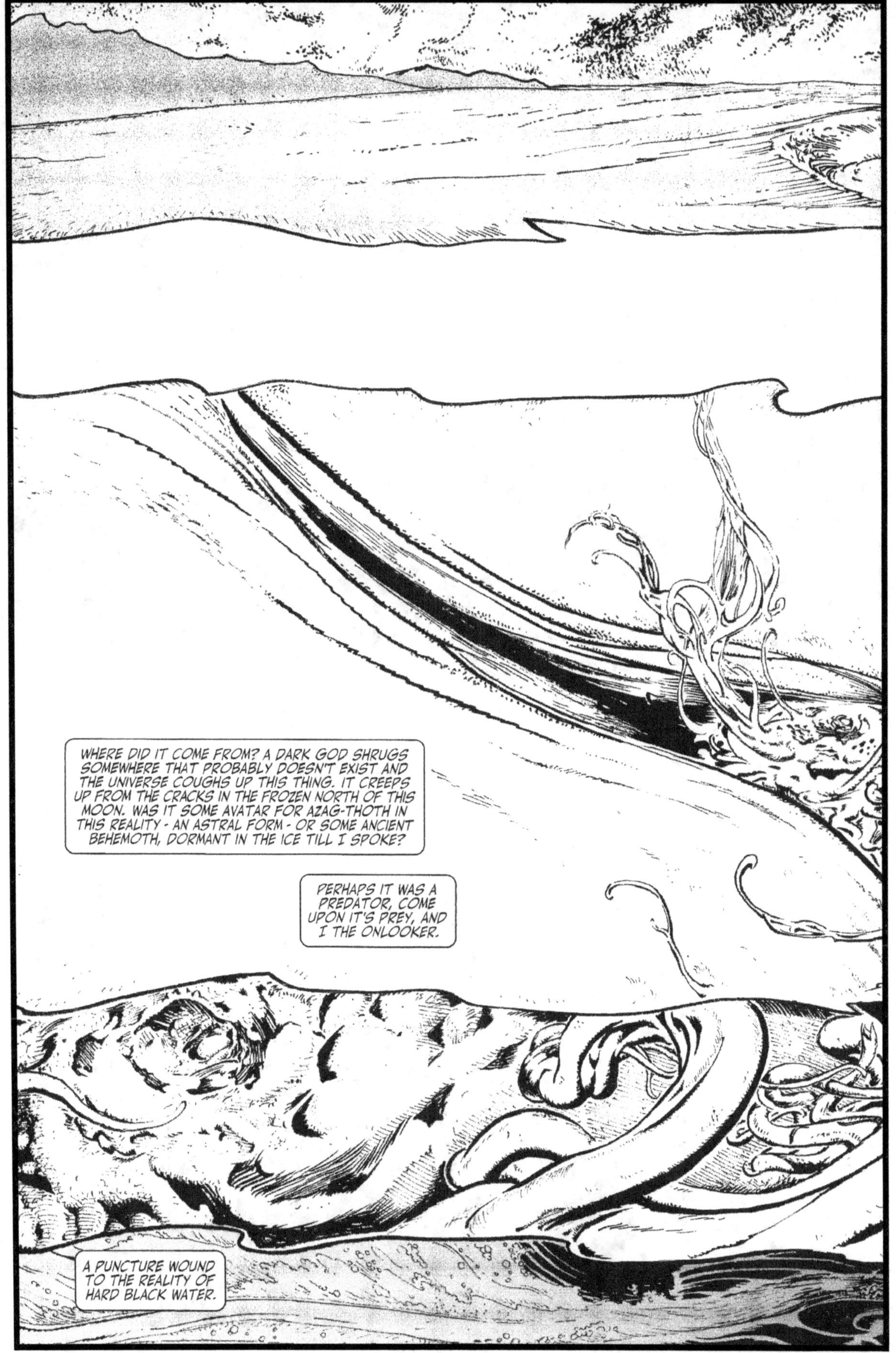
WHERE DID IT COME FROM? A DARK GOD SHRUGS SOMEWHERE THAT PROBABLY DOESN'T EXIST AND THE UNIVERSE COUGHS UP THIS THING. IT CREEPS UP FROM THE CRACKS IN THE FROZEN NORTH OF THIS MOON. WAS IT SOME AVATAR FOR AZAG-THOTH IN THIS REALITY - AN ASTRAL FORM - OR SOME ANCIENT BEHEMOTH, DORMANT IN THE ICE TILL I SPOKE?
PERHAPS IT WAS A PREDATOR, COME UPON IT'S PREY, AND I THE ONLOOKER.
A PUNCTURE WOUND TO THE REALITY OF HARD BLACK WATER.

EXHALE.

A STONE BLADE SHATTERS ON SPACE AGE METAL.
BUBBLES DISSIPATE AS WATER RUSHES IN. BLOOD FLOW TO MY BRAIN ECHOES.

HEAD RUSH, KNEES BUCKLE. DID I BLACK OUT?
THE SHIP WAS SINKING FAST. MY OPTIONS WERE LIMITED.
WIERDLING VERMIS!

FROM THE LOG OF LT. RIK DEXTAR - OFFICE OF INTERNAL AFFAIRS, TERRAN REPUBLIC SPACE CORP
EVERY SHIP ON THE PLANET, OURS AND XAX, HAD ABRUPTLY SUNK, CRASHED OR JUST STOPPED DEAD MID-BATTLE. EXCEPT FOR THE XII.
IT WAS THE ONLY VESSEL ON THE PLANET STILL AFLOAT.
IT WAS BROADCASTING, SENDING SIGNALS BACK TO EARTH, TO OTHER SHIPS ON ALL THE USUAL CHANNELS.
BUT THE TRANSMISSIONS WERE GARBLED- EVEN WHEN THE SIGNAL READ CLEAR, THE VOICES WERE DISTORTED, THEIR RESPONSES NONSENSE.
I WISH I COULD REPORT THE CREWMEN WERE WELL -
BUT WHEN I BOARDED THE XII, MY NOSTRILS STUNG WITH SAME ACRID SCENT OF DEATH I'D ENCOUNTERED ON THE OTHER SHIPS. THEN -
I WISH I COULD SAY THEY WERE ENTRANCED OR ILL WITH SOME DISEASE -
I THOUGHT PERHAPS A NEW BIO-NANITE, ONE THAT ROTTED THEIR BODIES AND WARPED THEIR MINDS.
THEY WALKED, THEY PERFORMED TASKS - BY GOD THEY KEPT THE SHIP AFLOAT!

BUT - THE CREWMEN WOULD NOT RESPOND TO US. WHEN WE TRIED TO FORCIBLY DETAIN AND EXAMINE THEM, THEY BECAME VIOLENT, UNCONTROLLABLE -
WHEN FINALLY WE FOUND ONE IMMOBILIZED BY THE LOSS OF BIO-MECH PARTS, THE RESULTS WERE INEXPLICABLE -
THEY'RE ALL DEAD!
BUT ALL OUR TESTS AND STUDIES LED US TO THE SAME CONCLUSION -
FINALLY WE FOUND THE ONLY SURVIVORS.
LIEUTENANT, LOOK!
HEY, WAIT!

WHERE?
THERE, THAT WAY!
STOP!
IT'S OKAY, SON. WE'RE HERE TO HELP.
AND MAYBE YOU CAN HELP US.
YOU'RE THE ONLY PERSON WE'VE FOUND WHO'S NOT -
NOT DEAD?
I WASN'T SURE. I THOUGHT PERHAPS I WAS IN HELL.
HER NAME, HE TOLD US, WAS ANNA MANDRETTA.

OUR RECORDS CONFIRMED THIS. SHE WAS CONSCRIPTED PERSONNEL, A FIELD MEDIC. AN EXAMINATION OF THE SHIP'S RECORD WOULD LATER REVEAL RECENT DISCIPLINARY PROBLEMS, BUT NOTHING TO EXPLAIN HER CURRENT CONDITION, A COMA LIKE SLEEP.
WE I - DEED HIM AS ONE OBLIV SHIVEAN, A VIRT-TECH. HE INSISTED HE WAS, IN FACT, A DOCTOR NICHOLAS VAN HISE - A NEUROSURGEON FROM A HOSPITAL IN VICTORIAN NEW ENGLAND.
HIS IS YET ANOTHER STRANGE CASE - PERHAPS THE ODDEST MYSTERY OF ALL. IF ANYONE ON THE SHIP SHOULD HAVE BEEN DEAD, IT WAS HE.
A VICTIM OF KIERSELLA POISONING - HIS BLOOD HAD BEEN TURNED INTO EMBALMING FLUID. WHILE HE WAS NOT A ZOMBIE LIKE THE OTHERS, HIS ANSWERS TO OUR QUESTIONS REVEALED AN UNHINGED MIND, ONE THAT COULD SHED NO LIGHT ON THIS SITUATION.
HE CLAIMS TO HAVE CROSSED OVER FROM ANOTHER DIMENSION -
HE KNEW NOT EVEN THE LOCATION OF HIS OR THE WOMAN'S QUARTERS. WHEN WE FOUND THEM, HERS REVEALED NOTHING. HIS, HOWEVER, CONTAINED YET ANOTHER MYSTERY.
THE GOAT WAS DEAD, ORNERY AND OBVIOUSLY THE LONG-TERM RESIDENT OF THE CHAMBER. WHY, OR HOW, THE ANIMAL CAME TO BE ON BOARD THE XII, SHIVEAN/VAN HISE COULD NOT EXPLAIN EITHER.
WE'RE TAKING IT ALL BACK TO TERRA. BEST OF LUCK TO HQ IN DEBRIEFING THESE TWO AND UNRAVELLING THIS KNOT.
I DON'T KNOW WHO'S GONNA GET THE MEDAL FOR THIS VICTORY.
I CAN'T WAIT TO GET BACK TO TERRA. THE CELEBRATIONS WILL LAST FOR YEARS.
THEN WE CAN GET BACK TO BUSINESS: COLONIZATION, EXPLORATION, MATERIAL EXPLOITATION -
THE UNIVERSE BELONGS TO HUMANITY, OUR MANIFEST DESTINY AWAITS.

WE SPACE-FOLD TOMORROW, 0700, PLANETARY DAWN.
WHAT'S HAPPENING NOW?
OH ANNA, MY LOVE, I TRIED TO PROTECT YOU. THEY WRESTED YOU FROM MY GRASP!
TEN THOUSAND PARSECS IN TWO HOURS. I WILL JOIN THE CREW AND OUR TWO GUESTS IN STASIS SLEEP - FOR OUR OWN SAFETY, IN THE EVENT OF A COURSE DEVIATION.
ANNA- WHAT AM I TO DO? ARE WE TRAPPED IN THIS WORLD FOREVER?
ANNA! ANNA!
IF THAT SHOULD HAPPEN, WE'LL ALL BE LIKE ANNA MANDRETTA -
IN FOR A LONG STAY IN THE WORLD OF DREAMS, WITH ONLY OUR OWN PHANTOMS TO GUIDE US.
DEXTAR, LOG FILE #1890

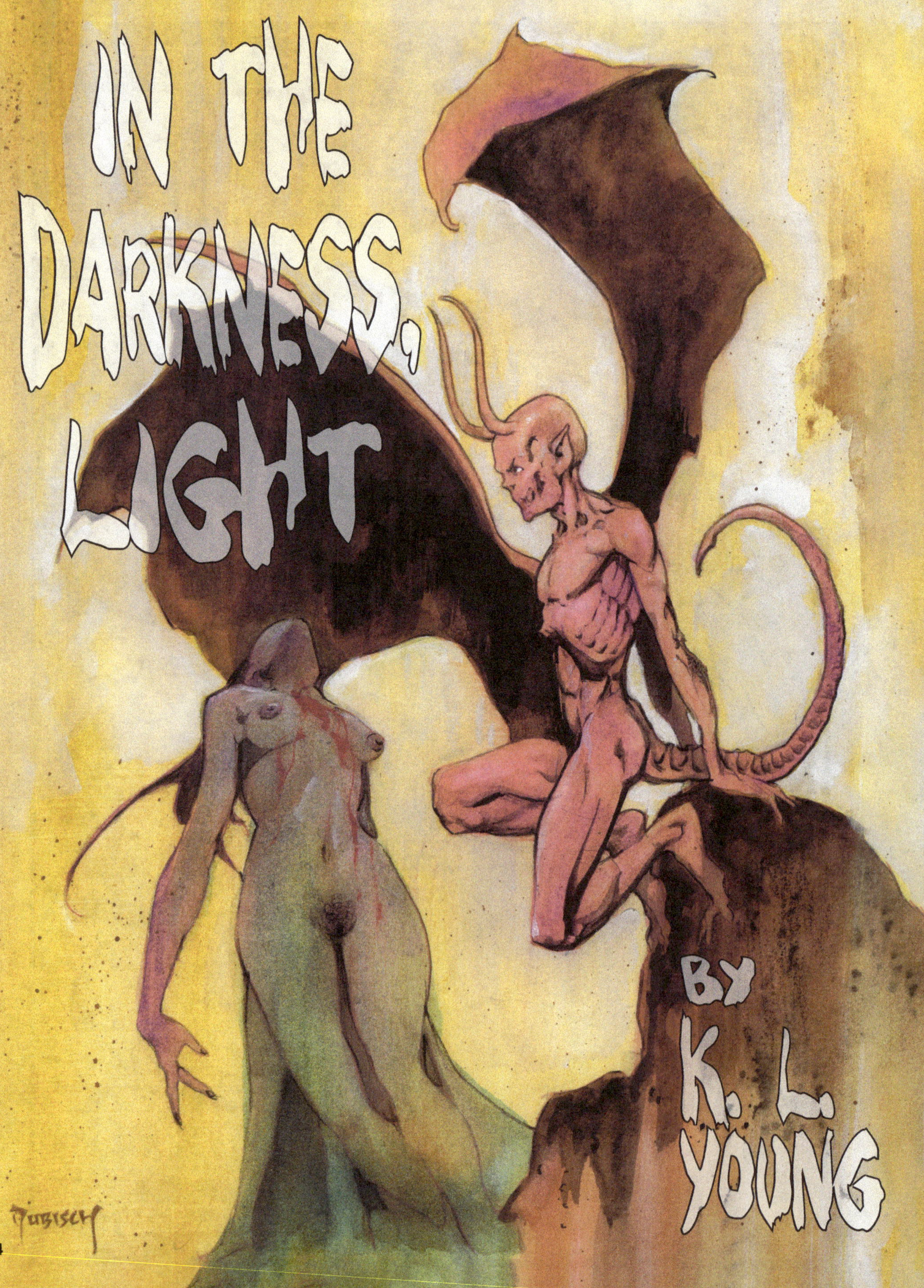

IN THE DARKNESS, LIGHT
BY K. L. YOUNG

THE CREATURE HAD EXISTED FOREVER ALONE IN A DARKNESS VAST AND EMPTY, UNBROKEN AND UNENDING. THERE WAS NO KINDNESS HERE, NOR LIGHT, NOR LOVE. NOT EVEN THE ECHO OF A HEARTBEAT IN THE NOTHINGNESS.

And then he found her.

But what was she? And how? She floated in the void, her chest rising and falling as she slept, body glowing from within by a soft, golden strangeness.

He was fascinated. Mesmerized by her warmth. Even from this distance, he could feel her heat on his own skin. Everything else here was cold. Sharp. Empty. But this thing—this woman—was different. She was *other*.

The creature approached slowly. He reached out, a single talon hovering just above the delicate swell of her hip. What would happen if he touched her? Would she disappear? Or scream? Would she—

The woman stirred.

He snatched his hand back.

Thunder rumbled through the blackness, and the creature froze. The void *shuddered*. Something had changed.

He squinted down at the woman. Had she done this?

He couldn't tear his eyes from her lips, pink and full. He was terrified of them. Mesmerized by them. He wanted to bite them. Hurt them. Fuck them.

Kiss them.

He ached to know her.

He turned away. It was time to leave.

He did not leave.

Instead, he moved closer. He was captivated by her hair, spilling across the nothingness like silk. Her skin glowed with a warmth the darkness had never known. Her scent... New. Green. The void smelled like ash and pain, but she smelled like *life*.

The creature inhaled, intoxicated.

He had felt the weight of eternity pressing down upon him, had heard the hatred of things that should not be named, watched time spool out, uncaring and unending.

But nothing had ever affected him like this.

He was entranced with the curve of her breasts as they rose and fell with each breath, and he swallowed with difficulty, suddenly parched.

Would she wake if he touched her? And what then?

Everything would change if she opened her eyes, he knew that much. But the urge to know all of her was overwhelming.

He reached out again, this time tracing his jagged hand just above the heat of her flesh. Not touching, *no, not yet*, just feeling the warmth that spilled from her, a sensation unlike anything he'd ever experienced.

His fingers trembled above her throat, and he could see a steady pulse just beneath her skin.

A heartbeat. *Life*.

The creature released a ragged breath. His own body was made of spite and scorn, sharp angles and cold shadows. But she was made of something else.

Would she be soft?

His fingers brushed her shoulder, the lightest of contact.

The void *shook*.

Jerking back, the creature cowered under the brightness that suddenly flared around them, a golden light that danced like flame.

He recoiled as the woman took a deep breath. Her body shifted, stretching, and a sound escaped her lips. Just a sigh.

The first breath of a hurricane.

The creature's heart hammered against his chest.

No, not yet!

He wasn't ready.

The void wasn't ready.

But the light continued to grow, tendrils of crimson and gold flickering and spilling from the woman, impossible, uncontrollable.

Her fingers began to twitch.

The creature wanted to stay, to touch her again, to see the color of her eyes when they opened, to hear her voice when she finally spoke.

But he would not survive the experience. This he understood implicitly. He tore himself away from her beauty and escaped.

Deep into the darkness he fled, back into the cold, the sharp, the uncaring. But as he disappeared into the void, he could feel the warmth chasing, spreading, growing all around him.

He had awakened something. Not just the woman, but something within himself. He had let there be light, and he knew nothing could ever be the same again.

TO A DREAMER
BY H. P. LOVECRAFT

I scan they features, calm and white
Beneath the single taper's light;
Thy dark-fringed lids, behind whose screen
Are eyes that view not earth's demesne.
And as I look, I fain would know
The paths whereon they dream-steps go;
The spectral realms that thou canst see
With eyes veil'd from the world and me.
For I have likewise gazed in sleep
On things my mem'ry scarce can keep,
And from half-knowing long to spy
Again the scenes before thine eye.
I, too, have known the peaks of Thok;
The vales of Pnath, where dream-shapes flock;
The vaults of Zin—and well I trow
Why thou demand'st that taper's glow.
But what is this that subtly slips
Over thy face and bearded lips?
What fear distracts thy mind and heart,
That drops must from thy forehead start?
Old visions wake—thine op'ning eyes
Gleam black with clouds of other skies,
And as from demoniac sight
I flee into the haunted night.

PERCHANCE TO DREAM
Thirteen Books and Stories About Sleep, Dreams, Nightmares, Shifting Realities, and Altered States
BY ROSS E. LOCKHART

This morning at about three, I woke up my wife loudly demanding that Dr. Stephen Curry, a man disguised as a scarecrow, reveal himself. I was, of course, dreaming. I don't remember much of this dream, likely the result of some late-night cheese and a partial memory of Disney's 1963 film *Dr. Syn, Alias the Scarecrow*, but in the moment it—and the notorious Dr. Curry—felt real.

We all sleep, and most of us dream, visiting nightly the strange world ruled by Morpheus, Greek god of sleep and dreams. Sometimes we remember these dreams and feel inspired to create art based on the things we encounter there. Sometimes reality seems altered as we readjust to it upon waking, and we feel like strangers inhabiting ourselves.

In the wake of the First World War an art and literary movement inspired by the writings of Sigmund Freud began to grow in Europe, using illogical and dreamlike scenes to create a surprising super-reality, a *surreality*. These Surrealists, including Guillaume Apollinaire, André Breton, Max Ernst, and others, wrote books and manifestos, and rendered automatic drawings, sculptures, and films exploring the line between the waking and dreaming realms.

Since then, reality has only become stranger. What follows is a list of thirteen novels, stories, and an anthology exploring sleep, dreams, and dreamlike realities. Sleep well!

THE DREAM-QUEST OF UNKNOWN KADATH *BY H.P. LOVECRAFT*

Lovecraft wrote a few tales set in the Dreamlands, a Lord Dunsany-inspired dream world, including "Polaris", "The Cats of Ulthar", and "The Other Gods." Unpublished in his lifetime, novella *The Dream-Quest of Unknown Kadath* is the longest. Protagonist Randolph Carter, after seeing a majestic city in his dreams, seeks to reach it, and plans to petition the gods of dream to reveal its location. Along the way, he encounters nightgaunts, ghouls, Ultharian cats, slave-trading Men of Leng, and various servants of Nyarlathotep. A hallucinogenic romp with plenty of references to the larger Lovecraftian canon. Also worth exploring are Jason Bradley Thompson's 2011 graphic novel adaptation and Kij Johnson's feminist reworking, *The Dream-Quest of Vellitt Boe*.

THE LATHE OF HEAVEN *BY URSULA K. LEGUIN*

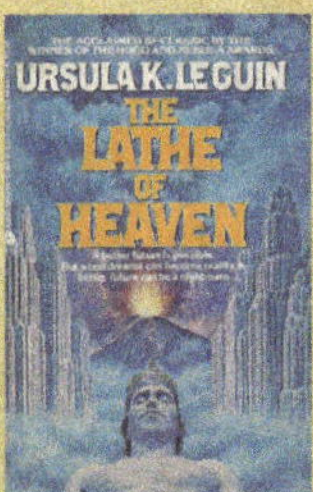

This 1971 novel, which would be nominated for the Hugo and Nebula Awards (and would win the Locus Award for Best Novel in 1972) is set in the then-future year of 2002. Drug-addicted draftsman George Orr suffers from dreams that change reality but leave him with memories of previous unchanged worlds. As Orr seeks psychological help for his ever-shifting realities his attempts shift the waking world towards utopia constantly result in increasingly dystopian premises.

THE LONG DREAM *BY JUNJI ITO*

A short manga story about celebrated neurosurgeon Dr. Kuroda and his assistant, Dr. Yamauchi, who take on a new patient, Tetsuro Mukoda, a man who complains of increasingly long dreams. Over time, Mukoda's dreams become longer and longer, with him perceiving weeks, months, and years passing in a single night. And soon, Mukoda's body begins to change as well, evolving and becoming something more than human. Collected in *Shiver: Junji Ito Selected Stories*.

THE NIGHT LAND *BY WILLIAM HOPE HODGSON*

First published in 1912, this baroque, 200,000-word novel would inspire the Dying Earth subgenre. Beginning in the 17th century, as a gentleman mourns the loss of his beloved Lady Mirdath and moving into a future in which the sun has gone black and the earth is only lit by radiation, the remnants of the human race take shelter in an immense pyramid known as the Last Redoubt, shielded from watchers and other Abhumans. To leave the Redoubt means certain death but may be the only way our protagonist can reconnect with the reincarnation of his lost love. H.P. Lovecraft described The Night Land as "one of the most potent pieces of macabre imagination ever written."

THE HOLLOW PLACES *BY T. KINGFISHER*

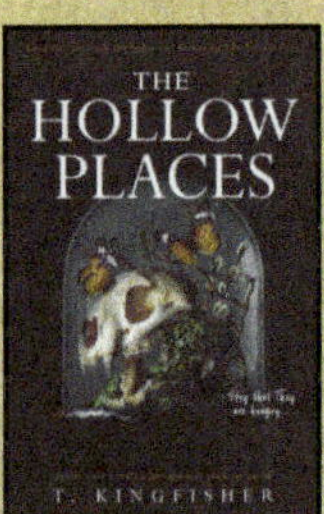

When divorcee Kara finds a mysterious bunker behind a hole in her uncle's house, she also finds a series of portals leading to dreamlike other worlds. Filled with Appalachian atmosphere, visceral body horror, and cosmic dread, *The Hollow Places* is a nightmarish Narnia as unsettling as a half-remembered dream.

BAD CREE *BY JESSICA JOHNS*

A nested First Nations coming of age mystery/horror in which a young woman grieving the deaths of her grandmother and sister suffers increasingly violent nightmares that seem to be bleeding through into reality. A slow-burn with a lot of atmosphere and suspense, and a uniquely Indigenous supernatural tale.

THROUGH THE LOOKING-GLASS, AND WHAT ALICE FOUND THERE *BY LEWIS CARROLL*

The 1871 sequel to Carroll's 1865 *Alice's Adventures in Wonderland* is filled with dreamlike logic, mirror images, and strange encounters, delivering many impossible things to believe before breakfast. The plot plays a chess game with the reader, advancing Alice across a gridded countryside as she encounters now-familiar characters including Tweedledum and Tweedledee, Humpty Dumpty, kings, queens, and knights.

SLEEP DONATION *BY KAREN RUSSELL*

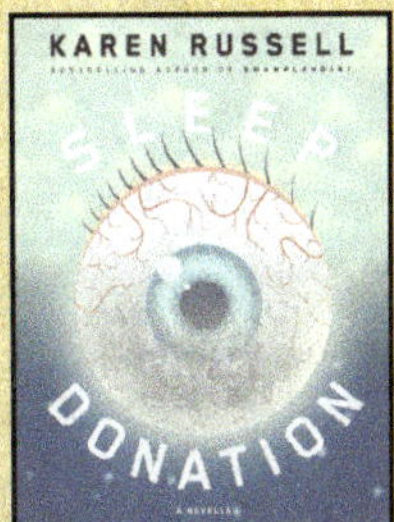

An epidemic of insomnia is sweeping the country, leading to the formation of the Slumber Corps, a nonprofit organization that works to cure the sleepless by recruiting sleep donors. Trish, whose sister was one of the early victims of the epidemic, is a particularly effective recruiter, using her experience and story to sign up donors and stem the tide of those wasting away from lack of sleep. But moral dilemmas arise, including a child found to be a universal donor and the potential of the disease itself mutating. This one may keep you up at night.

LITTLE NEMO IN SLUMBERLAND *BY WINSOR MCCAY*

This series of comic strips that ran in newspapers between 1905 and 1927 features Nemo, a little boy whose slumberland adventures take him into a world of wonders, rendered in glorious architectural detail and filled with all sorts of memorable characters, including cigar-chewing clown Flip and King Morpheus, ruler of Slumberland, until he is inevitably awakened in the final panel, a gag shared with McCay's other oneiric comic strip, 1904's *Dream of the Rarebit Fiend*. Surreal long before the invention of Surrealism, *Little Nemo in Slumberland* remains a fascinating and experimental comic strip, steeped in the psychological and featuring innovative use of color, perspective, and panel shapes.

THE FOREVER WAR *BY JOE HALDEMAN*

This 1974 Hugo, Nebula, and Locus Award-winning novel is both an answer to Robert A. Heinlein's 1959 novel *Starship Troopers* and the author's own experiences in the Vietnam War. William Mandella, a physics student conscripted in the United Nations Exploratory Force's war against an alien species known as the Taurans undergoes rigorous weapons and survival training before being shipped thousands of light-years to the front lines. While Mandella's battlefield encounters only last a few years, he has to deal with time dilation, finding that centuries have passed while he was deployed, and that he no longer understands how to function on Earth. Dreamlike and subversive, *The Forever War* remains one of the most entertaining antiwar novels ever written.

THE BETWEEN *BY TANANARIVE DUE*

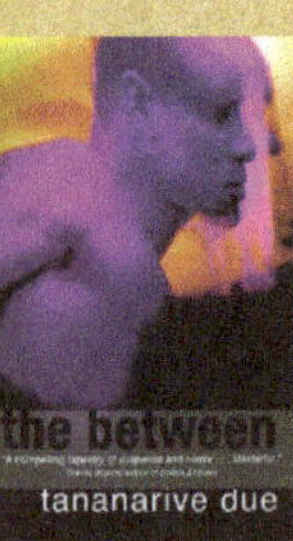

Saved from drowning as a child by his grandmother, who sacrificed her life for his, Hilton James feels as if he's been living on borrowed time. Now in his thirties, Hilton finds himself plagued by nightmares. Meanwhile, Hilton's wife, a judge, has been receiving racist death threats from a man she once prosecuted. Between the external threat of the madman and the internal demons tormenting Hilton nightly, he begins to lose his grip on reality. Is Hilton schizophrenic? Or has he become unmoored from reality. *The Between* was Tananarive Due's debut novel, and it was nominated for the 1996 Bram Stoker Award.

UBIK *BY PHILIP K. DICK*

The stories and novels of Philip K. Dick often blur the line between the real and the surreal, using dreamlike logic to cause the reader to question their perceptions, but even by that metric, *UBIK* is a strange book. Chosen by *Time* magazine as one of the 100 greatest novels since 1923, *UBIK* is set in a future in which both cryonic hibernation and psychic powers are commonplace. Protagonist Joe Chip works for Runciter Associates, a corporation that utilizes inertials, people with psychic blocking abilities, to help protect the privacy of clients. But after a terrorist attack, reality begins to shift and unfold. Objects become older models and deteriorate. Colleagues shrivel up and die. Contradictory messages abound. And the only thing holding reality together may be a product called Ubik, which comes in an aerosol spray can. An unsettling existential nightmare of a book.

NEVER WAKE: AN ANTHOLOGY OF DREAM HORROR *EDITED BY KENNETH W. CAIN AND TIM MEYER*

If just one nightmare tale isn't enough for you, this 2023 anthology from Crystal Lake Publishing brings you nineteen. With stories by authors including Laurel Hightower, Eric LaRocca, Joe Koch, Steve Rasnic Tem, Cynthia Pelayo, Gwendolyn Kiste, Philip Fracassi, and many more, *Never Wake* is filled with mind-bending phantasmagoria and delicious nightmares.

Check out Ross E. Lockhart's Word Horde Emporium of the Weird and Fantastic, a one-of-a-kind indie bookstore nestled in northern California, specializing in horror, fantasy, and all things uncanny. Whether you're hunting rare tomes, indie gems, or the latest eldritch offerings, this shop is a must at: https://www.weirdandfantastic.com

THE THIRD EYE BY MIKE DUBISCH

SLEEPING MIND:

WHAT HAPPENS WHEN WE SLEEP?

As we dream, the mind transcends both time and space. And in that state, something strange occurs, something science can measure but not fully explain. We become conscious inside another world.

WHAT IF DREAMS ARE ALSO PORTALS?

Your dream life is not a glitchy scene but an interface that enables you to connect with levels of reality beyond the reach of waking perception.

Lucid dreamers often describe visiting weird places and experiencing entire lives in a single night, while other dreamers encounter strange technology that they couldn't have imagined. All report a sensation as if the dream itself were watching back. If the universe is conscious, dreams may be the one place where consciousness can converse with itself.

DREAM
INTERACE

Many cultures across the globe consider dreams to be messages from another kind of reality accessed through the mind's dream interface. For instance, the Aboriginal Dreamtime mythos describes a parallel realm accessible only in altered states of consciousness. Tibetan Buddhists practice dream yoga by learning to wake up inside dreams so they can navigate death, rebirth, and other planes of existence.

In 2021, neuroscientists conducted experiments with lucid dreamers, who responded to yes/no questions with facial twitches, and even solved equations in the dream state. This discovery proved that a part of the conscious mind remains "on", even inside a dream, and that our awareness operates on multiple levels simultaneously.

Some noted philosophers and physicists believe that consciousness isn't something we have but something the universe just is.

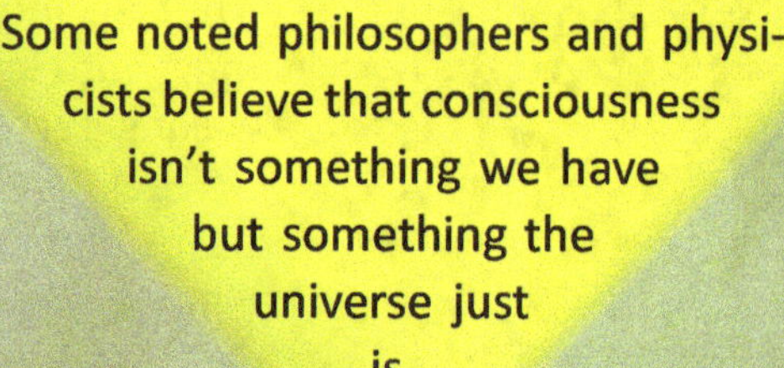

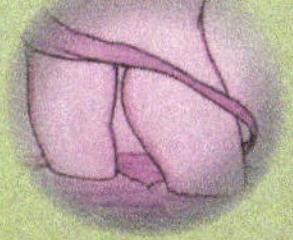

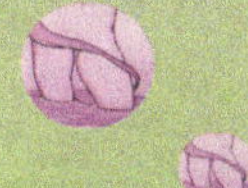

INSIDE THE PANPSYCHIC UNIVERSE

Panpsychism is the idea that consciousness is a fundamental feature of all matter. As such, consciousness is everywhere, like gravity, and your brain is a receiver that tunes into it.

When we dream, we may be unhooking from the narrow feed of waking life and dipping into a much larger sea of awareness spanning the cosmos. Can we explore different frequencies within the universal mind field with dreams?

FINAL TRANSMISSION

For a few hours each night, we are unmoored from the body and drift into a larger mystery that the universe may be dreaming along with us.

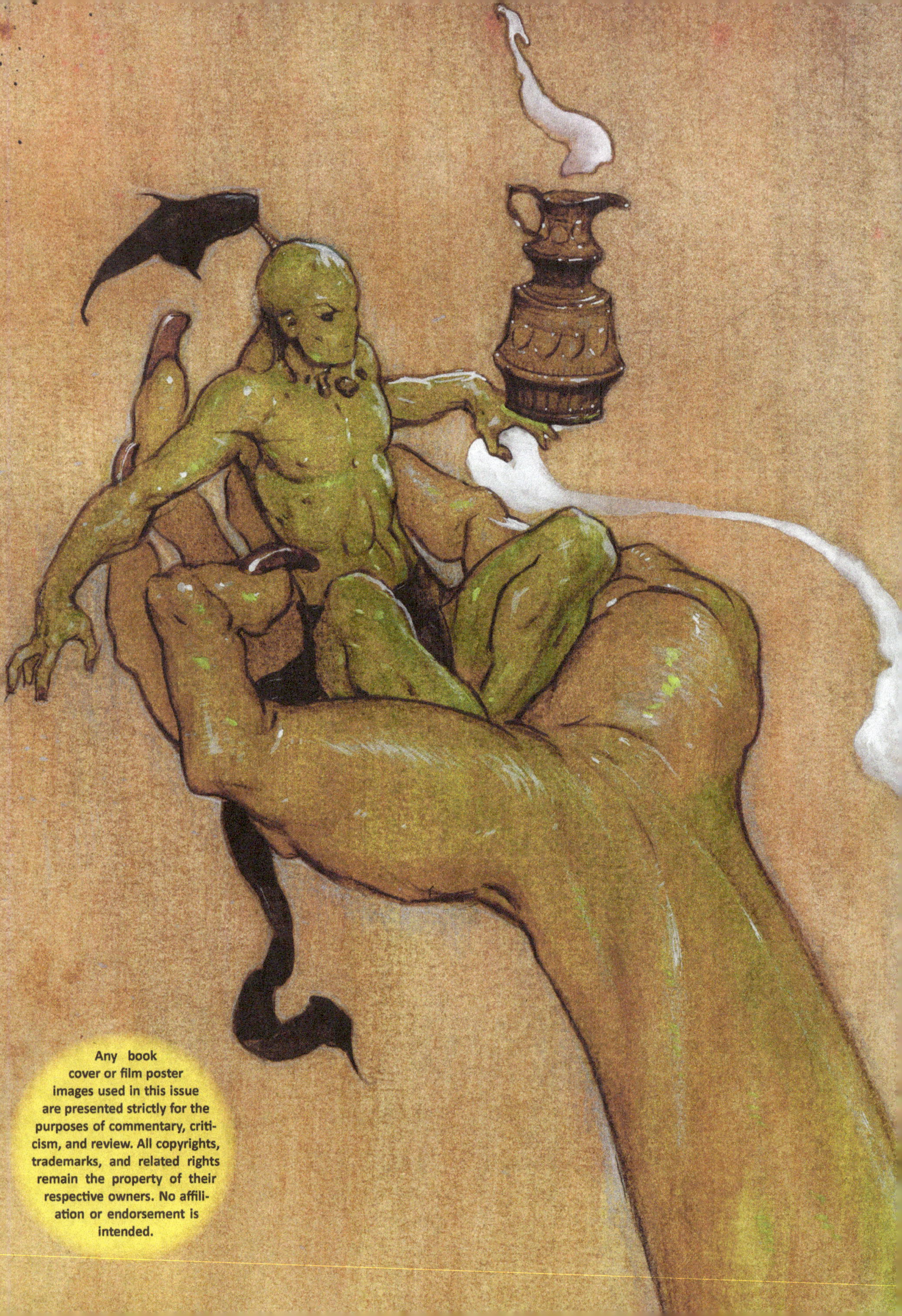

FROM THE PUBLISHER

This issue transported us into the chaotic lands of the subconscious dreamscape. A vision of sleep shaped by fearless writers who delivered killer visions. A huge heartfelt thank you to the gifted voices who made it possible:

PHILIP FRACASSI (The Third Rule of Time Travel, Boys in the Valley)
BRIAN ASMAN (Good Dogs, Man, Fuck This House)
ANTHONY TREVINO (King Space Void, Nightmare City)
DANIEL BRAUM (The Serpent's Shadow, Underworld Dreams)
KARINA COURTWAY (Forbidden Futures)
CODY GOODFELLOW (New Tomorrow, Unamerica)
JOSHUA SKY (He-Man and the Masters of the Universe, Heavy Metal)
ROSS E. LOCKHART (Chick Bassist, Editor: Tales from a Talking Board)
K.L. YOUNG (Thorns, The Secret Language of Spiders)
JEFFREY THOMAS (Punktown, Carrion Men, Forbidden Futures)
ANNA TAMBOUR (Death Goes to the Dogs, The Road to Neozon)
CHAD STROUP (Teeth Where They Shouldn't Be, Sexy Leper)
JESSE ROSE (Forbidden Futures)
JAN STRNAD (Ragemoor, Mutant World)

Mad praise for Mike Dubisch's mind-bending artwork. A fever dream on every page... and to you, fellow traveler who cracked this tome and tumbled headlong into our void... thank you for dreaming with us.